CHRISTOPHER BUSH
THE TRAIL OF THE THREE LEAN MEN

CHRISTOPHER BUSH was born Charlie Christmas Bush in Norfolk in 1885. His father was a farm labourer and his mother a milliner. In the early years of his childhood he lived with his aunt and uncle in London before returning to Norfolk aged seven, later winning a scholarship to Thetford Grammar School.

As an adult, Bush worked as a schoolmaster for 27 years, pausing only to fight in World War One, until retiring aged 46 in 1931 to be a full-time novelist. His first novel featuring the eccentric Ludovic Travers was published in 1926, and was followed by 62 additional Travers mysteries. These are all to be republished by Dean Street Press.

Christopher Bush fought again in World War Two, and was elected a member of the prestigious Detection Club.

He died in 1973.

CHRISTOPHER BUSH

THE TRAIL OF THE THREE LEAN MEN

With an introduction
by Tony Medawar

DEAN STREET PRESS

Published by Dean Street Press 2022

Copyright © 1932 Christopher Bush

Introduction copyright © 2022 Tony Medawar

All Rights Reserved

The right of Christopher Bush to be identified as the Author of the Work has been asserted by his estate in accordance with the Copyright, Designs and Patents Act 1988.

First published in 1932 by Lovat Dickson

Cover by DSP

ISBN 978 1 915014 84 9

www.deanstreetpress.co.uk

INTRODUCTION

CHARLES Christmas Bush was born on the 25th of December 1888 at Home Cottage in Hockham, a heavily wooded village in Norfolk in the east of England. Christmas Bush, as he was known as a child, was of Quaker descent and his family had lived in the area for over four hundred years. He was educated in the village school and, in 1899, won a three year scholarship to Thetford Grammar, where he gained distinctions in Religious Knowledge, English and Geography while winning prizes for English and German. In 1902 he won a further two year scholarship and in 1903 his Form Prize. Outside school, Bush was a competent sportsman, playing in competitive draughts competitions and opening for the village cricket team. He also sang with his friend Ernest Hensley at the Primitive Methodist Chapel alongside his sister Hilda and her friend Ella Pinner, whom Bush would eventually marry. In short, Bush appeared to be a model child so it is perhaps surprising to learn that on the day after his eighteenth birthday he celebrated by going poaching with his brother and Ernest Hensley: all three were caught and, found guilty, were ordered to pay a fine or undertake hard labour.

In 1904, despite his Quaker upbringing – and having lied about his age and the poaching conviction – Bush secured a temporary position as assistant master at a Catholic school in North Worcestershire, about which he wrote in an article, 'Life in the Black Country', published in the *Norwich Mercury* in March 1905. He returned to Norfolk to become an assistant master at Swaffham Boys' School. He also resumed singing at chapel and also played cricket, opening for 'Swaffham Singles' and, lower down the order, for 'Great Hockham Reading Room' a team that included his brothers in conviction, the two Ernests. Later that year, Bush matriculated as an undergraduate at King's College, London, where he studied modern languages, and on graduating, he returned to teaching, this time at a school in Wood Green, North London.

Around this time Bush also married Ella Pinner though what happened next is unclear. Curtis Evans, the authority on the Golden

Age of crime and mystery fiction, has determined that while the two remained married until Ella's death in the late 1960s, they do not appear ever to have lived together. Evans has also established that it was when Bush returned from four years military service during the First World War that he returned to Wood Green School and fathered a child by a teaching colleague, Winifred Chart. Their son, born out of wedlock in 1920 and largely unacknowledged, would grow up to become the composer Geoffrey Bush, co-author with Edmund Crispin of the excellent puzzle short story 'Who Killed Baker?'.

Romantic entanglements aside, teaching had always been Bush's ambition. However, he did not find it fulfilling and in the mid-1920s, as the result of a bet, he wrote a novel. To his amazement and delight, it was accepted and published. Set in 1919, *The Plumley Inheritance* (1926) concerns a treasure hunt and a mysterious murder, which prove – of course – to be connected. While not uncriticised by contemporary reviewers – "Mr Bush has two strings to his bow, and the story might have been a better one if he had restricted himself to one" – the book sold well. It was followed by *The Perfect Murder Case* (1929), whose manuscript Bush claimed the publisher had required him to halve in length, and then two titles in 1930: *Dead Man Twice* in the summer; and *Murder at Fenwold* for Christmas.

Buoyant, Bush decided in 1931 to become a full-time writer and he eventually produced over 80 books. The 63 he wrote as Christopher Bush, which are being reprinted by Dean Street Press, feature several recurring characters, most notably Major Ludovic Travers who appears in all of them. Many are set in English villages not unlike Hockham, but Travers also solves crimes abroad in novels like *The Case of the Three Strange Faces* (1933), *The Case of the Flying Ass* (aka *The Case of the Flying Donkey*) (1939) and *The Case of the Climbing Rat* (1940). Bush also wrote four excellent Second World War mysteries, including three – *The Case of the Murdered Major* (1941) and *The Case of the Kidnapped Colonel* (1942) and *The Case of the Fighting Soldier* (1942).

Writing success brough wealth and, in the early 1930s, Bush fulfilled a promise to his mother by buying the cottage where he had been born. He added two wings and a tennis court to transform it into Home Hall and it is now a boutique hotel. At the same time, he also bought 'Horsepen', a 15th century house in the village of Beckley in Sussex, to which he later moved with his long-time partner Marjorie Barclay. In 1941, while a member of the Home Guard, Bush made headlines locally for restoring the medieval wood carvings on the house's exterior, working to a Tudor design as specified by advisers from the Victoria & Albert Museum.

After the Second World War, Bush's novels took on more thriller-ish elements. For example, in *The Case of the Amateur Actor* (1955), Travers determines the connection between the disappearance of a teacher behind the Iron Curtain and the murder of a literary agent in London. However, while Bush is appreciated for the crime fiction published under his own name, he is known in East Anglia as 'Michael Home', author of 20 novels including nine set in Breckland, the vast and lonely borderlands between the counties of Norfolk and Suffolk. The series has echoes of Bush's own history, for example in the first – *God and the Rabbit* (1933), set in a thinly disguised version of Hockham village – a child wins a scholarship and becomes a schoolmaster while supporting his somewhat strait-laced mother from his dissolute and bullying poacher father. Curiously, Bush would claim that, as had happened with *The Perfect Murder Case*, the publisher had required the manuscript of *God and the Rabbit* to be cut by half. True or not, the novel was very well-received and a second followed quickly. *In This Valley* (1934) is a melodrama about a Methodist farmer and his son, an ambitious man with two women in his life and set on Fordersham farm, named for the ford near Bush's childhood home.

As well as the Breckland series, 'Home' also wrote an overtly autobiographical trilogy of novels – *Autumn Fields* (1945), *Spring Sowing* (1946) and *Winter Harvest* (1967) – as well as half a dozen "novels of military intelligence". These include a Buchanesque trilogy about an intelligence agent set in North Africa, the superb standalone thriller *The Cypress Road* (1945) and two novels featuring Major John Benham of MI5 who investigates a mysterious German prisoner of war in The Strange Prisoner (1947) and the disappearance of a collection of paintings during the Nazis' Occupation of France in *The Auber File* (1953).

'Home' also wrote a handful of short stories for magazines like *Good Housekeeping* and the *Illustrated London News*, as well as an annual called *Snapdragon* which raised funds for Norfolk and Norwich hospital. And, while living in Beckley, he was active in the social and cultural life of the nearby town of Hastings not least as a member of the Twenty Club "for men and women prominent in literature or art". He was also a popular speaker and a patron of local artists, on one occasion donating to an exhibition "a portrait of Mr Michael Home by Mr Christopher Bush".

But after his death it was revealed that Christopher Bush had another pseudonym. As 'Noel Barclay', a combination of the most common synonym for his given middle name and Marjorie's surname, he wrote *The Trail of the Three Lean Men* (1932). The novel is something of a Ruritanian thriller and has more in common with the Benham books of 'Michael Home' than the detective stories of Christopher Bush. It is nonetheless the author's rarest book and Dean Street Press are to be congratulated – and thanked – for making it widely available for the first time in a little under a century

In 1953, Bush and Marjorie moved from Sussex to the Great House in Lavenham in Suffolk where, while continuing to write, he again became a pillar of the community, opening art exhibitions and giving talks for example on the Breckland novels, and on how to be a writer. A modest man, he had no time for what he called "literary arrogance", seeing himself as simply "a public entertainer whose chief duty is to be thoroughly competent at whatever line of writing he decides to adopt". While never accorded the same respect by critics as, say, Christie or Sayers, he was elected by his peers to the Detection Club – an exclusive honour not accorded to as many writers as it is today. Many of Bush's novels have good ideas and interesting settings and he has been praised in particular for his ability to create and de-construct the unbreakable alibi, a trait shared with the "Alibi King" himself, Freeman Wills Crofts.

THE TRAIL OF THE THREE LEAN MEN

With Marjorie Barclay's death in 1968, Bush lost his enthusiasm for writing. He died at Lavenham on the 21st of September 1973, but he is still remembered today in Hockham where, in 1967, he unveiled the current village sign.

Tony Medawar

Chapter I
THE THREE LEAN MEN

SEEING Munro Burnside was a last resource. What I should have done if things had not turned out as they did, I haven't the faintest idea, but I know it would have been something desperate and foolish like joining the Foreign Legion – if they'd have had me. Not that I had a great deal to whine about compared with hundreds of poor devils who were in a far leakier boat. I did at least have that fifty pounds in the bank and was hanging on to it at the risk of emaciation, though I now knew the time had come when it would have to be broken into, and it had stood for me rather as a symbol than mere money; as something that represented the better days that would ultimately come and the better days that had long since gone. Moreover it was June, and one doesn't need a lot of clothes in June, or much food either for that matter, and if one wangles it circumspectly, even a bourgeois bed can be dispensed with.

In a way I suppose, I had myself to blame, since I was always an improvident bird; not from any spendthrift's make-up but because of a continually cheating sense of security. Let me explain that. An uncle brought me up and ultimately I went to Upton where I was a quiet sort of cove who might very well have dropped out without being much missed even if I did get into the second cricket eleven. In 1917 I was seventeen years old and though on the short side, had about me an air of young dignity and reticence that made me look not unlike the twenty I claimed to be when the doctor asked me my age. The first thing my uncle heard about it was when I wrote from a training camp, and then maybe he thought it was too late to do anything about it or else he guessed that with the incredible folly of youth that could see glamour even in a war like that, I should have broken from my hobbles again and joined up under another name.

The machine gunners licked some sort of shape into me and Providence saw to it that the bullet that knocked me out did its work cleanly through the shoulder. The same Providence ensured that I never went back to France but to Palestine instead, and there I was in time for Allenby's last show and went up to Damascus without a scratch. Being a bloke of no occupation I was not demobbed till the summer of nineteen – and with the rank of sergeant.

After that things were resumed for me much where they left off. I went up to Oxford and spent three drowsy years at Cranmer and there again I was a person of the supremest inconsequence and looking – so I was told – not a year older than when I joined up. Perhaps my five foot six and mournful, brown eyes had something to do with that, and my face was of the yearning type that suited admirably the wholly ridiculous poetic sort of soul who looked inanely at me when I performed my daily exercise with a razor. There was a time when I was so ashamed of this gutless looking self of mine that I dressed rather loudly and tried to grow a moustache, but the latter turned out such a romantic, Ronald-Colman-like streak that it made me more of a disembowelled poet than ever, and I shaved it off and took to smoking a perfectly monstrous pipe instead.

Three days after I came down, my uncle died suddenly and his affairs were so involved – farming ventures were responsible for the trouble – that all I found myself with was seven hundred pounds all told. I had never worried about what I was to do in life; we had never discussed it and I had always assumed that I should potter about peacefully and be much the same kind of gentle loiterer that my uncle was himself. But I had always had furtive inclinations towards journalism and now I saw my chance. I planned that I could live on two hundred a year, and I did. My rooms were in Hampstead and there I wrote three novels, only one of which was published and it brought me the sum of twenty-five pounds and the knowledge of what sort of agreements the unsuspecting and trustful author may sign. I also tried my hand at short stories, with what knowledge of life and with what qualifications heaven alone knows, and to this day I go red when I think of them. A dozen or so were printed in the cheapest of magazines, and as they were spread over a period of four years, they were for me what an occasional winner is to the punter – a will-of-the-wisp incentive to go on making a fool of myself. Articles of course I had a shot at, and I wrote a war play, and where they are now, unless it be in some pile ready to wrap up fish-and-chips or spring onions, I haven't the faintest interest or idea.

But I did grow up in those four years, and I even began to look something approaching my age. London is a great place for the unfrocked or uncloistered, and what the war mostly did for me, it rounded off. The day was my time for work, and my nights were spent everywhere – music halls, the streets, occasional theatres, at least two affairs with women – one, that looked like being too serious, I only escaped by a miracle, and that again I blush over to this day. I went to the Ring on Sundays and with a careless catholicity varied that with the Albert Hall. I did myself well in Soho restaurants and once ventured inside a night club. Then I had dancing lessons from a delightful woman at Earl's Court and joined a club which a casual acquaintance recommended, but I will say this for myself, I had no deceptions about being a great fellow in those days; I knew I should never be that, but I did get about a lot and I saw all sorts of people and I got plenty of local colour if I'd only had a gift for making use of it.

All the time, you see, I had nothing to worry about. There was still money in the bank and sooner or later I hoped I'd be making enough to live on. And then I had a tremendous stroke of luck. I tried the *Messenger* with an article on the Turk – it was one of those occasions when Turkey was prominent in the news – and to my enormous surprise I had a letter from Munro Burnside saying he would like to see me. It seems that he knew my uncle and had known me as a small boy, though I had long ago forgotten his name. One thing led to another, and to make a short story of it, I got a chance with the *Messenger*, and, more amazing, I must have made good. To this day I don't know how I did it. When I think of the self-conscious and decidedly nervous young person who sidled with curate-like modesty into the general room, I can't for the life of me conceive how I lasted more than a week. But I lasted longer than that. I was doing quite well in an unobtrusive sort of way, and once more I had no worries whatever about the future, even without the shelter of Munro Burnside's wing. I think too, I was fairly popular with the rest of the gang; I know I spent up as I went along and I still had a hundred in the bank.

They say that no man expects to die; the whole human race is bound for the ultimate and inevitable grave – but not one's self. That was the reason, when the news first got round that the *Messenger* was on its last legs, why I once more refused to worry. True I had never a relation or encumbrance in the world to worry about, but that was not the thought at the back of my mind. I knew I knew my job and I suppose Munro Burnside was somewhere in the distance of my assurance as a satisfying background, and I knew whoever failed to get transferred to the *Cyclone*, when it absorbed us, it would not be myself. But it *was* myself when the time came and that was the greatest jolt I had ever had. Munro Burnside of course went over to the *Cyclone* but I had no intention of getting back under his wing. Pig-headedness that was, and a certain resentful pride, and I also had the effrontery to think I could make good at the old writing game where I had left it off. But there were better men than myself adrift from the *Messenger*, and since my day there had been men at the other game who had got a firm hold and whose names were known where mine was not.

I stuck it for two years and then I began to be afraid. My suits had got down to one fairly presentable one and an unmentionable one, and the same with shoes, and my overcoat had lasted out till the April. Of my bank balance I had spent half and I was holding on to that last fifty as I told you. I weighed about a stone less and I couldn't well afford it, and I looked as little like a youthful poet as my wildest ambitions in my Oxford days could ever have dreamed. What had happened in those two years and the shifts I had been at don't matter. All I will say is that I was desperately scared, so much so that I made up my mind to do the unpardonable thing – make an excuse to see Munro Burnside.

It was a gorgeous afternoon of June, the kind of afternoon that always makes me think of a bed of stocks under a lozenge window; and I knew that Munro Burnside would be in Bouverie Street just before five, because I had made it my business to be dead certain of

5 | THE TRAIL OF THE THREE LEAN MEN

that one point. I'd invested fourpence on ammonia and had sponged my blue suit and altogether I wasn't looking too ravenous as I watched from the shade of Crome's doorway for his arrival. He came swinging along, prompt to time, wearing that light brown dust-coat sort of thing that he has on winter and summer, and ten minutes after he'd passed the swing floors I was inside too. The commissionaire handed me on to the waiting room and then a very handsomely dressed individual asked me if I had an interview, He rather irritated me, I don't quite know why,

"Yes," I said, and gave him a card on which I had the temerity to scribble "Personal," though that was to avoid filling in the usual form. When he'd gone I sat there and cursed myself for a fool.

And so I was, though not the way I'd figured it out. Things went well till I got inside that room where Munro Burnside came over to meet me with his hand out and a: "Well, how are you?" and then I knew not only that I was far too well dressed in that dim light that the drawn blinds made, but that I couldn't go through with it. Before I knew where I was I'd let him think it was a purely courtesy visit and I was airily explaining what I'd been doing and giving the reasons why I hadn't looked him up, though that seems cheek enough knowing just who the pair of us were,

"No hurry, my boy," he said, as I began the preliminary shuffle that showed I had to go and that he was busy. Then he shook his head. "I've always got ten minutes for your uncle's nephew though I'm not up to all this modern hustle. But you must come and have lunch with us. Let me see now . . ." and he began thinking forward while I sat there twiddling my hat and keeping the frayed side of the band towards me for all that.

"Thursday suit you? At twelve thirty?" he said, and went over to the window and drew the blinds. The room changed from dusk to midday in a flash and as he turned he seemed to see me for the first time – that is, as I was. He stopped short and gave that queer little sideways cock of the head with which the caricaturists always show him.

"You're much thinner than when I saw you last." If I hadn't been the fool I was, I'd have known he was taking me in from crown to sole, but I smiled at him brazenly.

"Oh, I don't know, sir. I'm perfectly fit and that's the main thing."

"Hm! yes." He nodded in agreement, then fired the question at me. "You wouldn't take a job – a beginner's job – on the *Cyclone* here?"

My face must have given me away. I flushed, I know that.

"Well, sir . . ." I stopped and licked my lips there, then I looked up at him. "I may as well tell you the truth, sir, but that's what I came to ask you this afternoon. I know it was an unpardonable thing to do – sending in that card. . . ."

There didn't seem to be anything else to say. He leaned back in his chair, finger tips together, and looked at me much as a kindly doctor might have looked at a poor patient.

"I know. They've been to me – dozens of them; as though I could do anything." He shook his head. "Things are bad – very bad. We've a waiting list as long as from here to Hyde Park and what I could do I did for men with families and so on. You see I didn't put you in the category of those in desperate need. You'll forgive me for saying that?"

"I'm not, sir. I mean I've not got down to bottom yet, but I don't think it's far off."

"I know." He nodded again. "It was a cruel suggestion for me to make, because I haven't anything to offer you. And yet I was thinking about you only the other day. Something you might perhaps do."

I looked up again quickly enough at that.

"That was an extraordinary good series you did for us," he went on. "I mean that series on London Streets. You'll pardon my saying so, but I didn't think you had it in you."

"Neither did I, sir."

He smiled. "It's good to hear you say that. But it was great work. The stuff that's always safe to print. Matthews could have done it better, so could Cope, but yours had something that sophistication might have left out. You never knew Tom Varlow?" He fired the question so unexpectedly that I couldn't have answered it, and in any case I didn't quite catch the name, and I told him so.

7 | THE TRAIL OF THE THREE LEAN MEN

"Tom Varlow," he repeated. "Taking him all round, the best youngster the *Messenger* ever had. But he'd be before your time and," he smiled dryly, "the old *Messenger* wasn't the kind of thing you people read at Upton."

He got to his feet again and stood with arms tucked beneath his coat tails and back to the fireplace as if it had been February.

"Tom was killed in the war. A clever youngster he was and he'd have gone far. Excellent linguist and so on – and an Oxford man like yourself. He did the most remarkable series – well, I can hardly call them that because they were too irregular in appearance – which he called by the lowbrow name of *Cuts from the Joint*."

Something stirred in my memory. "Excuse me, sir, but wasn't one of them a sort of skit on Barnum's circus when it was in England? Some imaginary collection of freaks?"

He laughed. "That's it. That's the kind of thing he did. There was one extraordinary interview he had – pretending to be a murderer – with a private detective agency. There was another about a man he heard in a church who sang each verse of the hymns in different voices – soprano, alto, tenor, bass. There was one about a suburban gardener who painted his garden roller – the roller, mind you, not the woodwork. Poor stuff as I outline it, but amazingly done." He laughed. "The funniest was about a man who was employed by a famous firm of scent manufacturers to beat the customs. He had a colossal amount of correspondence from readers about that."

"And how did he do it, sir?" I asked.

"Beat the customs, you mean?" He laughed. "That's too good to tell you. I'd only spoil it. What you must do in the morning is look up some of his work in the files. *The Man who Beat the Customs* that one's called. By the way you'll probably find they date a bit but you'll see the whole art of journalism in 'em."

"You mean, sir," I ventured, "that if I did something in the same manner – or near it – you could use it here?"

He nodded. "Yes, I think we could. It's worth a thought anyway. And send whatever you do to me direct; at my house, not here." He smiled. "But you're coming to lunch next week in any case. Bring a first attempt along then."

That may show you why Munro Burnside is what he is. What I felt at that moment I can't tell you but I got to my feet without saying a word. And as he came over he stopped at the window and glanced out. Then he went close and looked out. He stood there, head on one side, for a good two minutes, then his hand came out backwards and he beckoned me over without taking his eyes off the street.

"Look at those three on the pavement," he said quietly and almost as if they were three sparrows who might fly off at the sound of his voice or a sign of movement.

I looked at them. I couldn't have missed them, they were so unmistakable, and yet there was nothing obtrusive in what they were doing. Three men they were, each as lean as a rake. The first was at least six foot two and his face was the most mournful I have ever set eyes on. An artist would have hailed him for Don Quixote in one of his most lugubrious moments; and what was more, his was an inelastic melancholy; one that seemed fixed permanently to his face – a face that had never smiled since the day the midwife first beheld it.

The second man was about five foot nine; lean also and hard-bitten in a masterly, aristocratic way. His was the tanned leanness of the hunter; of the man who lives out of doors and wrinkles his eyes against the sun – and they were wrinkled up at the moment I first saw him for he was looking straight into the sun as he pointed out to his two companions the famous clock that hangs over the front of the *Cyclone* building, with its twin and hammered strikers and all the medieval artistry that Lord Ranksome transported from some German principality to adorn the outside of his new headquarters.

The third man was short; not more than five foot four, and his leanness was that of the jockey or the lighter kind of pug. There seemed to be something foreign about him too – or perhaps it was the sallowness of his face and the quick little gesture he was making with his hands that gave me that impression. And the queer thing about the three of them – I know it sounds silly to you as I write it – was that the three were so beautifully graded. A batten on the heads of the melancholy man and the jockey would have rested lightly on the head of the aristocrat, and their weights seemed graded in like proportion, and the whole appearance of them suggested to the most unnimble mind something of the queer and unusual.

Before Munro Burnside could speak, the aristocrat turned and the three moved off slowly along the pavement in the direction of Ludgate Hill, and it was only the short man who kept turning his head and taking things in, and talking excitedly to the others. Then the crowd covered them up.

Munro Burnside laughed gently to himself and gave them what seemed a series of valedictory nods. You'd have thought he'd forgotten all about me but he turned and took up the conversation where it had been left.

"I can see Tom Varlow handling that." He turned again for a last nod at the invisible three. "Amazing, weren't they? Like the three thin bears – the big'un, the middle'un and the littlest. Lean as rakes the lot of 'em. What a story!" Then he laughed. "And yet they might be three commonplace trippers who're just going to have a look at St. Paul's and then joining up with the rest of the party at King's Cross or Liverpool Street."

"But you didn't think that, sir?" It was a fatuous thing to say but I felt I had to say something.

"*I* didn't?" He smiled. "No, I don't think I did."

I was still standing there clutching my hat. "And what would Tom Varlow have done if he'd seen'em, do you think, sir?"

"I don't know. Probably followed 'em up and got all his colour and then made up some perfectly convincing and perfectly preposterous story about their being employed by a firm of slimmers. But I think I know what he'd have called it. The Trail of the Three Lean Men. He'd a great sense of titles had Tom."

He suddenly became aware of myself and the twiddling hat and all we'd been talking about, and the three lean men were forgotten.

"But about next week. You'll come to lunch? Thursday, shall we say?"

"That's very good of you, sir," I managed to mumble out. "I'll be very pleased if I can . . ." That trailed off into what I was thinking. He held out his hand.

"Come along – and bring anything you'd like me to see. We lunch at twelve-thirty by the way."

I was thinking so hard that instead of taking the lift I wandered down the staircase, still twiddling my hat, before I quite got where I was. Then I put on speed. Through my mind a medley of things were running – Munro Burnside who had spared me ten minutes of his time to talk to me as an equal so that the kindness of it and the understanding hurt more than any ingratitude could ever have done; the old days at the *Messenger*, I thought of them too, and of my uncle oddly enough; and floating across the sky of reminiscence would keep coming the thought of that man Varlow and his agile mind that could find a story in a painted roller; and as I became aware of just what I was thinking, I knew I was not hurrying along the pavement because I wanted to get back to where I had come from, but because of the three lean men.

St. Paul's, Munro Burnside had said, would be their next gazing place and that was where I was making for, and as I dodged this person and that and scurried for a few steps in the road itself, my mind was at work on just what I could make of those three when I had hung on their heels and heard them speak and got them as safely fixed in my mind as the view of the dome above Ludgate Arch. My mind, though I say it, had already placed them in the story that Tom Varlow might have written – some glorious and flamboyant advertising stunt with a droll and unexpected O. Henry ending, though that last would take some finding. And if things looked like working out well, I thought, that last fifty pounds might be drawn on – but not till I was reasonably sure. In the meanwhile the ten shillings or so of loose change that jingled in my pocket as I nipped along would last me out.

There was no sign of my men outside the cathedral front and for a moment or two there seemed to he no sun in the sky. Then I went up the steps and the sun shone again, for there, just inside the door the three of them stood, looking even more gaunt than they had done on the pavement outside the *Cyclone* building. Perhaps that was because they were standing stock still, letting their eyes roam round; and as their hats were off I could now see that the tall man was as bald as a badger and the short man had a frizzy mop of hair that his felt hat must have concealed. It was the short man who spoke first, in a sort of insistent, hurried whisper, that reached me clearly where I stood just two yards away. As he spoke I followed his pointing hand to the pillar on which a shaft of light fell, taking with it the red of the stained-glass window so that the stone looked splashed with blood. Also by some strange chance the stone was pitted and for a moment I almost thought that what he was saying was true.

"Say, Cap," he said, "take a slant at that. Don't it look as if some guy'd just been bumped off with a pineapple and mussed everything up?"

The middle man said something but it didn't reach me, and the three sauntered on. I moved on behind them and that began for me the trail of the three lean men.

Chapter II
THE FOURTH MAN

I FOLLOWED that party round as I said, without making myself too conspicuous, and in any case there were others trailing round – sightseers like those three – who covered me up. But I didn't get much for my pains. All that I knew for certain was that the middle man was English and the other two Americans, and I had more than a suspicion that both the latter were pretty tough.

When I got closer to the man they called "Cap," I could only wonder what he was doing in such extraordinary company, He seemed to be the perfect type of army officer in spite of the leanness that amounted almost to emaciation. His face was the red of an old farmhouse roof; hit narrow, clipped moustache outlined an upper lip that clamped down to form a mouth which was not in the habit of overmuch babbling, and the easy way he carried himself and the way he had of looking straight at and clean through things, gave him an air which the French would doubtless have called *formidable*.

Now I don't know that I have any cause to pride myself on the closeness or the accuracy of my observatory gifts, though in my job a man must naturally keep his eyes well open, but I will say that one or two things struck me as rather peculiar about the three of them, and let me add for the purposes of identification that it wasn't five minutes before I knew that the tallest man was called Spider and the shortest Marcel; and the Englishman, as I've already said, was Cap. Now the clothes of all three were brand new; reach-me-downs of the best class, in fact, and that in spite of that immunity from recognition which the full-page advertisements claim. Shoes were new and hats were new, and what seemed odd to me was that Cap was wearing a dark tie with his tweed coat and silver grey flannels whereas you'd have expected a man of his class to have on a sports' or club tie with a get-up like that. The other peculiar thing I noticed about him was that his hands were those of a man who had lately done hard manual work, whereas those of his companions were whitish and soft. Marcel indeed was so proud of his that as the party moved slowly along he produced a penknife and began cleaning his nails, thereby becoming I should imagine, the first to accomplish so blasphemous a piece of manicuring so unblushingly.

The Cap's voice, as you have doubtless guessed, had a resonance about it that was amazingly attractive. He didn't waste words either. When the party stopped before the tomb of a certain famous man, he merely let the general impression sink in, and his own contribution was: "You've read about that bloke in the history books."

"Sure," said Marcel. "I've read about him, Cap. Them Froggies bumped him off."

"Too bad," was Spider's only comment and as he said it you gathered that the expression was merely a stop-gap to fit the circumstances rather than any feeling of personal grief. I was to hear him use those two words hundreds of times, and he drawled them out with a long vowel in the second word, till with a voice less deep than his they'd have sounded like the bleat of an old, asthmatic sheep. His lips were tight too as the sounds escaped through the narrowest of openings, and the two words were the only ones I heard him use that afternoon, because when there seemed to be anything on which he wished to comment in a more happy way, he did so by a series of grunts, and they seemed incongruous too, coming as they did from the top of his lean, lantern-jawed length. And try as I might I couldn't place him; all I knew was that in his own country he would have made the prince of morticians.

Marcel reminded me of a sparrow, with the same liveliness and irresponsibility. I couldn't help smiling to myself as he moved unconcernedly along the aisle, trimming his nails with reverent care and pausing every now and then to look up or round and make some relevant comment. The very last minute I was close up to him was as they were coming out, and Cap halted them before Holman Hunt's picture of the Figure with a lantern knocking at the door. Marcel stood there, penknife poised and for the moment unused, his mouth slightly agape.

"Gosh, Cap; that's a swell picture! And who's that guy in the white shirt?"

The Cap explained, rather self-consciously, and Marcel immediately resumed his manicuring. Then he looked up again.

"I'll sure say he was some great little painter. Gosh! look at that moonlight, Spider. Don't it make you think of the night you and me was waitin' for Jim French's lorries? The way them lights was twinklin' over the lake?"

Spider grunted, then some personal memory rounded off the comment. "Too ba-a-a-ad."

"You two blokes had better lay off that personal experience business, or you'll be getting into trouble," said Cap quietly. "And come on! We'd better be moving back. Put that knife away or you'll be getting lockjaw."

Marcel put away the knife at once, and as the three moved on I thought I knew what they were; either an English rancher home from the States with two of his right-hand men, or else the English representative of a firm of liquor runners entertaining two of that firm's visitors to England. And then before I had time to do more than begin wondering which of the two was correct, I saw the thin, green package fall from the Cap's pocket as he pulled his handkerchief out and began rubbing it across his mouth. I was about two yards behind them then, and my foot was on the package and covering it long before the handkerchief was replaced.

Mind you, it was an unpardonable thing to do and all I intended was to keep it for a minute or so and make its return an excuse to get acquainted; so I stooped to tie my shoelace and slipped the package up my sleeve. As I rose again with a quick look round to see if the petty theft had been observed, I saw that my three men were already outside and I moved along after them.

By the time I got outside I saw them running, and I wondered why till they mounted the bus. I sprinted and caught it too, and followed them upstairs, but there I had bad luck and I had to sit in the stuffy inside, and in the middle at that, with an eye always screwed round to see if my men were getting off. Surreptitiously too, I drew the thin, green package out of my pocket and had a look at it.

I ought to have known what it was – one of its parts, that is – because many a time I'd carried one of those foreign railway tickets in my pocket, with the dark green cover and the apparently interminable sheets to be torn off; the whole held by the elastic band fastened in the stiff paper cover. This slim package consisted of four tickets, each for Levasque, or rather Montelle, and each ticket was a return. The route lay as I saw through Paris and Nancy, whereas one would rather have expected the usual one by Brussels. And who the fourth man was rather intrigued me. If he was to be as individual as the three I had already seen, then his company looked like being worth the seeking. And what my three friends were about to do in the tiny republic of Levasque was more intriguing still. They couldn't be going sightseeing because Levasque has little worth the seeing, unless it be the mountains, and Europe has enough of them elsewhere in all conscience. Indeed, the only thing with which I associated Levasque at all was its being the only corner still left in Europe where the laws of extradition were not accepted, though Greece, they tell me, is none too particular; and the way I knew that about Levasque was because of Blentner the bank swindler who skipped over there as you remember, and stayed there living like a lord till a decoy wench lured him just over the French frontier.

Opposite the Gaiety the three got off and made at once for a bus that was going up Kingsway. This time they were unlucky. It was the height of the rush hour and the three seemed disinclined to take their chances in the scrimmage. Then I heard the Cap say something and they moved off quickly. So fast did they hustle along Kingsway that I never came within listening distance. At Holborn they risked their necks with a dive across, and again at Southampton Row, and then at the Russell Street end I saw them disappear inside a hotel – the Mikado, on the right-hand side going up.

I went through the swing doors and nodded to the porter as if the place belonged to me. It was in any case that indeterminate hour between tea and dinner when hotel lobbies are usually deserted and except for a couple of old ladies chatting on a chesterfield there seemed to be no one about. But just at the end by the dining-room a man seemed to have been waiting for the arrival of my three friends; at least as soon as he caught sight of them he sauntered rather too unconcernedly towards the smoking-room and the three made a beeline in the same direction. I knew my whereabouts pretty well, having used the Mikado myself once or twice in the affluent days, and what I made for was the small drawing-room, hoping to heaven it too was deserted. It was, and I drew a chair up near the crack of the partition door and had an illustrated paper ready to hand. Then I listened unblushingly.

First I should mention what I had already seen of what I took to be the fourth ticket-holder. He was about five foot nine and thickset; not perhaps quite the aristocrat by the look of him but a man of taste in clothes, of ease in movement, and with an assured, masterly kind of way about him. In age he would be well under thirty, whereas the Cap was forty if a day, Marcel in the early thirties, and the lugubrious Spider anything up to fifty.

The first words I heard were: "Yes, Mr. Larkin." That was Marcel speaking.

"Damn you, Marcel!" came Larkin's voice: "How many more times am I to tell you to lay off that Larkin stuff? One more crack like that and I'll ship you home on the next boat or tip off the local police. Why don't you buy a bell and go round telling all the world who we are . . . ? The car all right?"

"She sure is, chief."

"And lay off that chief stuff too. Mr. Gimbolt to you and don't you forget it. Say 'sir' when you speak to me, wherever it is, and get used to it. You got that?"

"Sure I've got it, chief," said Marcel plaintively.

There was a kind of explosive, sardonic laugh, then: "Oh my God. . . . You're sure the car's all right?"

"It sure is all right . . . sir, and Mr. Lewis is all tucked up safely and . . . sure! everything's O.K."

"Good. Now you slip off upstairs and give Spider his French talk, then you two guys can get yourselves a feed and then turn in early. You got that?"

"Sure I got it."

"Right. Beat it."

There was the sound of the two disappearing, then Larkin-Gimbolt laughed gently. "Queer couple, aren't they, Prargent? How'd you get on with 'em?"

"Toppingly, thank you, sir. Interesting couple, as you say."

I should say that Larkin nodded there. "Capital. I'm glad you're doing that 'sir' business. You never know who might be around. We've got to watch our step from now on as I told that bonehead Marcel. You still think that's the best arrangement, for him to drive the car?"

"I think so, sir. He speaks the lingo and they're always less particular about a chauffeur. I think perhaps though, sir, I'd be ready for him at the frontier. A not too obtrusive use of backsheesh might do a lot."

There was an asseveratory grunt. "Hm! . . . Yes. We'll arrange all that. Now you'd better get into some black so as to look the part. I'll probably make a pretence of sending for you once or twice during the evening and you'd better take a suit or so down to the valet service. Oh, and you'd better give me those tickets before you go."

That was enough for me. In a couple of seconds I was out in the lobby and as I came to the swing doors I held the small, olive green package in my hand and showed it to the porter.

"I don't know whose this is but I've just picked it up. I rather think it belongs to the man in tweed coat and flannel trousers who came in just before I did."

The porter took it and had a look inside. His face brightened.

"That'd be it, sir. Mr. Gimbolt's valet. Mr. Gimbolt *is* going abroad to-morrow I remember, sir. Thank you, sir."

I smiled, nodded and escaped. A minute or two later I had cut back through Crevice Street and into Russell Square, wondering just what it was all about. Then I realised that I was decidedly hungry and turned into a tea-shop, and there over a cup of tea and a slab of their toast, tried to work things out.

Mr. Larkin-Gimbolt was one of my worries. Somehow I couldn't place him at all. He wasn't an American — of that I was sure — and yet there was something American about his choice of words and the very definite if fleeting accent. The man Prargent — Captain Prargent possibly — was of Larkin's own social standing and seemed to be treated as an equal although for the moment he was acting as Larkin's valet. Then there was the unknown Mr. Lewis who was all tucked up cosily, whatever that might mean — unless it was that he was a corpse who was being smuggled across the frontier. But it couldn't be that, because there were four tickets and Marcel, who was to drive the car across France, wouldn't be needing one.

Then what exactly was the game? Something big in smuggling? And why was it so necessary for them all to watch their step? Heaven alone knew the answers but there was one thing I did know, and I knew it in a sudden movement as my eyes ran round the slightly sniffy room where I was sitting, and the frowsty people and the hot, languid waitresses with perspiration on their faces, and the fly-speckled menu sheets and the saucer marks on the grubby table, and the smell of traffic that came through the open door. I knew that if I didn't make up my mind at once that the next morning would see me out of England, or on the way to Levasque – for that at the moment seemed the only alternative – something would go snap inside my brain. Whether I went under or not, I knew – and I knew with every feeling in me – that I must get out.

I think too that as soon as I realised that, I accepted it at once for a reasoned and certain happening, and if I had been challenged I could have found a dozen reasons for such an extraordinary resolve. After all, what was there left for me in England? Merely to try to fit into another man's shoes; to write as that Tom Varlow had done – that is, if one could, and I was a long way off being certain of recapturing the uniqueness that Munro Burnside had recalled so enthusiastically. But why worry about reasons? I knew that the morning would see me on the platform at Victoria, my fifty pounds in my pocket – or what was left of it – and my one suitcase in my hand.

As soon as I judged the evening conference was over I rang up the *Cyclone* and asked to be put through to Munro Burnside. They were rather perturbed about that till I told them that there'd be hell knocked out of somebody if I didn't get him quick.

"It's Don Temple speaking, Mr. Burnside," I said, my voice now meek as buttermilk, "I followed up those three men you saw from the window and there's something fishy going on somewhere."

It all seemed extraordinarily footling as I said it, talking to nobody as it were, and there wasn't anything but a grunt from the other end.

"What I was thinking," I went on, "was that I'd follow those three up, with a fourth man they met. They're going abroad tomorrow morning. To Levasque."

There was another little grunt from the other end, then a cool: "Why not? Got enough money?"

I gave a sort of sniff. "Oh, I've got enough money, sir. What I was worrying about was the visa. My passport's in order. I had it three years ago if you remember. I was wondering . . ."

He cut in there. He'd see everything was all right. The train left at eleven o'clock and I was to be at the *Cyclone* building at ten-thirty which would give me time. He'd also leave me some credentials which might come in handy – and once more, had I enough money? I said I'd plenty to get me there and back again, and then in the middle of my thanks he cut me off and I was left in the air with the receiver in my hand. And yet I was glad in a way because I should have babbled out something that would have sounded pretty poor thanks at the other end; not that Munro Burnside was the sort of man who liked being thanked.

The first thing I did then was to sprint to the Tube and make for the one room above Abram Gungelheim's furniture shop in the backwoods near King's Cross where I kept my belongings, and there I smartened myself up a bit and put on the hornrims which I use for reading, thinking they'd be some sort of disguise. The tiniest suspicion of darkening above my upper lip and a change of necktie, and I hoped that if the ubiquitous Mr. Larkin saw me that evening he wouldn't recognise me again when I was normal. Then I hopped a bus and made for the *Cyclone* building where I left my passport for Munro Burnside and then I made my way to the Mikado.

Already I was feeling quite a different man now I knew the step had been taken and I knew too that the change that had come over me was an extraordinary one, since I, as a newspaper man, was not in the least interested in the story that might or might not emerge from my absurdly hurried resolve. What I was interested in I hardly knew, but looking back on it now I rather think it was the cleanness of the cut that was seizing on my imagination. England had nothing to offer me except that extremely nebulous Varlow stuff which I was now sure I could never write, and there seemed moreover a fascination about going to a country so utterly different from all one's conceptions. And I had the hunch that my fortunes were bound up with those four men who also were going to Levasque; and suppose nothing came of that, surely, I thought, there must be some demand in a city like Montelle for English lessons, and there'd be a newspaper, and I'd at least stand the same chance over there as I had stood in London. In other words the change that had come over me was that I had suddenly become an optimist.

I waited near the hotel, till I saw the porter accompany a lady to a taxi and then I went through the swing doors. There's a public restaurant at the Mikado and I went through to the cloak-room and left my gear and then to the dining-room – dinner six bob. As I found I had seven and eightpence I hoped to see the evening out. Inside the room I looked about me and spotted Larkin at once at a corner table by himself, and by the time I had moved over to a table that got him in profile I saw he had just passed the fish stage. He was in a dinner-jacket suit and he had an evening paper propped up on the bottle of white wine that stood in the centre of the small table. He gave me a quick look as I took my seat and I noticed that all the time he was looking up quickly whenever people came in and that his table was the best in the room for that sort of thing.

All through the meal there was no sign of the other three and where they had their meals I don't know; and as for Larkin, the more I saw of him the more I began to like him. There was a something about him that was attractive; he smiled, for instance, at something he was reading, and the smile gave his face a charm which it lacked in repose. But there was nothing arrogant in his manner, even when he looked up or round; it was a quiet, reticent sort of watchfulness, and he spoke to the waiter like a man who has been accustomed to handling servants and who knows that one can unbend without losing caste. Hard as nails he looked too, and as healthy as a bullock, and for the life of me I couldn't gather anything else about him.

He had his coffee brought to the table and I noticed that he sipped his port before lighting the cigar. I had no coffee as my money wouldn't run to it, and when I had paid my bill and got out to the lobby, there was never a sign of him. In the cloak-room I removed the dirt from my upper lip and put my glasses in my pocket, then made myself come under the notice of the porter. He halted me at once.

"They *were* Mr. Gimbolt's tickets, sir. He's been looking everywhere for you to thank you. I'll tell him you're here."

"No, you won't," I said. "It's a pity I can't do my good deed for the day without being thanked for it. Besides, I'm not living here. I came in this afternoon to see some friends, and I've been dining here this evening. Mr. Gimbolt been here long?"

"About three weeks I think, sir."

"I see." I had half a mind to make some excuse and consult the register, but thought that would be rather too blatant.

"That valet of his," I went on. "There seems something familiar about his face. I'm sure I've seen him somewhere."

The porter nodded. "Quite possible, sir. The world's a small place as they say. He's only been here about a week, sir. Mr. Gimboldt's chauffeur and his odd man came when he did."

"American is he?"

The porter pursed his lips. "I should think so, sir. He has the look, if you know what I mean. What I always call a half Red Indian half Irishman look, if you get me, sir,"

I smiled because the description wasn't too bad. "I get you. You get plenty of them here I expect." Then I said I'd better be getting along and gave him a farewell nod. I ought really to have tipped him a bob, but I hadn't got it, and I knew, rather shamefacedly, that I'd never be seeing him again.

Next morning I was up with the lark. I paid old Abram a month ahead and arranged that if I wasn't back he'd look after my things till I rolled up again. That of course was after I had been to the bank and drawn out my balance. At the *Cyclone* building I was so early that I had to wait, but I got what I wanted, and when I opened the stout envelope in the taxi I found twenty-five pounds in notes to cover expenses. I knew that was Munro Burnside's own money and I knew I couldn't take it, so I scribbled some thanks on the back of the envelope and sent it back inside a registered letter. I suppose I was a fool, but how could I let the *Cyclone* grub-stake me in the hope of a strike when I didn't even know just for what I was prospecting? And as I had an extra five minutes I had the taxi halt at a men's shop where I got a thing or two for my wardrobe, and after that hopped in again for Victoria on the trail of the three lean men.

Chapter III
EN ROUTE

At Victoria I soon located one of my men. I had no seat reserved but it was not the time of year for continental travelling and I found a corner pew and put my case on the rack. Then I went along the platform as far as the engine and from there made my way along the corridor. Mr. Gimbolt-Larkin was in a first class corner seat with a newspaper shielding him from the platform. Where Captain Prargent would sit I didn't know but I passed him in the corridor, and not only was he wearing a black suit but he had shaved off his moustache. To be perfectly frank he looked not too unlike a butler. Where Spider was I hadn't any idea and I never saw him till we got to Dover, and as for the mysterious Mr. Lewis, I presumed he was on the king's highway with Marcel and the car.

There's nothing to say about the journey to Dover. All I did in my corner seat when I wasn't reading the paper or looking at the landscape, was to think of the wonderful things the clever people might have done; striking an acquaintance with Gimbolt-Larkin or Prargent, for instance, or even picking their pockets or removing their lighter luggage. All I could do was to sit there like a fool and do nothing; and then when we got to Dover and I was on the boat I had my first thrill for there was Marcel with a huge saloon car. It was black and with a bonnet that looked as long as a cricket pitch, and to my mind there was something malevolent about its rakishness. It didn't look a respectable car, if you know what I mean; it looked a pedestrian-slaying, massive juggernaut that could hurtle through a brick wall at ninety and never feel the shock. But the crane picked it up as if it had been a crate of oranges, with Marcel hovering beneath and swaying his body in sympathy with the twist of the chain. Spider was on the quayside too, looking after stacks of luggage, and when everything was shipped he and Marcel came aboard but I noticed that they gave no sign of knowing each other. As for Gimbolt-Larkin, he went below at once and Prargent must have gone with him for I saw never a sign of either after we moved off.

On the crossing nothing happened that would interest anybody and at Calais all I troubled about was getting quickly off the boat, so I mounted surreptitiously to the first-class deck in readiness to bolt down the gangway and get first to the customs, and there I rubbed shoulders with Gimbolt-Larkin, just behind whom was his valet with a couple of suitcases. I might have been mistaken but I thought he gave me rather a searching look, but as all I had to go by was the uneasy feeling that someone was staring at my back, I couldn't be any too sure. But I was in the first half dozen down the gangway and the first in the customs shed, and for a tip of five francs I again got a second-class corner – and in the through carriage to Levasque, though that latter was of no special importance since the carriage would be taken off the train at the Gare de l'Est and there hooked on the train for Nancy and Levasque, so that most people left the train at the Gare du Nord and dined comfortably in Paris, while those who preferred to stay in the train loitered for an hour or so along the Circulaire.

The carriage in which I found myself was a mixture, with two first-class sleepers, two ordinary firsts and the rest seconds. I was in one of the latter and it wasn't long before I discovered that Prargent and Spider were in another, and that Gimbolt-Larkin had a sleeper. I got myself some lunch at the station restaurant and made it do for tea as well, and then when the orange women had finished bawling and the engine had given about a thousand shrieks, we moved off and I settled to my pipe in the corner. And during that long journey to Paris only one thing happened. Prargent passed the door – mine was a window, not a corridor seat – and again I might have been mistaken but I could have sworn he had a good look at me, and within a minute of his getting back to his compartment, Spider came by and whether it was me he was looking at or not, he certainly stared pretty hard over at where I was sitting.

When we got to Paris, the two left the train and Spider was apparently in charge of the things on the rack. He had also provided himself with some dinner for I passed in front of his window when I got out to stretch my legs and there he was laying into a sandwich for all he was worth, with a bottle of something in the corner angle beside him. I sprinted to the buffet and got some odds and ends and made my meal in an empty carriage during that ghastly tour round the outskirts of Paris.

When we finally left Paris there were three people in my carriage besides myself – all of them French. I knew that my three friends were safely aboard and I spent my time looking at the landscape, till it began to get dark and then I dozed off. I think I must have slept pretty soundly because when I woke up the blinds had been drawn and the light was out, and everybody was asleep; as for the compartment it was so fuggy that the air reeked and my collar was soaked with perspiration. It must have been the braking of the train that woke me up as we slowed down at a station, the engine whistling furiously. Then the brakes began to drag and I decided we were going to stop, and to get a breath of air I made my way gingerly over stretched-out legs to the door and so to the corridor. Just past my door a man was standing, leaning on the rail, though what he could have been regarding through the window heaven alone knows, since it was dark as pitch outside. It was Spider, and if he had been placed outside my compartment to keep me under surveillance, he couldn't have chosen a better spot. He didn't even turn his head as I carefully closed the door after me; but then he hadn't any need, since the pair of us were so plainly reflected in the window.

The train came to a standstill and I saw that we were at Nancy. That might mean a goodish halt as our carriage would have to be shunted, so I got out and strolled up and down the platform. Except for the distant hooting and shrieking of engine whistles, everywhere was quiet. A few passengers descended mysteriously and furtively from the train as if afraid of waking the slumbering station, and I remember how deliciously cool everything was though there wasn't a breath of wind. Then I asked a porter how long we had to wait and he told me twenty-five minutes.

Just what happened then I can't say. I can tell you the unimportant things but when it comes to things that mattered, I know no more than you. I know I was looking for a lavatory, though why I patronised the platform one and not the train I don't know, unless it was that I didn't want to sniff the stuffiness again for a bit. But I found the place and a pretty dark spot it was. I remember looking up at the moribund gas jet as I stepped into the short passage that led to it, and just what happened then I had no idea. There was a thud at the back of my skull, and I remember a perfectly foul smell-and that's all I do remember. But I must have been carried from where I fell to the farthest and darkest corner of that filthy place or most likely somebody would have found me.

*

So much for the first phase. Altogether I was lying there for best part of half an hour. The first thing I knew was that I was still asleep in the carriage, and then I knew I wasn't – and several things told me that. Then I was violently and profoundly sick, and I was almost blind with headache. A minute or two later I managed to get to my feet and stagger out, and a pretty object I looked; my face white as a sheet and my clothes unbelievably filthy. At the back of my head was a lump that made me want to holler when I touched it – and then, with a suddenness that made me catch my breath I had a tremendous fear. I felt in my breast pocket – my trouser pockets – all my pockets. I had been cleaned out as thoroughly as if they'd gone over me with a Hoover. Financially and politically I was nude. Money, papers, everything had gone, and there I was on the other side of France with never a soul I knew.

I suppose I was feeling too ill at the moment to swear or do anything like that; it was like one more blow when you are numb with blows. I knew the train had gone for the station seemed absolutely deserted, and I remember I sat on a seat that was close against me and after a bit I noticed one of those small fountains set in the wall, and when I'd put my fingers down my throat and been sick again, and had had a drink and some sort of a wash, I felt a bit better. Just then too a train of sorts was due and a porter or two appeared. Before I could hail one of them he caught sight of me, and came along to investigate. A couple of minutes later I was in the presence of a *sous-chef de gare*.

You may think I was still pretty much of a fool but I didn't connect what had happened with any of my friends in the train. I had read of robberies in French trains and I suppose any foreign country after dark is naturally peopled in one's imagination with criminals of perfectly sinister appearance and possibilities. I thought some ruffian or other had been lying in wait on the off-chance, and I had been that chance. The station authorities were of that opinion too, and the police official who was called in at once, took all particulars and ended by saying he thought he knew who had done it. My French, I ought to have told you, is competent without any brilliant moments. My accent needs amelioration, as they say, but I can make myself pretty well understood.

All sorts of other things happened during that hour. They 'phoned through to the next stop – Santour – and asked for my things to be taken from the train.

I also had a tot of brandy and some coffee, after which I was unashamedly sick again and then I felt heaps better. I gave them my London credentials in case they wanted to make further enquiries, and I got permission to move on as far as Santour by the train that left at seven, and then, just when I was about to ask if they'd let me telegraph to London for money – that would have meant Munro Burnside – I had a thought that closed my mouth with a snap. There was another chance I'd take before I did that.

"Is it permitted to leave the station?" I asked.

"But certainly!" I was told. "But what does m'sieur wish to do? Everywhere is shut up."

I pointed out that the sky was already streaky and in a few minutes it would be light enough to see, and a walk might do me good. And so as to have a second string to my bow I asked if I might have coffee if I got back by six or so, as I had no money as they knew. Nobody offered me a loan but I was assured I could breakfast at the company's expense.

I waited politely for a bit before I did set off, and outside the station I began to feel more like myself again. Just at the foot of the hill was a square with a fountain in the middle and I had a surreptitious wash and dried my face on my sleeve. The sky was now lighting up and everything gave promise of a wonderful day, and as for myself, I walked on gingerly enough, my head feeling none too good, till I came across a gendarme and asked him where I should strike the route nationale from Paris. It seemed that I was on it, so I went on again, feeling the man's eyes following me, hatless as I was and with clothes on which the filthy wet was still drying out.

Just what I had in mind was the maddest of schemes but situated as I was I could see nothing else for it. All that would otherwise happen would be that I should collect my belongings at Santour – if they too hadn't disappeared – and then be transported back to England at the railway company's expense, and that was the very last thing I wanted. I was rather like a man who falls at the first fence and then follows the hunt on foot with never a chance of catching sight of it again but with some sort of satisfaction of going in the right direction, however slowly. I had made up my mind to get to Levasque and to Levasque I was going, even if I had to jump the frontier. And incredible as it may sound, I had still the hunch that my fortunes were bound up with the three men who had first set my feet on the road that led from England. That the police would ever recover my passport and papers I had not the faintest hope, and if they did, I could always send them word of my whereabouts.

I found myself in a straggly suburb long before I expected to be, and then came across the very place that suited my purpose – an extremely dangerous turn ahead of which round the corner one could see over a mile of straight road. By this time too I was feeling pretty knocked up and I sat down on the grass bank and wished that heaven would let fall a cigarette. It was a quiet sort of spot with only a villa or two standing back from the road, and there were trees everywhere to make it more countrified, and if only I'd had something to smoke I could have sat there till the time came to go back for my breakfast, whether Marcel came that way or not.

Before five minutes had gone I began to think it was a pretty forlorn hope. For all I knew there might be a special road that avoided the town, or Marcel might have taken quite a different route, or he might even have passed through the town long ago. But that I hardly thought possible. I doubt if he could have left Calais till well over an hour after our train left and since then we must have travelled at a speed that was well above his average. And while I was trying to work that out, what should come in sight but a car; a large one too that was coming on at a tremendous pace. Almost before I was aware of it I was out at the edge of the road with my hand stuck forward, but as the car drew near I knew I had made a mistake. It was too late; the car drew up with a skid of the brakes and the driver put his head outside.

"Vous voulez quelque chose, m'sieur?"

"I'm sorry," I said. "I'm waiting here for a friend's car and I made a mistake. I'm very sorry."

He nodded, then bent down to the gear lever. Then he straightened himself again.

"M'sieur est anglais?"

I wasn't in the least annoyed that he should have guessed that, though perhaps it wasn't so much my accent as my absence of hat that led him to make the attempt; and before I could say I was, he was showing me his knowledge of English.

"Walk, eh?" He waved his hand at the sky. "A fine morning, eh?"

I grinned and said it was, and as he seemed so friendly I thought I might as well try him for a cigarette, so I fumbled in my pockets as a preliminary, and then asked him in pidgin-English if he had one. In a moment he'd produced a packet of Maryland and then a match.

"Smoking good, eh?" he said, and smiled idiotically. Then as his vocabulary failed him he felt for the lever again, and said good-morning very slowly and precisely. I did the same and wished him good luck and we parted with a couple of dazzling smiles.

I sat down on the bank again, smoking my cigarette very slowly, and took out the letter I had written in the office of the *sous-chef de gare*, on official paper with the best purple ink.

> MARCEL,—This guy is one of us. You're to bring him to the frontier by my orders. His baggage has gone on.
>
> L.

Given the fifty to one chance that Marcel came that way, I thought that letter would fetch him, and once I got within reach of the frontier I could always make a get-away, or if I cared to bluff it out I could go to the end of the journey and tell my story to Gimbolt-Larkin and see what happened. And just what else could I tell Marcel? I began to think it over, and then all at once I saw another car, or rather I heard the blare of its horn in the distance before I saw the car itself. Then something told me that this time there was no mistake and from where I sat I could almost discern that wicked looking bonnet as the car hurled itself on down the straight slope. Again I stepped to the edge of the road, my hand held out, and a hundred yards away the car slowed up to take the bend and I walked clean out in front of it with my hand up. The bonnet stopped a foot from my belly, and I moved back again to the grass verge. Marcel stuck his head out just sufficiently to see me in the open and he kept his hand on the wheel. He was wearing a chauffeur's coat and cap and he looked smart enough in it though his face was grimed and his eyes were dark underneath.

"Eh bien, m'sieur? Qu'est-ce qu'il y a?"

"You're Marcel?" I asked.

His small, black eyes narrowed as I fired the English at him, and he hesitated for a moment before he answered.

"Sure I'm Marcel."

"I thought perhaps you'd think something was wrong on the train," I said, "but there isn't. Everything's going O.K. . . . And here's some new orders for you."

He gave me another wary look as he took the letter and when his other hand left the wheel it went to his pocket.

"You don't want a gat," I said. "This isn't a hold-up."

I stepped back clear so that he could read, and that took him only a couple of shakes once he'd slit the letter open. He looked at me and then he read the letter again. Had he seen Gimbolt-Larkin's writing before – or hadn't he? I held my breath . . . but he hadn't.

"Who gave you this letter, mister?"

"Doesn't it tell you that inside?"

That rather took the wind out of his sails for a moment, then he gave me another look that was meant to show what a smart fellow he was.

"Maybe it does; maybe not. Only you'd better say who the gent's name was that wrote it."

"What name's at the bottom?"

"It's an L and maybe you know what that stands for."

"It stands for all sorts of things," I told him, still standing well back from the car. "It stands for Levasque and it stands for Larkin. That good enough?"

His eyes opened as I said that last word and he made a movement to open the door. Then he hesitated again.

"And you say the big boss gave you this letter. Where'd he give it to you?"

"On the station platform where I met him. He expected to see me at the frontier but the cops were after me – or we thought they were – so he said you were to take me along."

He glanced at the letter again and you could almost see his brain working it out – the heading on the paper, the early hour of the morning, the fact that he hadn't been in communication since Calais, and all the rest of it.

Just then a lorry came into sight from the direction of the town, and I stepped forward angrily.

"Look here now; am I to get in this car or am I not?"

The look he gave me this time was from the collar of my coat down to my knees but there was never a bulge to disturb the neatness of the outline. Then he opened the door.

"Sure. Park yourself alongside me, mister."

I parked myself alongside with an assumption of deliberate nervousness.

"I say; if I'm going to sit here instead of out of sight at the back, hadn't you better find me a hat of some sort?"

"Sure." He nodded for me to get up, lifted the seat and found an old cap in the locker. It was miles too small for me but I balanced it over my eyes and got well into the corner. The car moved on. I don't know what the urge was to add to the genuineness of my already accepted credentials but all at once I thought of something and I said it.

"What about Mr. Lewis? What's happened to him?"

He stared round at me so quickly that for a moment his hand was off the wheel.

"So the boss let you in on that, did he?"

"Sure," said I. "There's things I could tell you if I wanted to open my mouth – which I don't. And got any cigarettes? If so you might give me one – and a match."

He lighted one for himself and then passed the packet over. I got my own alight and as we were now in the outskirts of the town itself, drew back into my corner.

"You'd better get a move on," I said. "We're a goodish bit late."

He glared round truculently.

"Am I drivin' this car, mister, or you?"

I puffed away unconcernedly. "And lay off the 'mister,'" I told him. "My name's Temple – Don Temple – and you can make it either."

A person of less terrifying appearance there couldn't have been found that morning in the whole of Nancy but there must have been something in my unconcern that came to him as a bewildering climax to the bewildering events of the last five minutes. Possibly he glared at me again; I don't know for the cap was well over my eyes and by the tilted peak all I could see was a narrow angle through the window.

Then to my surprise he came out with an, "O.K., Mr. Temple," and his foot trod on the accelerator.

Chapter I
JOURNEY'S END

As soon as we got through the town, and since the roads were clear that took us no more than ten minutes, I took off that cap Marcel had given me and got my head well into the corner. It was not aching now in the headache sense but there was a soreness that made the head numb, and if I'd been an honoured guest instead of what I was,

I should have tried to get off to sleep. As it was I watched Marcel, and the car, and the countryside.

The chauffeur's face looked less rat-like when you saw it in profile, and lost the hatchet effect which the cheekbones accentuated. In spite of the smartness of his get-up he was looking more of a gamin than ever, and once we were in the open country he began singing softly to himself, and of all the incongruous things – *Auprès de ma Blonde*. I had almost a mind to ask if he were French or Levascan, but thought the time not propitious for making conversation. His driving was magnificent and his nerves were chilled steel, and his judgment of curves and distance was superb. Once I thought we were for it when he seemed to be cutting in between a lumbering ox-cart and an oncoming car but he calculated it to a nicety without acceleration and the driver of the car didn't even curse at us. Once we touched eighty but most of the time we were doing round about sixty and we roared through most of the villages as if we'd been a visitation of the devil.

The country was all new to me and it wasn't very thrilling at first since we followed the river valley, and that phase lasted for a couple of hours. Then we began to climb and got to a sort of plateau from which we had a view of fields like an immense patchwork quilt, then we got more inland and the landscape was much more uninspiring, with vines terraced in the hillsides and patches of vegetation till we might just as well have been anywhere in the hill country of France instead of what should have been new and individual ground. Most of the hills we took in top and when we changed down it was fascinating to watch Marcel's shoes; vivid yellow with the narrowest of welts and absurdly pointed toes.

The clock on the dashboard showed seven-thirty when we suddenly slowed down just before what looked like an insignificant hamlet, and Marcel drew the car in at a tiny café-restaurant which stood back from the road. He nodded over at me.

"Come on, Mr. Temple. We'll rustle some grub in this joint."

That was good hearing but it made things awkward for me and for a moment I was tempted to say I wasn't hungry, then I tried a bluff.

"You'll have to pay then," I said. "Didn't I tell you all my money was in my things on the train? Damn it, I haven't even a cigarette."

He seemed perfectly unconcerned. "Sure. I'll pay."

He waited for me and we went over together. A woman was already at the door. Marcel strutted up as if he owned the car.

"Vous avez des brioches, madame?"

No *brioches*, she said. They were only for Sunday, but she had *petits pains* and in five minutes we were sitting outside in a sort of arbour place which sheltered from the sun, with a dish of café-crème apiece and a plate of rolls, and a small slab of butter for me. Marcel didn't trouble about butter; he dipped his rolls in the coffee and sucked off the ends, and the surplus which ran down his chin he kept wiping off with the back of his hand. There was no conversation till the meal was nearly over, and then I ventured on a question.

"Won't they be at the frontier long ago?"

"Sure," he said. "That's all arranged. They're stayin' this side till we get there, then we're goin' on together. Say, didn't the chief tell you all that?"

I said he might have done but I'd had plenty of time to forget it. Then he got up and called the woman and as soon as he'd paid up we got in the car again and set off. While we were sitting there over our meal I had noticed for the first time the two huge trunks strapped on the carrier, and the long, flat one on the roof, and though the easiest thing in the world is to draw conclusions, I took that as a sign that the party would be staying in Levasque some time. Then Marcel passed his cigarettes across and the matches, and as soon as I settled to my corner again, he began to talk.

"I reckon you've known the chief some time, Mr. Temple."

"Sure." The word slipped out, and it seemed to cover the ground. And it made him think for it was a good minute before he was ready with the next question.

"Then you must have had all this fixed back there in London."

"Sure," I said again, and then I knew I had dropped a brick and tried to cover it up. "That was after you left with the car yesterday morning."

That puzzled him again. "You came over in the same train?"

"Didn't I tell you so?" I said with exaggerated patience. "Didn't I leave all my stuff in the train at Nancy when I had to get away? You see it was this way," I went on. "I got out of the train to stretch my legs, and when I was down the platform I caught sight of a detective I knew, peeping into the carriage I'd just left, so as I knew all about you I tipped a porter to take Mr. Larkin a note I'd scribbled and I lay low till he brought the answer, and that letter I showed you this morning. You see," I explained elaborately, "if I'd only had the time to think I'd have asked him to send me some money too, but you know what it is when you have to make a getaway in a hurry."

He grinned. "Sure I know!" His face for a moment looked just like a monkey's, then it straightened. "I guess you've got acquainted with Spider."

"Spider?"

"Sure. The long guy with legs like one of them trees." He nodded over at the pollarded poplars with which the road was now lined. Then he grinned again. "Guess there ain't nothin' that guy don't know about a gun. He sure cut his teeth on one. Say, Mr. Temple, if you was to stand one side of the road and Spider was the other and you was to designate any particular hair on your head you'd like him to clip, he'd take out that hair like you was pickin' it out of soup. Yes sir! And you wouldn't know nothin' about it neither."

"I guess I shouldn't," was my comment. "Only you wouldn't think it to look at him. Not a very talkative gent, is he?"

"Him!" His face wrinkled up again. "Guess if you're playin' Spider for a sucker you've got a kick comin'. That's all a stall, see? The chief told him to keep his mouth shut and Spider's keepin' it shut. The chief's got a swell society act all fixed up for Spider." It seemed to me he was going on with some interesting revelations but he suddenly stopped talking for some reason or other and confined his attention to the car, though the road was fairly obvious. When he spoke next it was with another question.

"When we was way back there at Nancy, did I hear you askin' how Mr. Lewis was?"

"No," I said. "What I asked was where he was."

I don't know why but he seemed extraordinarily struck by that. He repeated the question in rather a different way. "Say, you're kiddin'. Didn't you say to me, 'How's Mr. Lewis?'"

I shook my head. "I don't give a damn how Mr. Lewis is. Why should I?"

He didn't say a word to that, but kept his eyes fixed on the road ahead. It wasn't a minute later when we began to go through a wood, thick with trees and undergrowth, with the sprawling hedge coming right to the road. Then for some reason the car began to falter. He did things with his feet but the speed slackened to almost nothing. He drew her in.

"What's up?" I asked. "Out of petrol?"

"Can't say." He got out and I heard him doing something at the back of the car, then he came round to my window.

"Guess you'd better lend a hand."

I got out at once and followed him round to the back of the car. What I had in mind was that we'd stopped at the very place for me to make my getaway. There to hand was the wood through which he daren't follow me and if he had a gun – and I was pretty sure he had – I'd be out of sight in the undergrowth long before he had time to use it. And the frontier was close enough if that line of mountains were what I thought they were. That was what I was thinking as I followed Marcel, and I was looking away to the line of mountains and then at the hedge for a handy gap when he spoke with a suddenness that made me start.

"Stick 'em up!"

There he was with a gun not a foot from my ribs and his face about as pleasant as a hyena's. My hands went reaching for the sky almost before he had finished speaking.

"What's the idea?" I began.

"Turn around."

I turned around and squinted at him over my shoulder, and I began to feel most damnably afraid. I could see both ways and there wasn't a soul in sight, and I suddenly went chill all over as I listened for the roar of the gun and my muscles quivered as I felt the thud of the bullets.

"Stick them hands down. . . . Now stick 'em behind . . . thumbs together."

He had my thumbs lashed in a couple of jiffs, then he lashed my wrists; after that he prodded me in the back.

"Get in the car!"

His dirty hand reached in front of me and opened the door. Inside the roomy back he made me lie down; then he lashed my feet and tied my wrists to my ankles. He didn't worry about gagging me for I doubt if I'd have been heard if I'd let out the devil's own holler from where I was lying. I couldn't see what else he was doing but he put a rug over me and then I felt him doing something else to my ankles and when he had shut the door and the car was moving off again, I found them tied so that I hadn't a chance of moving from the floor. It was cool enough there and not too uncomfortable if you weren't liable to cramp, and the only thing that troubled me was the bristles of the foot-mat that rubbed against my face and mouth.

I must have been right about the nearness of the frontier because in about ten minutes as I judged, I heard the whistle of a train and we passed under a bridge and the car began a violent downhill run that lasted another five minutes or so. Then I began to hear the noise of traffic and voices and long before I was ready for it the car made a sharp turn and the light was blotted out. By using my teeth on the rug I had now got my head clear and I wondered if I dare let out a holler, and then Marcel began the most noisy sounding of the horn as if he were summoning somebody to wherever it was we were. I heard two voices almost at once; one of them French and the other English.

"All right. All right!" the latter said. *"C'est moi qui attend monsieur. Allez vite chercher mon valet."* The voice came closer and I knew it was Gimbolt-Larkin. "Gee, Marcel. Where in hell've you been?"

It seemed as if his voice broke off and I guessed that he and Marcel were whispering together, and then I heard Marcel say: "Take a slant in there."

The door opened and the rug was whisked off me and there stood Gimbolt-Larkin with it in his hand. I lay with my back towards him but I twisted my neck till I could see him and I must have looked like a snared rabbit looking up at the man who's going to twist its neck. His face was absolutely impassive in the moment I saw it and then the rug was whisked over me again.

"That's the guy. Hop in behind and if he lets out a yell, sock him on the bean."

The door opened again and Marcel trod on my legs unconcernedly as he got into the corner seat by my head. I heard him give a little chuckle as he felt down for my head and drew the rug tight to leave a clear outline, and then with his heels he pressed me close in to the seat.

There was about five minutes of that and then more voices were heard; Gimbolt-Larkin returning and Prargent's low-pitched baritone and Spider's petulant bleat.

"You in the back with me," said Gimbolt-Larkin.

"Get to the wheel again, Marcel, and you two keep your mouths shut till I speak to you. Stop where you said, Marcel."

There was the sound of more luggage being placed on top and then the two got in where I was, treading well away from me and then hooking me back with their legs as Marcel had done. My head was now covered again and I hadn't any idea of where we were going; all I knew was when the road went up or down and for the most part it went up. In less than no time the noise of traffic had ceased and at any moment I expected the car to stop just short of the frontier barrier, though how I should be explained away I didn't know, unless the four were going to accuse me of trying a hold-up – in which case I might spend the rest of the day in gaol. But the car didn't stop. It went on for what seemed an interminable time – over an hour I knew afterwards – and most of that time we seemed to be going steeply down or up. Then the car did halt but only for a moment or two, and then it turned sharply and began to bump. That went on for a hundred yards or so, then it stopped altogether. There was silence for a moment, then the rug was pulled up off me and Prargent stooped down and cut the rope that held my wrists and legs. He also pulled down the folding seat opposite where he sat and I managed to get to it, looking sheepishly about me.

"Sit there," said Gimbolt-Larkin curtly, and before I had time to chafe my wrists: "What's the idea of this following us from England? What's the game?"

There wasn't much chance there for me to be heroical even if I'd had the inclination, and my tone was conciliatory enough.

"I haven't been following you from England – and there isn't any game."

"Where's your passport?"

"I don't expect you to believe me," I said, and I must have cut a pretty poor figure, "but it was stolen from me at Nancy." I bent down and showed the back of my head and rubbed my finger over the bump. "I was attacked at the station and the train went off and left me –"

"Too bad!" came a voice from behind me.

"Shut up, you!" I took a peep at Spider and saw him turn his face. Opposite me Prargent was sitting regarding me with never the movement of a muscle. I might have been a fly on a sheet of paper.

"Go on with what you were saying."

"Well, I was left on the station with all my money and papers stolen, as I said, and it so happened I'd heard Marcel call you by the name of Larkin –"

"Where'd you hear that?"

"In the Mikado the other day. You see I happened to be behind this – er – gentleman here, and the other two when they entered the hotel and I picked up a packet of railway tickets they'd dropped and I handed them to the hall porter, but before that I happened to be right against where you two were talking and so I went out. You see I didn't want to overhear your business, though it has happened to come in jolly handy."

He gave no sign as to whether he believed me or not. "And you just happened to be coming to Levasque too."

"That's right," I said. "I'm a journalist and I'm going to do a series of write-ups." An extraordinary good idea flashed through my mind.

"My editor had the idea of sending me out to write up the stories of – and of course I'm to try to get in touch with – various noted people who're sheltering here from the law. He thought that'd make a most original feature. There's Gorland who did that bank robbery and murder, and there's –"

He cut me short. "I see. And what's your name?"

"Donald Temple. Munro Burnside of the *Cyclone* is who I'm taking orders from about this."

I looked at Prargent as I said that, but for all the attention he paid I might as well have kept my mouth shut. Gimbolt chewed the cud of thought for a minute or two, and he scowled to himself like a man who finds thinking pretty hard work.

"You're expecting me to believe that?" he said at last. "You're actually having the nerve to say that you weren't interested in us at all?"

I think I was beginning to get my nerve back. The mere fact that I was allowed to talk at all made me surer of myself.

"I'm not such a fool," I said. "Of course I was interested in you. How could I be anything else? Wasn't it an amazing coincidence that I should be the one man in London to recover your lost tickets – I mean because I happened to be going to Levasque myself? Of course I was interested in you. If I hadn't been an Englishman I'd probably have introduced myself at Calais, only I didn't want to force myself on anybody. And if it comes to that," I went on, and this time I gave him look for look, "what law is there that forbids me to come to Levasque the same day as your party? Doesn't it strike you that you're making yourself very conspicuous by all this secrecy as to your movements; I mean this holding me up and tying me up – and all this questioning you're doing now? You must be up to something remarkably shady yourself to be suspicious of me."

His eyes narrowed. "Keep the conversation to yourself and leave me out of it. You poked your nose into my affairs most unwarrantably and you jumped my car by a cheap trick." He turned to Prargent. "What shall we do with him? Hand him over at the frontier?"

"I don't give a damn what you do with me at the frontier," I broke in. "I don't think I'd try a bluff like that if I were you. If you stop to think, all I've got to do at the frontier is to ask them to enquire what happened at Nancy. In the meanwhile I can wait this side till money and fresh credentials reach me from London. That may take a week or more and in the interval I promise you I'll send my paper the full story, *with names*, of just what happened to me."

That caught him clean in the wind. He thought for a moment, then got out of the car. Marcel got in alongside me and Gimbolt-Larkin and Prargent strolled on a few yards out of earshot. As I craned round I could see that we were up in the mountains in a side road that ended just on at the edge of a precipice; a road in fact constructed roughly for a car to turn, and out of sight from where we were, of the main road. Marcel offered me a cigarette friendlily enough and lit it for me, and in two minutes the two were back and the car was reversing to the main road.

Gimbolt-Larkin took something from his pocket and handed it to me.

"This your passport? We found it on the platform just before the train went."

I looked at him and then at the passport. It was mine all right and I didn't quite know what to say about it. When I looked up again the two were regarding me in the friendliest way in the world, and though there was nothing patronising about the way they did it, I felt a quick suspicion.

"One good turn deserves another," said Prargent in his charming voice. "You found something for us and we return the compliment."

Again I could find nothing to say and Gimbolt-Larkin chimed in.

"We're perfectly willing to take you over the frontier, by the way, if you'll give us your word you'll go with us to where we're going and make no attempt to leave the car before."

In spite of the way he said it and the way Prargent was smiling benevolently at me, I had the idea that if I'd have said no, they'd have had me trussed up again in a jiffy.

"That's good enough for me," I told them. "And if you'd like any more information about myself you can have it for what it's worth."

"That's all right," said Gimbolt-Larkin soothingly. For the rest of the journey till we came to the customs barrier, you'd have thought we were bosom friends though the conversation was of the stilted kind that marks Englishmen who have a horror of being thought too talkative. Prargent said what a jolly waterfall it was, and the other agreed, and I remarked on a peasant woman with her steep, crowned cap, and the others echoed my sentiments, and that was how we progressed for the next quarter of an hour.

At the barrier we drew up just short and all got out except Marcel. Half a dozen Levascan officials in peaked caps and with a profusion of that yellow adornment that one sees everywhere in that one-horse country, came fussing round. We passed through a wicket gate before the sentry-box sort of office and our passports were examined and our persons glanced at. All I could see, once I had got through, was the amazing figure of Spider. He was wearing horn-rims and a suit of grey plus-fours, and with his felt hat well over his eyes, looked as much like the undertaker of St. Paul's as I'm like Carnera. He looked indeed for all the world like a college professor taking his Sabbatical year, and he had a newly acquired way with him. When he said, "American," the official bowed. Prargent said, "English," Gimbolt-Larkin said the same; Marcel said, "American," and added something in dialect at which the official laughed.

I thought of the Forest of Arden and, "Now am I in Levasque the more fool I," and then wondered if when I was at home I really was in a better place. Out of the corner of my eye I saw Gimbolt-Larkin stroll over to where the luggage was being examined, and I saw him take out his pocket-book. Prargent stood with his elbow touching mine and I wondered what would have happened if I'd flicked my forelock politely and moved off.

In ten minutes we were away again with a chorus of, *"Au revoir, Messieurs,"* in our ears. Straightaway we were in a little town and then we climbed to the hills again. Ten kilometres perhaps and I caught sight of a cathedral tower and the smoke of what could only be a city of some size, but just then we left the main road and took another that descended to a roughly metalled track. We crawled along this for a further kilometre or two, and then came to a wide valley. Across this was what looked like a farm, with white walls and flat roof and vines everywhere on the slopes. We came to it from behind, as it were, through an avenue of ancient olives – the first I'd seen in that part – and the car was stopped in a spacious courtyard, with cobbled stones overgrown with grass among which innumerable fowls were scratching. Long before we reached it Marcel had let out a series of gurgles from the horn and an old man and woman were standing outside the door peering at us through the glaring sun. Marcel got out at once, face wreathed in smiles, and made for them. I heard him say what sounded like: *"Eh, la tante!"* as he threw his arms round her neck. Then Gimbolt-Larkin got out of the car and I made as if to get out too, but Prargent jabbed his elbow into me and wedged me in the corner.

"You stay where you are, Temple."

I glared round at him with a: "What the hell do you think you're doing?" but all that happened was that I missed the introductions and when I looked out again, everybody had gone into the house. In a couple of minutes, however, Spider put his head outside the door.

"The chief says for you to bring him along, Cap." Prargent took my arm and out I got.

Chapter V
MR. AND MRS. LEWIS

We went across the cobbled yard, the hens hardly troubling to get out of our way, and mounted the three tiers of brick steps that led to a stone-flagged corridor. Marcel was standing in a doorway that was just inside and he cocked his head upwards.

"The top of the stairs, Cap, you was to bring him."

I didn't wait for instructions but went on up the stone steps and just as we reached the top, Gimbolt-Larkin came out of the door at the head.

"Come along in here," he said and it rather sounded as if he were trying to be jocular. "Take a chair, Mr. Temple, will you. We'd like a little more of that information you were talking about just now, if you don't mind."

The room was a huge bedroom with the bed away in the far corner. The walls were whitewashed, the green shutters were just enough open to keep out the sun and let in the air, and it was a room I wouldn't have minded spending quite a lot of time in. A table had been drawn back from the wall and Gimbolt-Larkin took his seat behind it. Spider was seated behind it too, back on the left, and Prargent took a chair and mounted guard just inside the door.

"What's all this?" I said flippantly. "A viva voce examination?"

"Perhaps it is," said Gimbolt-Larkin, perfectly unruffled. "The point is this and I don't know if you realise it. You've virtually threatened us, and that's a dangerous thing to do."

"Surely that's an admission on your part," I said. "If you're afraid of me it means you've got something to conceal."

"That's not it. I admit we've got something to conceal, and I admit that if you wrote to your paper what you said you were going to write, then things mightn't go so smoothly for us as they look like doing. Mind you, I don't say there's anything to be ashamed of in any way. You might make things awkward and that's all." Then he gave me what was meant to be a remarkably expressive smile. "I suppose you don't know your whereabouts?"

"Not exactly," I said. "I know we're not far off Montelle."

"You're five and a half miles, to be exact, and you might as well be five hundred. If we wish we can keep you here just as long as we like. Nobody'll be a penny the wiser."

I showed an amusement I was far from feeling.

"Come now: you mustn't talk like that, Mr. Larkin –"

"Gimbolt, please."

"Well then, Mr. Gimbolt. There are people in Montelle who expect my arrival and they'll make enquiries, and my editor will want to know why he isn't hearing from me."

It was his turn to smile. "Wondering what's become of you, and finding you, are two different things. Still, we're getting nowhere like this. What we want to know is where we stand."

Spider cut in there. "What I say is, treat a square guy square. If he double crosses you, sock him on the bean."

"Though the latter remark doesn't quite go with Mr. Hobart's elegant line in pants," said Gimbolt gravely, "it sums up the situation. I don't say you're going to double cross us, Mr. Temple, but I'm not altogether happy about your story. To be perfectly frank you don't talk like a reporter for one thing. You'll pardon my saying so but you seem a different type."

"Oh, I know I'm a dud enough reporter," I said. "When I was on the *Messenger* there were men who hadn't had a tenth of my chances and who were ten times better journalists."

"Exactly." He leaned forward confidingly. "You wouldn't like to tell us some more about yourself?"

"I wouldn't mind in the least if it interests you," I told him. "Where do you want me to begin."

"Wherever you like."

"Very well then. An uncle brought me up after my parents died and I lived with him in Cambridgeshire. I went to Upton and joined up from there in seventeen. I was in the machine gunners all my service, and I was wounded in France –"

"Where?" snapped Prargent.

"Givenchy brickfields," I said, and he nodded reminiscently. "Then I went to Palestine –"

"Division?"

"Fifty-fourth."

"Brigaded with?"

I told him that too.

"Sorry, skipper," he said. "You carry on."

I glanced at Gimbolt and went on with my story; at least I got so far as to say I went up to Oxford, when I was interrupted again.

"What college?"

"Cranmer," I said.

He raised his eyebrows. "Cranmer, were you? What schools did you read?"

I ought to have given a start there but I managed to show no surprise. Modern languages I'd gone in for principally, I told him, and then he began firing more questions.

"Who was your tutor?"

"Henshire principally."

"Who was president of the J.C.R.?"

"I forget for the moment," I said, "but I think it was a bloke called Frent or something like that."

"And who was your scout?"

I smiled patiently. "A nasty, little bloke called Beedal. Chap with a game eye and always reeking of the bottle."

I saw him smile at that and that made me think a lot more. "And where were your rooms?" he went on.

"On the ground floor near the Memorial first," I said. "Then I got the chance of better ones at the top of the stairs."

"Any distinguishing feature about them?"

"I don't know that there was," I said. "There was a rather jolly window seat that looked over the High."

He nodded. "That's good enough. And what happened when you came down?"

I spun him all that yarn, with of course the same edition of the reason for my presence in Levasque. I did admit that I was damnably hard up and that I had to make good in the show or go under. When I'd finished he sat thinking for a bit, then got up, nodding to Prargent as he went out. Mr. Hobart stayed with me and as soon as the door had closed he took Prargent's chair by the door. It rather looked as if he wanted to try out on me that swell society act that Marcel had been so tickled with.

"So you lost your roll, young man," he began, and a college professor never spoke with a greater air of unbending.

"Roll?" I said. "Oh, you mean my money. Yes, I did. Whoever it was took every cent I had in the world."

"Too bad. And now it kinda looks as if you're in a tough spot."

"You think so?"

"Well, it looks mighty bad to me." He put up a lean hand and rubbed his bald skull, then he nodded at me. "So you was at one o' them Oxford colleges. Education's a mighty fine thing, young man. And you was in France too. Guess you was in some pretty tough spots out there."

"Guess I was," I told him. "But I had plenty of luck."

He nodded at that. "Sure you did. Education and all that punk don't cut no ice if you don't get the breaks. I reckon you know a lot too about them machine guns what you was handlin' out there."

The look that accompanied that was a pulling one. It was something like that of a small nephew who says: "Have you been in an aeroplane, uncle?" and there was also in it something dryly ironical.

"Well, I know a bit about them," I said modestly. "Not so much as you do about a gat of course."

He waggled his long jaws at that and I had to laugh. Then Gimbolt and Prargent came in again and Spider Hobart moved back to his own seat.

"We're going to put all our cards on the table, Mr. Temple," Gimbolt announced straightaway. "You give us your word that what's going to be said is entirely without prejudice?"

"Certainly."

"Then, frankly, are you prepared to come in with us? I gathered that you're in need of money, and the job you'll have to do will be a perfectly clean one. Why not drop this writing business if we make it worth your while?"

"Depends on a lot of things," I said. "The job, for instance, and what I get out of it. I'm none too squeamish, I might tell you, but I'd just like to know."

"That's fair enough," he said. "Still, I told you we'd put our cards on the table and we'll do so. It's like this. I'm an Englishman who was brought up in the States. I was at Oxford – at Cranmer – till a year ago –"

"Pardon me," I put in, "but I knew that. I mean, I guessed it when you recognised old Beedal."

"Yes, I suppose I did cut those questions pretty fine. Still, I'm in this show up to the ears and Captain Prargent here is too. Hobart's also in the know and so is Marcel. What we're after is a concession. This place where we are now belongs to Marcel's uncle and some extraordinarily valuable springs – radio active – have been discovered. We've had expert advice and we know we're on a good thing. There'll be a spa here and probably a casino. The air's as fine as any in Europe and the scenery can't be beaten anywhere. There's a fortune in it if only we can get the concession from the government, and the trouble there is that one other party is after it too."

It wasn't the lame way he made of explaining it all that made me doubt his story but the sight I had of Hobart's face. His jaw sank and his eyes bulged when Gimbolt came to that concession business and it was only too clear that he and I were both hearing the story for the first time. Perhaps that was why he cut in suddenly at the end with: "Sure it's a good thing!"

"I haven't any doubt of what you say," I said frankly. "Only, where do I come in on this concession hunt?"

"Ah," said he. "There we become intricate. We came to Levasque, as you know, by a roundabout way, so that we shouldn't be known. We didn't even cross the frontier by the Montelle route for the same reason but by where we did, and that was where Marcel had friends. We even took an extra ticket so that we could explain away the car and say Marcel came with us. Also we're splitting up here into two groups because there's going to be wheels within wheels. I'm going to a hotel with Hobart, who's acting as my uncle. Captain Prargent is going to a villa we've taken, and he's going to be just what he is and no more. What we were thinking was that – er -you might act as his valet – purely pretence, of course, though you'd have to take the trouble to know all about it."

He gave me quite an anxious look as he said that.

"And what about the pay?" I asked bluntly.

"That depends," he said. "If you're with us, all in, and scrap your newspaper work altogether, and give us your word to do anything you're asked – provided it's perfectly honourable – then we'll pay you a hundred quid a month with a bonus of a thousand if things turn out right. Pay to be in advance and you get your hundred now."

"Any written agreement?"

He shook his head. "You'll have to take our word. As you're being paid in advance, what's it matter? Besides, you'll also get your expenses from England to here, and that thirty quid you lost at Nancy."

"Sounds good to me," remarked Spider.

I laughed and that relieved the tension. Everybody laughed too.

"Right-ho," I said. "I'll take your offer. Trot out your money and don't forget to allow for what clothes I'll have to get."

Before I'd finished speaking he'd pulled out a wad as thick as a coffee-stall sandwich.

"We'll say a hundred francs to the pound and that'll save trouble. Your hundred – and fifty – and another fifty all told; you to get your own outfit." He told off twenty thousand-franc bills, all clean and new, and laughed as he saw my questioning look.

"It's all right. They're perfectly good." He put the wad away, and it didn't look any thinner for what had been stripped off for me. "That suit you all right?"

"Suits me all right," I said, making a small wad of my own. "I give you my word here and now to do my part of the job." And as I put the wad into my breast pocket with elaborate care I couldn't help a dig at Spider. "And if Mr. Hobart doesn't mind my saying so, if he should happen to want my roll I hope he'll ask for it politely and not sock me on the bean."

Spider grimaced sheepishly at that but Gimbolt seemed immensely tickled. He even hooked his arm through mine as we went out of the room, and then at the top of the landing drew me aside to the window to see the view. It was fine enough, I knew that, with most of the colours of the rainbow in its composition, from the purple black of trees to the snow still capping the distant peaks, but it didn't cut no ice with me as Spider might have said. I did ask if the mountains were in Levasque or out.

"They're twenty miles away from the far frontier," he said, and then laughed. "Levasque isn't so small as that, you know. It's larger than Yorkshire."

"And what's the population?"

"Rather dense," he said. "Just under a million, and a hundred and fifty thousand of 'em are in Montelle." He took my arm again. "We'll have a freshener and then you and Prargent had better be pushing on."

The freshener was a white wine of the country, of which we each had a glass. Marcel's relations were not in evidence except when his aunt produced the bottles, and after we'd drunk somewhat self-consciously to the success of the venture, the bags were brought in and some of the contents sorted out, and Prargent's share was ready to put in the car.

"Just a minute while we're all here," said Gimbolt, and ran his eyes over the lot of us. "From now on, what I say goes. Everybody get that. You, Marcel, keep that tongue of yours under control and think before you speak – and then don't! My name's Gimbolt to everybody and I never had any other. Spider's Mr. Hobart, and don't forget that, Marcel; and the same goes for you Temple. Prargent's 'sir' to you and so am I and so's Spider, and that goes with you, Marcel. Don't forget, the lot of you; one false move or one damn-fool slip and we take the next train for home. And lay off the booze the lot of you, and you, Marcel, lay off the women. You can all get tight as fiddlers' bitches when this show's over and you can all have harems for all I'll give a damn. You got anything to say, Prargent?"

"Don't think so," said Prargent.

"Right then. You two push off. And get that car well in the back way, Marcel, and then come back here for me."

Marcel got the bags out and the others came to see Prargent and myself off. Just as the captain was getting into the car, Gimbolt let out a yell.

"Blast you, Marcel! Is that how you've been told to let your passengers get in the car? Get out of that seat. And touch your hat, blast you!"

He made us draw back to the kitchen door and Marcel, without showing the least malice, held the door open and flicked his finger to his hat as Prargent entered. Then we moved off, backing out of the courtyard and along the same rutty lane till in about five minutes we rejoined the main road again.

The road was now uninteresting and in less than no time we were in the suburbs of the city, with gay little villas dotted on the slopes. If the approaches to Montelle reminded me of anything it was Toulon, and there was the same immense square sparsely bordered with trees, and the same clangy little trams. The only difference was the people who seemed shorter and darker, and the costumes seemed quaint with the men wearing those braces-like things over their shoulders and the women with flowing linen caps. Then we came to the first big shops and hotels and for the life of me I couldn't see any difference between the boulevards we were now going through and those of any considerable French town. Then when I could see that we were coming to an important crossing with a yellow-trousered Levascan cop on traffic duty, the car suddenly took a sharp turn and began to climb the slope. In a couple of minutes we were among the villas and looking down on the town, and then long before I expected it, the car stopped and Marcel nipped out like a streak and opened the doors that led to the garden behind a villa whose flat roof was all that could be seen from where we were. We passed through into a garage that seemed ridiculously long and no sooner were we through the doors than Marcel nipped out again and locked them behind us. He flicked his hat to Prargent.

"Everything O.K., sir. Want the baggage off?"

"Yes," said Prargent, and I knew that whoever else Marcel was free and easy with it wouldn't be with him. I noticed too that Prargent had a sudden feeling of uneasiness when the baggage was mentioned. He turned to me.

"You lend a hand too . . . Donald. That'd better be your name while you're here. Make a note of that, Marcel, and don't let's have any slips."

The inner doors of the garage opened on a small courtyard, paved with immense flagstones, in the middle of which was a huge plane tree with a wooden seat all round it. The back of the villa was the precise counterpart of thousands of other villas; walls a pinky, anaemic red, and shutters a vivid green. A couple of shrubs in tubs flanked the back door and a vine trailed up the space between the windows. Inside, the house was stone flagged too on the ground floor, except for a species of drawing-room, and along the whole front, which faced due south, ran a stone verandah with glass top. The garden, which seemed about a cricket pitch in length, fell away sharply down the hill towards the town, and below it lay more and more villas, and then the town with the cathedral standing clear in the great square, then more villas dotting the far slope, and then the distant line of hills through which the river could be seen like a white snake in a trough of green.

There was nothing special about the bedrooms except that a narrower verandah ran in front of them too, only it had no roof. Mine was a tiny room facing west but a pill-box would have held all my luggage, and I remember that when I thought of that I felt my fob pocket instinctively to see if my wad of notes was safe. Then when the luggage had all been brought in we stood for a minute just inside the back door and I wondered what we were waiting for. Marcel gave Prargent a quick look.

"All right," said Prargent. "Come along Donald. You'll know about it sooner or later and we might as well start now."

Inside the garage Marcel did something to the side of the bodywork just above the petrol tank, and when he'd done the same to the other side a metal covering fell clear and he thrust his arm in the space. What he brought out, one after the other, were a couple of machine guns and half a dozen trays and what would probably amount to some hundreds of shells. When he replaced the metal cover, I couldn't for the life of me have found the joints.

"We had that made in London specially," said Prargent, looking down at the heap on the concrete floor, and when I caught Marcel's eye I'll swear he gave me a wink. "We didn't know if we could get anything of the sort here."

"I see," I said, and saw nothing at all. "I suppose the idea is that when you get the concession it'll have to be protected."

"That's it," he told me. "This is a pretty long way off the map, you know."

I nodded for the want of something better to do, then pointed at the guns. "Where do you want these put?"

But Marcel knew all about that and we carted the whole lethal collection to a cellar that lay beneath the dining-room, with steps leading down from a trapdoor under the carpet. Then Marcel expressed the opinion that he'd better be pushing on again and I had to watch outside by the road and give him the signal everything was clear, and when he swung the car out he roared off with never a stop. Then Prargent locked the outer doors again and when we were back in the house he dropped into a wicker chair in the dining-room and offered me a cigarette. We smoked for a minute or two, looking at that wonderful view across the valley, and then I ventured on a feeler.

"So that was Mr. Lewis, was it?"

He smiled. "You've got it. How'd you tumble to it first? Hear us talking at the Mikado?"

I owned up.

"Pretty lucky break for you, wasn't it?" he went on. "If you hadn't asked Marcel that damn-fool question you'd never have got a ride in the car."

"Sort of password, was it?"

"Yes," he said. "Sounds silly, doesn't it, when you think of it here in cold blood. Only Gene – sorry! – Gimbolt wasn't taking any chances. If anybody approached Marcel on the journey while he was separated from us, he'd know if that person was genuine if he mentioned Mr. Lewis. Marcel had to say Mr. Lewis was safely tucked up, and then the other would ask about Mrs. Lewis too. That's where you went wrong when Marcel gave you the twice-over."

I said I certainly had been lucky and I knew I didn't mean it. As a matter of fact I hardly knew what I did mean with everything so strange – Prargent himself, the villa, my own circumstances with all their uncertainty, and above all the utter incredibility of the Balkan-like landscape at which I was looking. Then I realised that I was most damnably hungry.

"Want that 'sir' business kept up?" I asked.

"After to-day most certainly yes," he said. "The cook comes in late to-night. Name's Moulines, a widow, so I'm told. She cooks and you do the housework between you."

"And what about rustling up something now?"

I asked.

He glanced at his watch and seemed surprised at the time. Then he found me a hat which fitted pretty well and as it wouldn't do for us to be seen together, I went out first by the door that was let in the wall by the garage. So long as I was in by eight that night everything would be all right and after my meal I was proposing to do a bit of shopping and then look over the sights.

Prargent had a last word with me as he prepared to shut the door after me.

"There's a rather swagger restaurant place in Granard Square – the Café-Restaurant Granard it's called – you'll find jolly good for meals. I'd rather like to hear what you think of it."

"You be there too?" I asked.

"Maybe. Cut me dead if I am."

"You bet your life I will . . . sir." A dry smile passed over his face when I said that and I had an idea that things with Captain Prargent weren't going to be so bad after all.

Chapter VI
THE RESTAURANT GRANARD

The alarm clock woke me at seven o'clock the following morning and I tumbled promptly out of bed. There was no hardship in that because the sun was shining out of a clear sky and it wasn't long before I learned that the morning up till about ten o'clock was the best part of the day. The clothes I donned were black and I had a little white apron to put on when I took off my short jacket to do housework. Captain Prargent liked his early morning cup of tea and I made it for the pair of us. When I said: "Good morning, sir," he gave me a: "Good morning, Donald," with a naturalness that would have made one think I'd been in his service for years. Then I filled the bath with cold water and made my way back to the kitchen where Mme. Moulines was already at work.

She was short and asthmatic; distressingly so in fact. When she first spoke to me she wheezed so badly that I thought for a moment she had suddenly been taken ill. But she was a good-hearted soul and as placid as they make 'em, and I never saw her ruffled, but I learned later she was a distant relation of the Marcel family and that may have had something to do with her rapid settling down. And one thing I soon learned was that Prargent's airy distribution of work had been all wrong. Mme. Moulines' place was the kitchen and the whole of the housework was mine, and every morning at eight-thirty she waddled forth to some market or other and returned at about ten staggering under a bag or two of purchases.

At eight up went the captain's coffee and rolls and while he was dressing I had my meal in the kitchen with madame. Then I made the beds – but not hers – and got rid of any dust I saw about. There were shoes to clean too and general valeting to do and I learned to put a crease in a pair of bags by the aid of a wet towel and a hot iron. Sometimes I did things with vegetables and I set out the table for the captain's lunch and cleared away when he had finished.

At one-thirty came the siesta when I stripped entirely and lay on the bed with a towel under me and another round my middle.

THE TRAIL OF THE THREE LEAN MEN

At four o'clock precisely I had to take the captain a cup of tea to his bedroom and then I was free whether he was dining in or not. If he was dining out it didn't matter when I got in, but if there was a meal to supervise I had to be in by seven at the latest.

That first day Prargent was out to tea and dinner so I had plenty of time to myself, but before he went he gave me two things: a key of my own and an entirely new passport which had been amazingly well made up from the one I had given him the previous night. Who did it and where I haven't the least idea, but it was the very spit of my old one except that I was therein described as a gentleman's servant. I did see that my photograph had been removed from the old one and put on the new, and everything else, including the pontifical flourish of His Majesty's Principal Secretary of State for Foreign Affairs, was in to the last curl and comma. I took it and said nothing. Twenty-five quid a week – payable in advance – was meant to cut out questioning.

Not that I hadn't done the devil of a lot of questioning to myself, mind you. What my twenty-five quid was for and what the idea of the whole show was, were things that weren't often out of my mind during those first twenty-four hours. Granted that the concession scheme was all bunkum, I didn't quite see what was to take its place, and where Mr. and Mrs. Lewis came in was more puzzling still. I did try to fit in a bank robbery and a train hold-up but neither filled the frame. Still, I wasn't worrying. As Hobart might have said, I was sitting pretty. I had over a hundred and seventy-five pounds in thoroughly good money and I was fitted out with clothes, and what was far more to the point, whatever the gang was up to affected my ultimate safety little. I had only to call in Munro Burnside – however far off he might seem from Montelle – and prove my identity as a pressman – tell the whole story in fact – and I didn't see how I could be held as an accomplice. Not that I should have given anybody away; I couldn't have done that and kept my word, but I should have played the innocent; and remember I had a face that would have convinced any examining magistrate of my liability to be led astray.

That afternoon therefore, when my master had gone out, I had a cup of tea myself from the same pot; changed – which means I put on a coloured necktie – and made my way down to the town. Our street was the Rue St. Paulette and the villa was the Villa Marguerite – a hackneyed enough name in all conscience. The way to the town was all downhill and to reach the Place Granard took just ten minutes. I went straight to that restaurant where I had had lunch the previous day, and I went there for more than one reason. When I got in the previous night Prargent and I had had quite a long chat before we turned in. It was a sweltering night in any case and it was good to sit out on the verandah and smoke in the dark with nobody to distinguish us as master and man. He told me never a thing about himself; what he was interested in were my wanderings of the afternoon and evening, and especially he seemed anxious to know what my impressions were of the Café-Restaurant Granard. I don't mean to say that he showed deliberate interest; it was that in that quiet, fatherly, good-of-the-regiment manner of his he introduced the subject and kept it to the foreground. As for my general wanderings, all I could tell him was that I thought the cathedral magnificent outside and tawdry in; that the shops were as good as most of those in the largest French provincial cities, and that the Musée would probably be the place where my spare time would often be spent.

As for the Restaurant Granard, all I could say was that it was a colossal place, evidently *the* place, and that I had an excellent lunch there for a reasonable price. When Ed dropped in again just before seven o'clock, it had been full. A sort of cabaret was going on and what I didn't tell him was that a most charming looking girl had sung three songs, and had caught my eye for some reason or other and had answered my tentative smile.

Then, as I said, he asked me all sorts of questions about it, the people there; any Americans, for instance, or English? What he was getting at I didn't know and I'm afraid I wasn't much use to him; still, you see there was some reason for my making a bee-line for the Restaurant Granard that afternoon, and my experience of it was to be better than I could have thought. For one thing the sliding glass panels were all drawn back and the long facade was open to the street and shortly after six, when the really fresh breaths of air came

57 | THE TRAIL OF THE THREE LEAN MEN

down from the hills the whole population of the city seemed to be promenading before where I sat. Before me was the huge Place with its enormously wide pavement surround, and along this everybody went, round and round; fat little civil servants gesticulating; young bloods in berets and sports' clothes; graver officials; some of the military in the eternal yellow trousers; women of heavy virtue and many of lighter; children with and without their parents – in fact the most varied and inexhaustible pageant went by my seat, and all the spectacle cost merely the price of a drink.

Then I heard the small orchestra tuning up in the large hall behind me and I made a move in their direction in the hope of seeing the girl who had smiled at me so unexpectedly twenty-four hours before. I never had been much of a chap for women and it was the unexpectedness of the thing that had intrigued me, and I was in any case making sure that nothing should come of it in view of Gimbolt's famous final speech on the parade ground about laying off the women.

As soon as I got inside the hall the first person I caught sight of was Hobart, tucked away in a corner where he could see everything and not be too well seen. His felt hat was well over his eyes and he was wearing enormous hornrims, and when I entered he gave a quick little look and then paid no more attention to me. But whoever came in he did the same, and then he'd busy himself with the paper he was supposed to be reading, and he'd sip the drink that stood at his elbow. And I'll say this for him – he wasn't aggressively American in appearance; indeed, but for the hornrims he might have been one of the middle aged gentlemen of solid social standing who were promenading so resolutely round and round the Place Granard.

Though I didn't know it at the time, things were to happen to me that evening that would change everything in my hitherto humdrum life. It's funny how things happen, how one thing leads to another. Just before I left England I was talking to a man who bought a small place in Sussex with an orchard behind, and he'd told himself that that was all the land he wanted. Then he cut down the hedge that grew into his orchard trees and saw the meadow beyond them for the first time, and being afraid somebody should build on it and spoil his view he bought the meadow, only to find that people came in Spring into the wood beyond it to pull the bluebells, so he bought the little wood too. That was how it was with me that night though I didn't know it, as I said.

First of all, while the orchestra were playing an extract from *Turandot*, an artist fellow came and sat down alongside me on the red plush seat, and opened an enormous portfolio. What I didn't like was the way he took me for granted, with his pidgin English and his assumption that all English were inartistic fools. I had a glance at the horrors inside the portfolio and told him I wasn't a buyer. When he began to expatiate on their merits and pester me, I turned my back on him and listened to the orchestra.

The curious thing about him was that I ought not to have been taken in by his appearance for if ever a man stepped straight out of *La Bohème* it was he, with his enormous, slouched hat and velvet jacket and baggy breeks and flowing black tie. When he'd left me I watched him out of the corner of my eye and saw him going round the hall, and more than once he did a bit of business. It was only when the waiter brought me my next bock that I noticed the card he'd left beside me – M. Etienne Monard, rue Montguichet 24.

Then another man came and sat down beside me for the hall had filled up and by now there weren't many vacant seats. I took a peep at him and liked the look of him. He was wearing dark clothes and a broad, black hat and his dark, firm-looking face was clean shaved except for a thick, badger moustache that covered his upper lip and stopped short at the ends of his mouth. It was a quiet, scholarly face and there seemed something patrician about his reserve as he sat there without calling a waiter or drawing attention to himself. But a waiter soon saw him and came bustling across, face wreathed in smiles. They spoke German and I couldn't gather what they were saying but I could see the waiter was enormously and affectionately deferential and the other was gracious and friendly.

Beer in a long glass and the current *Impression* came for my neighbour and a minute or so afterwards I felt pins and needles in my crossed legs and unhooked them, and kicked his shins in the process. The English words popped out before I knew it.

"I say, I'm awfully sorry."

"That's all right," he said, just like that, and smiled at me gently. "Not much room under these tables, is there."

I smiled too. "You'll pardon me," I said, "but aren't you English?"

He shook his head. "Afraid not. I'm German – at the moment. I'm getting naturalised here in a month or so."

I was extraordinarily surprised. We hear all sorts of rot about foreigners speaking English perfectly, but this man didn't speak English perfectly, if you know what I mean. He *was* English from all you could gather and he spoke the English that has an English background to it. I think he must have noticed my surprise because he began to explain. "You think I speak English well?"

"If you'll pardon my saying so, you speak it just as well as I do," I said. "Why, you must have spent years in the country – and even then you couldn't have done it."

"Oh, I don't know," he said diffidently. "Those things help a lot you know." He noticed my empty glass. "You'll have another drink?"

"Very good of you, but I won't," I said. "I'm going in to dinner in a few moments." I don't know why I told him but I did. "The fact of the matter is," I said, "there was a girl singing here last evening and I rather wanted to hear her again, or I'd have been in to dinner now."

He nodded as if to himself. "You mean Mademoiselle Lucille Brock?"

"I don't know what her name is," I said, "but she was a jolly pretty girl. Awful good voice too. And by the way she looked as if she might be English"

He nodded again. "She is. She came over with a French company that got stranded in Montelle and she got a job here. Two months ago, that was. I know her well."

There was no particular pride in the way he said it; it was merely a statement of fact, but it interested me.

"How topping!" was my remark, and the fatuity of it was drowned by a sudden burst of clapping and I looked up to see on the low platform the very girl we'd been talking about. My neighbour saw her too and swivelled himself round sideways to me.

She was shortish and slim and with a young figure as taut as an ash-plant. Her hair was fair and though you couldn't have called her beautiful she had the jolliest smile and the most laughing pair of eyes you'd ever wish to see. Her cheeks had just a touch of colour in them and when she smiled she showed the whitest row of neat little teeth, and two dimples came in her cheeks just above the corners of her mouth. I noticed all that because the song she was singing was in German and I didn't understand a word of it, but there was a burst of clapping when she finished the first verse and people came crowding in from the pavement tables and craned their heads at the end of the hall.

But even if I couldn't understand a word she was singing, I knew she had that one thing which makes every song intelligible – a perfectly attractive personality. She had all sorts of little gestures that took the audience into her confidence, and she would nod at them and laugh and shake her head as if she were telling them something intimate and personal, and when the song suddenly left the almost talking voice she had used and finished on a clear top note, there was a roar of cheering and I clapped my hands as frantically as the best of them. My neighbour smiled at me and clapped gently too.

Next she sang a song in Levascan dialect and in the middle of it he bent forward and whispered to me,

"I taught her that." From which I gathered he had taught her the words and the pronunciation, but whoever was responsible for it the audience took it rapturously and she had to sing it twice. Then she came forward and spoke.

"I will now sing a song in English – a song of my own country. It is a love-song – what you call a *chanson d'amour*."

She had a beautiful speaking voice with never a trace of affectation in it. I wondered what she was going to sing and when the piano struck the first chord or two I knew. It was "Annie Laurie" she sang this time and she sang it without a gesture in a voice as sweet as a robin's in October. I sat through it hardly daring to breathe and my

61 | THE TRAIL OF THE THREE LEAN MEN

neighbour leaned forward, face cupped in his hands, as if he didn't want to miss a syllable, and as for the hall, it was quiet as death till she had finished and then it burst into a perfect frenzy of cheering and she had to sing the last verse again.

When at last she'd gone and the orchestra broke into a waltz, my neighbour turned to me.

"You liked her?"

My face beamed. "Topping, wasn't she. Jolly fine, don't you think, to see an English girl like that out here? I mean, sort of doing credit . . ." I broke off, but not before the brick had been dropped.

"Sorry! I forgot you weren't English yourself."

He smiled. "That's all right. I see what you mean." Then he nodded his head and gave a wry sort of smile. "I think I have some English blood in me somewhere or I shouldn't admire your people as I do. And I'm always getting the most tremendous longing to go to London – though what I'd do if I got there I don't know, except see the sights."

I was simply bursting to ask him all sorts of questions but just then there was a voice at his elbow and there was the girl who had come through the side door by where we were sitting, and I knew just why my neighbour had chosen that particular seat.

She said: "Ah, there you are then, Herr . . ." I didn't catch the name but it ended in 'mann.' Then she caught my eye as I looked up and drew back a little. He turned to me.

"You didn't tell me your name."

"Donald," I said, and blushed, I don't know why. "I mean that's my surname."

He introduced me and we nodded and smiled at each other.

"You staying here long, Mr. Donald?" she asked.

"I can't say," I told her. "It might be a month and it might be much longer. . . . Perhaps I shall see you again."

I got up to go as I said that because I guessed they'd want to talk to themselves. The way she smiled at me you'd have thought I was her brother.

"Of course we must see you again. You must come and have an ice with us one morning. We're always here at eleven; aren't we, Herr Feuermann?"

I caught the name all right that time and I stammered out that I'd be glad to come some time if I weren't in the way. Then I shook hands solemnly and made my way to the dining-room. The waiter who came to me was one I'd seen in the hall and after he'd brought me my soup I asked him who the gentleman was I'd been sitting with. He seemed surprised at my ignorance.

"That was Ernst Feuermann, sir," he told me. "He used to be manager here till Monsieur Destordi came here and then he went to his villa to take charge there. Monsieur Destordi is very wealthy," he added for my gratification and his own. "He owns the Restaurant Granard."

So much for that and I own I was rather disappointed, for my man had seemed quite a different type from that. I should have put him down, in fact, as a lawyer or professional man of some standing, even if the managership of so swagger a place as the Restaurant Granard wasn't to be sneezed at. And then I laughed to myself at my snobbery. It had been a good thing they hadn't asked me what I was doing in Montelle and a pretty flush of colour or brazenness would have gone over my face when I owned up I was a gentleman's valet.

Nothing else happened there that evening and I made my way home just after nine, and the thermometer as I went through the door stood at over ninety and I loosened my waistcoat as I trudged up the hill.

I was thinking all the time about Feuermann and that girl and it was the absent-mindedness that did me a good turn for I overshot the mark at the turning to our tree-bordered avenue and it was the sudden turning back that made me aware of the fact that I was being shadowed, for the man, whoever he was, nipped into a doorway and kept out of my sight till I'd turned into the rue St. Paulette. Then when I got a short way along the road I took out the tiny mirror I carried in my waistcoat pocket and there he was coming along behind me, so I passed our door and then turned again, whereupon he crossed to the other side and when I was sure his back was turned I slipped through. But I watched him turn again quickly as soon as I disappeared and finally he shuffled off the way he had come. When I mentioned the matter to Prargent that night and told him I'd seen the man before, he only laughed at me, and when I reported the same thing a day or two later be didn't seem any too interested.

Chapter VII
A BUM BREAK

Things went on like that for best part of a week and I was beginning to think I had dropped into the softest job in the whole country of Levasque. First of all, going back to that adventure of mine in the Café-Restaurant Granard, I hadn't been able to follow anything up in the mornings. At the time when Lucy Brock and Feuermann were having a chat and an ice, I was going round with a feather duster and playing Hercules among the women, but I got down once or twice in the evenings and though I never got the same seat again, I spoke to Feuermann and I had more than one smile from the stage.

But all that seems unimportant compared with the stagnation that had settled on the affairs of the four lean men – that means myself as one of them. It was not for me to ask questions, or even enquire after the health of people, and so I never heard a word mentioned about Gimbolt or Hobart or Marcel.

I hadn't even any idea where they were living and I knew no more of what they were doing than the man in the moon.

Prargent and I did have a chat or two about generalities and he told me a good deal about Levasque, and Montelle particularly, but where he spent all his time I had no notion whatever. My own idea of him and Gimbolt was that they were going round making useful contacts, and when they had all the information they needed they'd begin some real business; all the same, why that required so much secrecy and why I was being paid a hundred quid a month, were things that I couldn't fathom, and I own up I didn't let them worry me. To tell the truth I was having the time of my life. I was fed like a Surrey chicken, hopelessly underworked, slept like a top both at night and in the afternoon, and had heaps of leisure into the bargain. How long it was all going to last I hadn't any idea. Then came the afternoon when I went out at about four-thirty and was due in at seven.

I had run out of tobacco and though I had cigarettes in the house it wasn't the same as my pipe. Prargent had gone out just before me and Madame Moulines was doing nothing particular in the kitchen, and was moreover expecting a niece of hers who had been recently coming in for company. As I swung along down the hill the sun was as hot as ever and the mountains beyond were merely a grey background. The short outing I'd planned was to get my tobacco first, then have tea or an ice at the Granard, and then be early for one of the backed seats on the Place to watch the fascinating panorama of the promenade. The tobacconist's I had in mind was one in the Place itself. There is no tobacco monopoly in Levasque, and this shop was the most aristocratic of its kind I have ever run across. That sounds absurd perhaps, but you may guess what I mean. There was a thriving dignity about it; its fittings were palatial; its stock was miraculously complete, and the place itself was long, narrow, deliciously cool and fitted with divans at the ends, and there was a smell about it of priceless cigars and aromatic snuff. The prices, I admit, were stiff for English tobaccos, but that didn't worry a man with twenty-five quid a week and nothing to spend it on.

Perhaps I ought to tell you first something of the geography of the Place Granard. It was huge in extent and surrounded entirely by vast hotels, beneath which were shops. At the back, facing south, was an equestrian statue of the great Duc de Granard, in whose family the duchy had remained till the postwar revolution. At each corner was a kiosk, and there were long flower beds, and by way of contrast, three of those foul-smelling public conveniences that leave exposed the legs of their users. All round too, shading the wide pavement, were false-pepper trees and eucalyptuses, sheltered by the hills to the north, and the air in the cool of the evening seemed full of the most elusive scents, once you got high enough above the eternal whiff of tobacco.

I came then into the Place Granard at the northwest corner and the bare extent of it all glared so dazzlingly that I was glad I had put my sun glasses in my pocket. Then just as I slipped them on, I saw Hobart in front of me on the pavement. Where he had come from so suddenly I didn't know but it must have been one of the hotels whose porticos ran out between the shops. He went on perfectly unaware that I was a few yards behind him and I drew back to keep my distance. Not having seen him for some time I was naturally interested and not a little curious.

Once more I must repeat that he was looking a vastly different person from the one I had seen on the pavement staring up at the *Cyclone* clock. He had on a light grey jacket, and light grey flannel trousers that gave an air of distinction to his long, skinny legs, and his snap-brimmed, grey hat was turned up elegantly at the back, and altogether there was an appearance of affluence and standing about him. Then, all at once, he stopped in his tracks and flapped his jacket pockets with his hands. Then he felt in them and I could almost hear the click of annoyance that he made as he realised he had left his makings behind, for Hobart as I should have told you, always rolled his own cigarettes and he did it like an expert with never a look at the process till the finished article was ready to wipe along his bluish mouth.

It was by chance that his eyes fell at that moment on the tobacconist's where I was going, and he went straight to the window for a look. I stooped down and untied my shoe-lace, and I saw that the Place was deserted on the west side except for a gendarme who was standing in the shade and looking the other way. By the time my lace was tied, Hobart was in the shop and I don't know why I did it but I followed him.

When I entered he was alone, and he was leaning over the counter, hands on the brass rail, as if to crane along to the rear premises to see if anybody was about. There was a carpet on the floor and he didn't hear me, and I went past him to the far divan which formed a kind of inset and there it was as dark as dusk and an electric fan was going.

What happened then took place so quickly that I can't describe it at all. As I tell it it might have been five minutes from start to finish, whereas I doubt if it took more than half a minute all told. How I describe it then is in a kind of slow-motion.

First of all a man appeared from somewhere beyond the long passage that ran behind the counter. He had on a black waistcoat with a gold chain elaborately braided through and arranged over his fat belly, and he was in shirtsleeves with the white cuffs rolled up. His face was fat and red and he had a moustache like the horns and centre tuft of a buffalo. Hobart was still bending over the counter and as the man approached him he drew back.

"*B'jour, m'sieur. Fait chaud.*"

"It certainly does *fait chaud*," said Hobart drily, and he got out his handkerchief from his trouser pocket and mopped his forehead. It was then that the man must have recognised him, for I heard Hobart's: "Say, have you any of that English tobacco . . ." and then came a something that startled me.

"Christ! It's Spider!"

What I then saw was the man with his hands reaching for the ceiling. Hobart had his back to me but he must have had a gun trained on that fat belly.

"Sure it's Spider," he said. "Only I wouldn't holler it if I was you, 'cause this gun's liable to go off. . . . What are you doin' here, Greasy? Come over with Destordi?"

A smile spread over the other's face and he showed all his teeth. I could see them under that black moustache like a row of palings.

"You've got me all wrong. I wasn't sittin' in on that." He broke off and though I didn't know it at the time, he was working the old trick. Spider told me he stared behind him, and then smiled.

"You'd better put down that gat. We've got you covered, Spider!"

Hobart gave a quick look round. It wasn't a look really but a movement of the head that didn't take a hundredth of a second, and as he began it, down went Greasy's hands and he ducked. And he stayed there on the floor behind the counter for Hobart's shot got him just above the eye.

Again just what happened I don't know. Hobart was at the door like a streak and I was ready to bolt too but Hobart came back quicker still, leaned over the counter and sort of dragged himself over. I didn't see him after that but he must have gone out of sight on his hands and knees. But before he'd hit the floor I was darting across the shop and out at the door, and it was there that the gendarme collared me.

It was sheer bad luck that he should have happened to be within earshot when the gun went off, became it didn't make too much noise within the confines of the shop and in any case it might have been mistaken for the backfire of a car. It was bad luck too, that I should have removed my sun glasses when I got inside so that when I bolted out I felt dazzled by the glare, and it was that which gave me an appearance of guilty confusion when the gendarme gripped my arm. And I didn't understand his Levascan. It took me quite a minute to explain that I was English and would he speak French, and that very slowly.

I told him what had happened. Hobart must by then have been clear of the premises, and I said that just as I entered I had heard the shot. I saw a man fall behind the counter and the man who'd fired the shot had vaulted over it and disappeared. As I said that I was probably nearer death than I'd been for a good many years. The gendarme still gripped my arm and drew me to the door where he hailed a colleague who came over at the double. The two jabbered away in Levascan to each other and then the first one asked me to describe the man who'd fired the shot. It took me some time to translate my thoughts into French.

"He was a short man," I said, "about as high as I am; with a black beard. Perhaps he was about thirty years old."

"And his clothes?"

As far as my vocabulary permitted I described an apache. Then with a sudden brain-wave I picked up one of the earthenware spittoons and drew a picture of him on the unglazed bottom. After that there was more conferring in Levascan and then the second man ran his hands over me from top to toe, perhaps in the hope of finding the gun. Then one of them held me and the other pulled up the flap which gave an entry from behind the counter to the customers' side, and the three of us passed through.

I know I'm making an awful fist of telling what happened but you must know just what that counter was like. There were two flaps in it, one by the entrance and the other at the far end where we went through. By some ingenious arrangement, when you lifted the flap, the front panel slid back too to give access, and when it dropped the panel moved back to preserve the continuity of the handsome front of polished mahogany, and under the counter then there were two little cubby-holes, and when I thought Hobart had gone on his hands and knees through to the back of the shop I was wrong. He had been in the hollow nearest the door.

But to get back to when the three of us went through to behind the counter. Hobart's shot had been a clean one and Greasy must have been dead before he hit the ground. There he lay on his back, mouth agape, staring at the ceiling. The younger gendarme made sure he was dead, then said something to his colleague and went along the passage and through the door at its end. We stood there, the other gendarme at Greasy's head and I at his feet, and I daresay if I'd tried I might have made a bolt.

It was then that I saw Hobart's head come furtively out of his hole and I looked away at once, and then with a sudden desire for conversation began to talk.

"Vous le connaissez cet homme-ci?" I asked, pointing to the dead man.

The gendarme said he knew him all right. He was a Levascan who had made money in America and had come back to settle in his native country. His name was Gustave Berousse and he went on to talk about America and the money there was to be made there. All the time I was in a state of panic for Hobart had raised the flap with his arm and was making his way through. I guessed he knew I was keeping the gendarme engaged but at any moment the other might have come back and there was always the chance of a customer entering in spite of the fact that the town never woke up till about five o'clock. So acute was my discomfort that I had to look round at the door along the passage as if to listen for the return of the other gendarme, and the next thing that happened was a sharp rap on the counter and there was Hobart, tapping away and looking mightily annoyed that nobody was attending to him.

"Say you!" he called. "How long am I going to wait here while you guys are talkin'?"

The other gendarme came back at that moment and there was a regular argument for a minute or two, with myself as interpreter. The door to the back premises of the shop had been open – Greasy having been apparently in need of air – and there was a door leading to a side street and through this the murderer had apparently gone. I described to Hobart what the fellow had looked like and his face showed an enormous surprise. One of the gendarmes asked me what he was saying.

"He says it's a pity you didn't tell him sooner," I said. "Just before he came in here he saw the man running along the street."

Hobart was asked to go at once and show where he had seen all that, and the other two of us were left in the shop. My particulars were taken and my passport examined, and the gendarme made copious notes in his book. Then I had to explain that he wouldn't find Captain Prargent at home if he went there, and the upshot of it all was that by the time the other man – minus Hobart – got back, it was decided to take me to police headquarters, and the younger man took me off while the other remained in charge of the scene of the crime.

It was all very friendly but very tedious. First of all I had to give my statement, and then I was told to wait. Half an hour or so later I was shown into another room where an imposing gentleman in civilian dress and with a yellow button in his lapel was seated at a desk. I took him to be the examining magistrate but he gave no explanations. All he did was to hold my statement in his hand and question me in pretty bad English, Just before that ended who should turn up but Captain Prargent. He told me afterwards that Hobart had tipped him off as soon as he'd left the gendarme, and he'd thereupon gone straight to the Villa Marguerite to await the inevitable visit of the police. His French was much better than mine and I heard him giving me the best of characters. Then he congratulated the presiding gentleman on his English and when I was finally turned adrift it was with the most cordial of farewells. Prargent told me rather loudly to get back to the house and when we were outside, said he'd be along later. I had the presence of mind to get some tobacco after all, but when I next passed the door of the fatal shop it was closed and another gendarme was on duty outside, and just twenty yards away the crowd was circulating round and round the Place Granard.

I took it very steadily up the hill that evening and what I was thinking I hardly know. I ought to have been incredibly shocked, but things don't happen quite like that. It wasn't as if I'd seen blood all over the place and a man hacked to death or blown about. The death Greasy had died had been as quick and painless as a pole-axed bullock and he hadn't been a sympathetic character in life for me to brood over his death. I think it was the inexplicable in it all that got me most and of course the fear that I might now be implicated. It hadn't been for me to tell on Hobart. It was the job of the police to discover the murderer and besides I didn't know what lay behind it all. If I had known the facts I might even have killed the man myself, at least that was the sop I gave to conscience. And about my being implicated, I couldn't help thinking that Hobart had been worse than imprudent in having the effrontery to act as he had done when he crawled out from under the counter.

I think perhaps, the nearer I drew to the Villa Marguerite, the more I began to feel something of fear. Hobart I couldn't place but I now knew him for a killer who would look at you with those dead grey eyes of his and let a bullet into your guts without a tremor. Then there was Marcel who'd as soon blow the innards out of a man as he'd look at him. There was the unknown Gimbolt and there was Prargent, the man who kept his own counsel and looked through you rather than at you, and when he was being friendly and intimate, always left you with the feeling that his brain was unaware of what his tongue was saying and that the more you saw of him the less you knew.

It was just as I reached the door that I had the sudden temptation to bolt at all costs. I had my passport, the clothes I stood in, and my wad was safe in my pocket. I think in that mad moment I should really have gone and it was only the most ridiculous of occurrences that stopped me – the sight of my Café acquaintance, the dud artist whose name I'd forgotten, sitting just above the villa on the slope painting for all he was worth. I stopped then and had a look too across the valley and a fine enough view it was. Somehow too I got to thinking of Feuermann and that girl in the café, and before I knew it I was through the door and in the courtyard.

Prargent said nothing to me at dinner but when I brought in the coffee he told me to sit down.

"A pretty bad business of this afternoon," he said. "What happened exactly?"

I told him the whole story and he didn't make a comment till I'd finished, then he passed me over his cigarette case.

"Damn good work on your part," he said. "Cool customer, Hobart, what?"

"Cool, I grant you," I said, "but he's damn bad medicine that chap. And don't you think you owe me some sort of explanation? I mean, is it part of my contract to run up against things like what happened this afternoon, and be expected to go on here dusting furniture and being a dummy?"

He didn't say anything for a moment, then he hid behind a platitude.

"You've been in the army, you know, Donald," he said. "After all I'm in much the same boat as yourself. We've got to do as we're told and keep our mouths shut. Gimbolt's handling this."

It all seemed extraordinarily unreal, we two sitting there so calmly talking about the murder of a man as if he'd been no more than a trodden-on beetle. And looking out of the window at the valley and the sun still on it, I felt a sudden rebellion like that of a kept-in schoolboy.

"Well, I feel like being through," I said. "I'll keep my mouth shut with anybody, as this afternoon showed, but I won't stand for being kept in the dark any longer. If you people don't want me, let me go. If what you're doing is good enough to tell me, then I'll come in properly, but I'm not going to run any more risks without knowing where I stand and what I'm up against."

"But we told you. That concession. . . ."

I laughed. "My God, Prargent! you must think I'm a fool. Leaving out all that bunkum about radium and spas and casinos, who the hell in Europe has got money to put in that kind of thing, even if it existed?"

He didn't turn a hair at that. That was the strong thing in his make-up; an almost terrifying reticence. It wasn't that he was cold in his aloofness – you felt him friendly enough – but just that there was something of the passionate sense of duty that made his stoicism that of the fanatic. Paradoxical perhaps, but it's the best I can do.

All at once he turned on me. "Look here," he said. "You prepared to go the whole way in this?"

"You heard me when we first made our bargain," I told him. "I said I wasn't too squeamish – and I'm not. Also, whatever you care to tell me is as safe as if it hadn't been said. I give you my word for that."

You'd have thought he hadn't heard me. "Know the Hotel des Alpes?" he asked.

"I don't," I said, "but I can find it."

"It's plumb behind the Granard statue," he said, "and there's a back way which you can't help finding. If you don't hear from me by nine-thirty, be there at ten o'clock sharp, and I'll have a man on the look-out for you. Mention no names but just show yourself at the back door. And don't be too conspicuous in getting there."

I meant to say, "Right-ho," but I found myself saying, "Very good, sir," as he got up. Prargent was like that. In his presence I felt it quite a natural thing that I should be a valet. What generations of breeding and soldiering went to that aristocratic face of his I don't know, but with him I always felt like a subaltern in the presence of a general or a small boy with the captain of his school eleven.

When he'd gone I went down to the kitchen for my meal. Madame Moulines wheezed out the question as to what the police had been after, and I told her I had witnessed an accident and had been detained in consequence. As I sat down she poured out my soup and squeezed out something into my ear.

"Des accidents? Eh bien, oui. Il y en aura beaucoup, bien sûr."

It was the way she wheezed the words into my ear as well as what she said that made me draw back.

"What do you mean, 'more accidents?'" I said.

She shrugged her fat shoulders and said she had a premonition, and that was all I could get out of her until the end of the meal and then she made the remark off-handedly and as if to give the topic its final quietus.

"On n'aime pas la police chez nous," she said. *"Ça annonce."*

I couldn't help laughing at that, though why her people had no use for the police and just what it was that the sight of them foreshadowed, I hadn't the least idea. And then I thought I might learn something about that at the Hotel des Alpes.

Chapter VIII
KILLING NO MURDER

I DON'T know who the indoor servant was who was waiting to spot me but as soon as I approached the back door of the hotel he came out, and I was taken through the back premises to some back stairs at the head of which we came into a wide corridor. Just along this my guide knocked at a door, drew back to let me enter and then closed the door on me.

Inside the room were Gimbolt and the three lean men, all in shirt-sleeves, for the evening was a sweltering one, and with glasses handy, and though the windows were open the blinds were closely drawn. Gimbolt himself hopped up as soon as I entered and came across to meet me, and the quick glance round showed me that everybody was going to be friendly.

"Come and sit down, Donald," he said, and drew me over to a handy seat. "That was great work you did this afternoon. Have a drink."

I said I didn't mind if I did, but with a lot of soda. Marcel shoved a packet of cigarettes under my nose and old Hobart craned his skinny neck towards me.

"Guess, Mr. Donald," he said, "I was plumb right about you. I know a right guy when I see one."

"Then it's a pity you didn't have a good look at me before you gave me that sock on the bean at Nancy," I told him.

Everybody laughed. "Too bad," said Hobart, shaking his head till his Adam's apple wobbled like the bubble in a spirit level. "You've sure got me all wrong."

"Well, you can't blame me for that," I said, and everybody laughed again. It was strange how we were all keyed up, but a little, footling joke like that made all the difference and we were like five old friends before I'd got through my drink.

"We'll get straight down to business," Gimbolt announced. "As a formality, Donald, we'll ask you to give us your word that nothing of what's said gets outside this room."

"That's all right," I told him. "It'll go in one ear and there it'll stop."

"Right," he went on. "First a pertinent question or two. Are you prepared to inform us if everything you've told us about yourself is implicitly true?"

You may find it hard to believe me but I knew as sure as I was sitting in my chair, that I was in for a straight deal. There was a difference in the atmosphere that a fool could have sensed, and I thought I knew enough about Prargent to be certain he would stand for nothing crooked.

"Well," I said, "I think that's a fair question. I don't mind saying that nearly all I told you is perfectly true. I'll admit there's one or two bad spots – though not so many as in your own account of yourselves."

There was a little chuckle in the room. Gimbolt smiled gently. I think that was the first time I had really seen him, and in that light his face looked almost dark against the white blondness of his brushed-back hair. His expression changed to the serious again.

75 | THE TRAIL OF THE THREE LEAN MEN

"Well, all's fair, they say. Would you care to – er – point out the spots? . . . your own spots?"

I pointed them out. First of all I gave him my assurance that what I was about to say was implicitly true and he could rely on it, and then I told him the tale of the death of the *Messenger*, and what had happened to me, and Munro Burnside and the *Cyclone*, and what happened on that afternoon. The story perhaps was unusual, but it held them, and when I'd finished there was a nodding of heads like elders sitting in the market-place.

"The trail of the three lean men," said Gimbolt slowly. "And it's landed you in this room."

For a moment I felt a quick alarm, but there was nothing to be alarmed about. He nodded once or twice.

"We're grateful to you, Donald, and we'll be equally frank. After I've finished you're free to get up and leave the room, because we know" – and there he looked round at everybody – "that you're absolutely square. What I rather think though, is that you'll come in on this deal. Our story, I may say, is even more unusual than your own. We're here in Levasque for the express purpose of killing a man!"

My eyes almost popped out of my head.

"You mean . . . a political assassination?"

He smiled. "Lord no! A purely private killing. What the law can't do we're here to do. Still, I'll begin at the beginning, and remember that what you're about to hear is gospel truth though we haven't too many documents to prove it."

As he was talking he pulled a handful of papers from his pocket and began sorting them out. He put two or three aside.

"First myself. My name's Larkin – Gene Larkin. My father was a Suffolk man who went to the States when he was a boy. My mother was an Englishwoman whom he met and married when on a trip back home. He got in on the ground floor of a real estate firm and made the devil of a lot of money. I don't say he made it all on the square, but that's neither here nor there. His home was Cicero, by the way, a town you may have heard of before. When I tell you that Spider Hobart was his bodyguard, and that when he died he left me seven million dollars salted away in English banks, you'll probably guess that his hands weren't any too clean as judged by the law and the prophets.

"I do know this, however. He was in various rackets because he had to be. In England you can't understand how a man can be jockeyed into rackets; all the intricacies of protection, political jobbery, graft, and so on. But I will say this for my father and I can prove it. He was never a party to the death or maiming of a man, and he was killed because he refused to stand for something of the sort. In fact he said – and his word was known to be good – that if certain actions were followed he'd tip the parties off."

He passed me over a couple of newspaper clippings. "Read those and you'll see the kind of man he was. Flatfoot was his nickname, because he had a saying: 'I've got my foot down flat and nothing's going to move me.' He thought the world of my mother and a better father never lived. As far as I knew he never did a dirty trick, and he gave money away in fistfuls where he thought it'd do good. I won't say he was popular with the religious crowd but they took his money all the same –"

"They sure did!" broke in Hobart dryly.

"The situation's hard for you to follow," went on Larkin. "You can't understand how a man can be so highly respected by a community and yet be well outside the law. You see what those clippings say. The whole city was in mourning when he went west, and his funeral wasn't a gangster's circus either. Still, I guess you don't want to hear any more about him, It was myself I started out to explain.

"My mother had a fad for my being educated in England and living there near her people. I went to an English school – Headborough, to be precise – and by special arrangement I used to spend a very long holiday at home in the States, from mid-July to early October. Later I went up to Oxford as you know, and I used to spend the whole of the Long Vac. at home. My mother died two years ago, and after I came down I thought I'd make the Grand Tour of Europe before going back home for good. I was in Paris when I heard of my father's death."

He passed me yet more clippings.

"The whole story's there. What happened exactly Spider will tell you if you ask him. It was at what you'd call a country house on the Lake that it happened. My father was down there for a few days, and Spicer and Marcel were with him. I don't mean that there weren't other servants, but I mention them as corroborative evidence. Spider always shadowed him and the reason they slipped up was that the trick was a new one. There was no pumping lead out of a fast car or throwing a pineapple. What was done was a fellow threw a fit outside the gate as he and Spider came through, and they carried him into the garden. While Spider nipped into the kitchen for help, the fellow let off his gun and then legged it. There was a fast car just away in the woods we found out afterwards."

He paused for a moment but not for any theatrical gesture. He gave just a little shake of the head and then went on.

"That brings us to the real point. That bastard who shot didn't shoot to kill outright. He pumped the lead into the old man's belly and it took him quite a few hours to die. Marcel got him later so he'll never tell you why. When I got to New York I met Spider there and we decided we could do more good if I kept out of the way. The gang wasn't wise to me, and Spider thought he'd better drop out too, so I employed the finest detective agency in the States and gave them a free hand to get me the inside dope. When we knew the man who did it, Marcel as I've just said, gave him the works – so to speak. But, and this is the point I want to make; by the time we knew that Tony Destordi was the man higher up, it was too late. We were almost certain, mind you, but we wanted to make dead sure – and we did. By that time Tony had some idea of what was coming to him, and he made his getaway. He was a Levascan and he made for home. I should say that in the States he was known as Tony Short. He assumed his real name over here. He wasn't able to bring the whole of his wad but he brought enough to make him a mighty big guy in this one-horse country. He's wanted by the Federal authorities back home but he can sit back and put his fingers to his nose. He's safe here for life and he can't be touched. Not only that; he consolidated his position since he's been here. Levasque isn't all that different from Cicero."

He leaned forward and there was a silence in the room. I anticipated his question.

"And he's the man you've come here to kill?"

"Exactly." He leaned back and there was like a deep breath in the room. "We won't labour the argument. Here are the rest of the clippings and you can read the facts for yourself. All I say is that Tony Destordi gave the order for my father to be shot as he was; and that as the law can't line him up, we will."

"I see." I grunted to myself and pulled a long face. The thing had come too suddenly and I wanted time to sit and ruminate. Hobart helped me out.

"Guess Mr. Donald ain't got no use for this strong-arm stuff. Hadn't you better wise him up to the break what you've give Tony?"

"Yes," said Larkin as if he'd just remembered it. "What we did was this. We got Destordi safely tracked down, and as soon as we'd got our own plan of campaign worked out I did a foolish thing. I think I was just swanking, as you call it. I wanted to show what a sportsman I was, so I had Destordi warned we were coming. A message reached him in the name of Frank O'Brien, who was an associate of my father – we'll call him that to avoid complications – to the effect that Frank was coming for him. Needless to say Frank knows nothing about it, though he'd worry none if he did. After a suitable interval we sent him a second warning, this time from Brussels, to show Frank was on the way. I think that explains to you why we had to be so secretive about our movements and why we didn't cross the frontier where he'd expect us." He gave a wry smile. "I guess if I'd had any sense I'd have slipped over here nice and quiet and seen him decently buried without bothering all you people."

"Aw, don't talk thataway, Gene," chimed in Hobart. "You wouldn't hog a thing like that to yourself. I reckon I've got a kick comin' to me outa that guy." He got to his feet and I could hardly see him through the haze of smoke, then he sat down again. "Guess I can talk just as well sittin' as standin'. What I want you to know, Mr. Donald, is that what Gene's been handin' out is the straight dope. I knew Flat-foot Larkin like as if he was my own pap and he was a straight guy.

They don't make 'em no better. That guy Destordi ain't no better'n a snake what don't even give a rattle. Here, take a slant at his mug."

He lugged a photograph out of his breast pocket. It had been clipped from a newspaper and pasted on cardboard, and I didn't have to look at it more than once to see the rattlesnake allusion. It was a lowbrowed, oily, sensual face that stared at me, and if only a corner of the mouth had been twisted it'd have been so like the face of a typical movie gangster as to be laughable. But there wasn't anything laughable as I looked at it then. It was merely repulsive. I handed it back to Hobart with the remark that it wouldn't have been any great loss if he'd been trodden on when young.

"You've sure said it, Mr. Donald," and he came as near to smiling as I ever saw him. "I've carried that picture around plenty since I lamped it in the *Sentinel*. Guess I take a peek at it most days," and he shook his head as if the photograph were his wife's. I caught Gene Larkin's eye fixed on me.

"I don't want to rush you into anything, Donald," he said, "but you've heard most of what we've got to tell you. I may say there's no danger in it for anybody. It's part of the contract, and I insist on it, that if we do this job and we don't get clear, I take the whole responsibility. They won't be able to hold you for anything. And if there's any other questions you want to ask – shoot!"

"I don't know that there are," I said, and hesitated because I knew there were dozens. "About the man who got hurt this afternoon. He was one of Destordi's gang?"

"Oh no! Spider was as surprised as anybody when he saw him. If you mean, is he in Destordi's gang over here, then the answer's yes, to this extent. He was a fellow countryman of his and knew him back in Cicero, and though we don't know everything yet, we know Destordi put him in that nice little shop where he's making – or *was* making – money hand over fist. You bet your life if he could have got to a 'phone he'd have put Destordi wise to the fact that Spider was in town and that'd have queered the whole pitch."

"I see," I said, and it was my turn to smile ruefully. "I'm sort of half way in this killing already."

"Oh no!" He rounded on me quickly. "You have my word that you can pack your bag and get out whenever you like and there'll be nothing left against you here in Montelle. I'll see to all that."

"You seem to be trusting me rather a long way," I said.

"Perhaps we are. You mayn't believe us but we liked the look of you the first time. And we've made enquiries."

"Enquiries? Good Lord! Who from?"

"Your friend Munro Burnside for one thing," he said. "Merely a business reference, so to speak. And there were others."

I rather looked down my nose at that. "You seem to be doing this thing pretty thoroughly."

"Why not? I've got the money to burn and I'm going to burn it."

"And what about Hobart?" I said. "Isn't he running a risk being here? I mean if Destordi saw him he'd spot him at once and he'd have him bumped off."

"Destordi, as far as we know, doesn't know Spider any too well," he said, "and his real name's not Hobart. Also we took extensive precautions – Spider lost his life in a motoring accident two months ago, and you'll find an account of it in one of those clippings – I told you we were doing this thoroughly. And there's one difficulty I ought to have mentioned to you and didn't – I see now what a damn fool I was to warn Destordi at all. We're here surveying the ground the last few days and he's made that villa of his a little fortress. Also he's got two of his old friends over as bodyguard, from the gang that used to operate in New York, so you see we're not going to have a walk-over –"

Prargent spoke for the first time.

"Don't you think Donald might sleep on it and tell us in the morning? As you said, we don't want to rush him into anything."

"Just a minute," I said. "I grant you that I would like a night to sleep on it, but we haven't yet got to the point, which is this. Suppose I come in with you, just what am I supposed to do? Perfectly frankly I'll tell you here and now that I don't feel like killing anybody. I'm sympathetic, mind you, but it isn't as if I'd seen a man murder your father. If I'd have done that I'd have followed him to hell and all to put a shot in him. Only, you see, as far as I'm concerned it's all too impersonal – I can't get away from the idea that I'm committing cold-blooded murder myself –"

"But we've warned Destordi that we're coming!"

"I know that," I said, "and I hate to be so argumentative, but you ought to see my point. In any case what is it you'd want me to do?"

He rubbed his chin. "Frankly, there you've got me. We don't want you to fire a shot or do anything like that, but we jolly well know you might be useful. Prargent's useful as a certain type of Englishman – the pukka, military type – because he can make contacts with those who might be helpful. Spider's the same. You're the same, though we don't see at the moment how. Still, we'll fit you in." He leaned forward again. "You wouldn't mind, for example, keeping an eye on the Lewis guns?"

I smiled. "Not in the least. I'll see they're ready if they're wanted and if one goes wrong I'll put it right. Only, I'm to assume you want them for partridge shooting or something like that."

He nodded. "That's all right then. And something else you can do. You've made one contact already that's likely to be useful. You've met Feuermann, who's Destordi's major domo. We'd like you to keep in touch with him because . . . well, it's obvious why."

"I don't know much about Feuermann," I said, "but he struck me as a decent sort and provided he isn't hurt in any way I don't see why I shouldn't do that. And by the way, isn't there a lot of risk in your proclaiming yourself American? I mean, won't Destordi have spent money to be supplied with the descriptions of all Americans that cross the frontier?"

He smiled. "That may be so, but he'll have the devil of a job. Seven hundred Americans entered Levasque last year as you'll be told if you enquire at the Salle d'Initiative. Besides, he's keeping tabs on Frank O'Brien. And Spider's dead. And when I was home I was always at the country place and everybody knew I wasn't of much account. The only danger is another adventure like this afternoon's – and there isn't likely to be another like that." He shrugged his shoulders. "It's all in the game."

"Tell him what the rake-off'll be, chief." That was Marcel.

Larkin smiled. "I don't think that'll influence him very much; still if you'd like to know, Donald, you'll be paid like everybody else. Expenses now and fifty grand when the job's over – whoever does it."

I shook my head like the puritanical fool I was.

"I don't want to insult you but it sounds too much like blood money to me. What I will promise you here and now is this. Keep me on at my present job as a blind, and I'll do what I said I'd do – and anything else in reason. And when we leave you'll do your best to find me a job elsewhere."

Larkin got up out of the chair. "You take a night to think it over and then see how things look. Just another spot?"

I had another spot, then the bell was pushed and I left the conspirators' den to find my guide outside. Five minutes later I was making my way up the hill, and for the life of me I couldn't believe that I'd spent the hour as I had. The only thing that was real was the face that Hobart carried in his pocket, and as I thought of it I had the sort of shiver that some people get when they see a rat or a snake. Curiously enough too, when I got through the door and into our little courtyard it felt just like coming home, and inside my tiny bedroom I had a feeling that was remarkably like security, not unmixed with affection. But I didn't undress. Prargent I knew would soon be in and he'd want to speak to me. And I wanted to talk to him.

He came in a bare five minutes after I'd got back and we went out to the balcony. He poured out drinks for it was a thirsty sort of night and bed was the last thing to think of.

"I thought you were very reasonable," was the first allusion he made to the earlier evening. "If I'd been in your place I'd have done the same thing. By the way, you didn't know how moderate Gene was being about things."

In the dark I gave a rather cheap, ironical smile. "Strikes you as moderate, does it?"

"You're mistaking me," he said quietly. "I'm not talking about the killing; what I'm referring to is his presentation of the case. I could tell you things about Destordi which would have made you jump clean in with the rest of us. For instance, you've read a lot about American justice?"

"Afraid I don't get you."

He explained. "At home we think any crook or gangster can wriggle clear if he's got the money to pay shyster lawyers or grease other palms. My question's merely this. If Destordi's definitely wanted by the State authorities who'll send him to the chair, then what must his record be?"

I couldn't answer that.

"The man's not fit to live," he went on. "Isn't it an affront to every justice – and justice is a divine thing, mark you – that a man like that should live here on the fat of the land after what he's done? Aren't you and I committing an offence against justice if we permit such a man to go on living?"

But I wasn't to be convinced – at least at that moment, and I said so.

"I'm a coward, and that's frank," I told him. "I don't mind sheltering here and doing donkey work but the other's going too far for me at the moment. I know I'm equally in the boat with you others in a way. And I feel very unhappy about it – I mean being such a coward."

He slapped me on the back as he passed to refill his glass.

"I wouldn't worry about that. They also serve, you know."

I smiled. "You've wrenched that quotation well out of its context! And how'd you get in all this, by the way?"

He waited till he'd got back to his chair.

"How'd I get in it? I don't know. Commuted my pension after the war and had the hell of a time after I lost all my money – like yourself. Then I spent my last quid on a Bulldog Drummond sort of advertisement. You know – do anything, go anywhere, no scruples, and that sort of thing. I was terrified when Larkin sent for me."

I wish I could have seen his face but it was too dark for that. All I know is that at that moment I felt for him such a sudden surge of affection that I knew that what was good enough for him would be good enough for me – killing or no killing.

"You see," he went on, "I was squeamish to a certain extent and to a certain extent only. I was desperate; never a relation or friend I could call on, and I didn't see anything for it but a deep breath and a jump over the Embankment. As I told Larkin, I'd never stand for smashing out a baby's brains against a wall, but I drew the line at nothing else."

"And you're prepared to kill Destordi?"

I could imagine how he smiled at that. "Kill him? My dear fellow, there's only one thing that's annoying me – that Gene insists on doing the job himself. So does Spider. Between them I'll never get a look in."

Chapter IX
DESTORDI

I TURNED in that night well after midnight and I was out of bed as usual at seven in the morning and I don't think I had a couple of hours' sleep. What I dreamed about doesn't matter, but I dreamed plenty, and yet the curious thing was that when I finally woke up after an hour's sleep, that came at the very end of the restless night, my mind was quite made up.

I rather think Prargent slept restlessly too for he was sitting up in bed reading when I came in with the early tea. We gave each other the usual good mornings, and then he fired the question at me point-blank.

"Made up your mind what you're going to do?"

"Yes," I said. "I'm coming in with you. I'm not doing no killing, mind you, but I'll go the rest of the way."

"That's good enough," he said. "I'm not doing any killing myself if it comes to that, but I'll go so far as to hold the gun for the man who is. Want a morning off?"

The question was so unexpected that I stared at him.

"Now you're in the show, you might as well know," he went on. "We're overhauling the machine guns this morning. After to-day there won't be a time when the house is alone. Marcel'll be lying handy for a gun in a place we're making here in the bedroom."

"A gun?"

He got out of bed at that and called me over to the side window.

"See that grey sort of house down there on the left? Like a castle? That's Destordi's place. We got this one so as to overlook it, and we do to a certain extent as you see. Behind those wooden shutters he's had steel sheets put up, and there's barbed wire all round the inside of the garden walls."

"You mean he's gone to earth?"

"More or less," he said. "He goes to see some of his pals occasionally and he's paid one visit to the Granard since we've been here. The trouble is, of course, that we don't want to involve anybody else. I don't mean those two gunmen he's imported as bodyguard; I mean bystanders and all that, or we'd have pumped lead into him the other day. Spider cursed hell out of Gene for not letting him do the trick in the Granard, but Gene's got some fool idea that before Destordi's done in he's going to have a personal word with him and tell him who he is. Sporting and all that, but what I say is, if there's a job to do, get it done and make your getaway."

"Then what's the idea of Marcel and the gun?"

"That's complicated," he said, "and if you ask me just a bit silly. Gene says he doesn't give a damn what happens after he's had his personal word with Destordi. How he's going to get it, Lord knows, but there we are. The telephone's going in to-day and there may come a time when he can ring us up that he's had his word and Destordi's on the way home, and then Marcel'll get him as he comes in. If we can't get the lower part of the house we can get the road up to it as you see. Something else. See that villa at the end of our garden?"

It was the one straight below us down the bill that he was pointing to, and its garden was so long and so thick with trees that even from where we stood only the flat roof was visible, and that was a couple of hundred yards away.

"Gene's bought that villa," Prargent said. "A pal of Marcel's from the country is being smuggled in there to-day and he's going to cut a communicating door through from their side to ours, out of sight behind that shrubbery, which means we'll all be together whenever we like. There's a nice quiet entrance to it in a side street and you'll notice it enfilades Destordi's place from slightly below. Old Hobart's going to have the other gun down there."

"They're leaving the hotel?"

"That's right, but they're doing it in conjunction with the hotel, if you know what I mean; Gene's having one of the waiters – the chap who showed you in last night, and they're lending him a young chef for a bit. He's absolutely lousy with money, you know."

That was all for the moment but as I was going out I remembered to ask him what time he wanted me back.

"Doesn't matter," he said. "I'm being in till late in any case, and as I told you, after to-day one of us must always be in." He lit himself a cigarette and I knew him well enough to be sure something was coming.

"You see, we're anxious for you to keep in touch with Feuermann," he said. "You told me, I think, that he was always at the Granard at eleven."

It was on the tip of my tongue to tell him that I wasn't going to stand for bringing a man like Feuermann into it, but I thought I'd hold my tongue instead, and after all Feuermann himself might volunteer some information that would come in handy and that would let me out. But I had to say something to Prargent and I got off my chest what had been worrying me ever since that night at the Granard.

"Don't you think," I said, "that I might let Feuermann get the impression that I'm ... well, not a valet but a sort of travelling friend of yours? He's not likely to see my passport and he'd probably open out more than if he took me for a gentleman's servant."

"Hm!" he said. "I don't see why you shouldn't. And by the way, I'd be rather careful how you opened out with that girl, if I were you. Excuse my mentioning it but Gene had you tailed until he was sure you were all right." He caught my look. "That's right. The fellow you said was following you round."

I think I looked several ways a bit of a fool, though he did put that advice about the girl quite decently; but I hadn't any idea of chattering to her, and that I told him. All the same I didn't feel quite so elated as I thought I should have been as I went down the hill to the Granard that morning. There was a vague uneasiness somewhere that would keep popping up and disturbing things. Then, under the trees in the Granard garden, where the morning society of Montelle rolled up regularly for music and ices, I had quite a different feeling – the one that comes in a strange place that holds the promise of adventure. And almost as soon as I'd found a shady seat Feuermann appeared. He caught sight of me at once and came over, holding out his hand.

"Very nice to see you again," he said with that shy sort of smile that went so well with that attractive diffidence of his. "We began to think we'd offended you."

I protested vigorously and while the waiter was bringing another seat, Lucy Brock arrived. I call her that already because that was her name, and before the half hour was gone she was making me call her Lucy, for the quaint reason that I looked far too boyish to be called anything but George. I had to give her that name because George Donald was the name on my passport. She was looking most amazingly cool in a frock of what I took to be flowered muslin, and the three of us chatted away over our enormous ices like children at a picnic.

"Know yet how long you're staying?" she asked.

"I don't," I said. "The man I'm doing this holiday with – a Captain Prargent – has business over here and I promised to stay till he'd finished. I expect it'll be some weeks. We're at the Villa Marguerite, rue Paulette." It seemed most natural at that moment for us all to be asking personal questions or I'd never have put the question to Feuermann. "And where do you live, Herr Feuermann?"

"Quite near you," he said unconcernedly. "At the Villa Martine. A rich Levascan came here some months ago and offered me the complete charge of the place and I took his offer." Either it was my imagination or he said that with a certain regret. Then he smiled. "I act as butler, caterer, general adviser and everything. We have some indoor staff, and a gardener or two."

"It must be a pretty big place?"

"Yes," he said. "It used to be a monastery till the usual banishment took place after the revolution. It's been modernised since. The gardens are very fine though they're small."

"I think Herr Feuermann's simply wonderful," said Lucy. "Do you know that just after the war he started in this hotel as an ordinary waiter and rose to be manager, and now he's . . . well, he gets a fabulous salary. And you can see what everybody here still thinks of him."

He looked rather self-conscious at that outburst and turned to me.

"Miss Brock exaggerates but we'll excuse her. And what do you do when you're in England, Mr. Donald?"

"I'm connected with the Press. The *Daily Cyclone*. Ever hear of it?"

"The Press!" he said. "That's curious."

But he didn't say why, and then Lucy Brock rose to go. She had some new songs to run over with the orchestra and she said it was just like me, coming to the Granard the only morning in the week when she had rehearsals. We watched her pink parasol disappear and then sat down again, and the waiter brought us two iced mangoes, which Feuermann recommended.

"If it isn't rude of me," I said, "just what did you mean when you said it was curious my being connected with the Press?"

He looked up and frowned to himself and for a moment I thought I'd offended him.

"I don't think I should have said that," he said. "Still, there's honour among thieves, so they say, so there's honour among pressmen and you won't give me away."

"But you're not. . ." I began.

He smiled. "No. I'm not a pressman, but I write sometimes. You acquainted with Levascan politics?"

"I'm not," I said. "But if they're anything like French, don't try to teach me because you'll never do it."

He chuckled at that. "Ours are far easier. There's the Agrarian Party, which is also identified with the exiled Jesuits and the old Catholics, and there's the Nationalist Party, which is the party of the Revolution. Country and town you can call them for convenience. The Nationalist Party," and I couldn't help noticing how his voice fell, "has established a Dictatorship, and it controls the army, which may be only two thousand all told, but it's the only army we've got. It controls the elections and it therefore controls the Assemblée Nationale. It also controls the Press."

"Then you must be for it," I said.

"What's that?" He looked at me. "Oh, I see what you mean. But you're wrong. The two papers are government ones, I know, but there's also another which is published surreptitiously. *La Terre*, it's called, and it's been dislodged three or four times already and two of its editors are still in jail." He smiled dryly. "But it's still going strong."

"Good luck to it!" said I, and nodded a health over my spoonful of mango. "And do tell me. You're in sympathy with it?"

He leaned over in the funniest way in the world and whispered confidentially.

"I write an occasional article for it!"

He resumed over his mango, and by the way he said it, nobody listening could have guessed what he was referring to.

"I'm afraid I'm an awful dud but they seem to like it – and it's a hobby. There's a spot of adventure in it too."

I lowered my voice there. "You mean the danger?"

He nodded. "I don't say I'm without friends here but I wouldn't like anything to get out. It might be awkward."

"I think it's wonderful of you," I told him, and I meant it. "And you did me a great honour in telling me. You bet your life I'll never give the slightest hint, even to my friend Prargent."

He leaned forward again. "Why shouldn't you do something for us?"

I stared at him. "I? Good Lord! What can I do?"

"Do?" He smiled. "Do us an article on your country's part in the crisis. Follow it up by one on the freedom of the Press and what England has done to dictatorships. Follow that up with a simple account of your system of government and then with the position of religious bodies. You up to it?"

"Well, I might do it," I said, and I spoke with deliberate flippancy. "They say a good pressman can write about anything. But would it be quite fair to my friend who practically got me here?"

"But he needn't know. There'd be nothing underhand about that." His head came close again. "Draft us out something and let me have it. If you'll permit me I'll translate it for you or get a friend to do it. That way, you see, you'll be absolutely safe."

"I don't know that I want to be safe," I said, but that was more cussedness than anything else. "But I will draft you out something. The freedom of the Press, shall it be?"

He beamed at me. "Anything you like. Let me have it some evening when you're here, or slip it to Miss Brock You'll like to see our little – er – headquarters? We've only a hand press, you know, but you might give us a tip or two."

"That's very good of you," I said. "I certainly would like to have a look; only I shan't be of any use to you technically."

"That's all right," he told me. "They even find me useful so you'll be a godsend." He took a card from his pocket and wrote something on it in pencil, then slipped it across to me. "Know the jail?"

"I don't," I said, "but probably shall do before I'm much older."

He smiled gently. "There'll be no risk for you – and what would life be without risks in any case? But the jail's just past the Hotel de Ville, in the Cathedral Square. Next door to it as you go to the bridge is a florist's shop. A cripple and his sister keep it, and all you need do is to walk in and ask for three white roses with long stalks, then you'll be shown down to the cellar if the coast is clear. When you get down there, show Crevelle the card. He speaks English of a sort." He held out his hand. "Afraid I must go. . . . We're going to be very grateful to you."

I began a deprecatory speech but he smiled at me and hurried away. I looked at my new watch and found it twelve o'clock, and just then the cathedral clock struck the hour. But I was in no hurry and sat on in the pleasant shade. Feuermann had made a tremendous impression on me, there was no doubt about that. Never in my life had I been so attracted by the charm of a personality as I was by his.

I felt in him a strength of character that made for implicit trust, and there was a natural dignity and a likeableness about him that gave me something of the feeling that a young monk might have for his Abbot. Such men as he, I thought, have always been in the background of revolutions; biding their time and choosing it, unknown until the moment of tremendous failure or success, with the alternatives of a brick wall and firing squad or maybe a president's desk.

I was sitting there thinking high-faluting stuff like that when I became aware of a stir going round the garden. A couple of women sitting near me craned their heads round first and when I followed suit I saw that people were staring and turning round to watch the progress of four people who were making their way towards where I was sitting. In front walked a pluggy individual, with the rolling gait of a bruiser. His nose was askew but I couldn't see his ears for they were hidden beneath an enormous Panama hat, but his hands were set tight in his jacket pockets.

Then came a man and a woman. The man I knew at once and he was uglier than his picture. He had a beefy, sagging jowl, and the colour of it was an indigo blue that looked purple against the saffron of his cheeks. He too wore a Panama hat and a cigar was fixed in the corner of his mouth. In height he would be about five foot four and he weighed thirteen stone if he weighed a pound, so that I thought instinctively of the greasy proprietor of a Soho restaurant or an organ grinder run to fat. As he walked he gave quick little glances from his pig's eyes, and he kept close to the woman.

She was not more than thirty and dressed to kill. I put her down as a fourth-rate actress and I wasn't far wrong. In a hard way she was a good-looker, and she knew it, for every step and look was an affectation. Languidness was her strong suit from the droop of her parasol to the drawl of her voice.

Close at their heels came the other man and he looked most uncomfortable in a dark suit and black bowler. He stood about six foot and seemed as tough as his partner of the vanguard, and his hands were deep in his jacket pockets too. I don't know why I was amused at the melodrama of it all but I was, and when I saw yet another man,

I almost laughed, for he was the manager by the look of him and he was fluttering just in the rear, trying to be helpful and deferential without having a ha'p'orth of attention paid to him.

The woman was not five yards from me when she spoke. I suppose she took me for a Levascan for my face was pretty brown and the clothes I was wearing were Levascan all right.

"Now, don't that make you tired? What did that guy want to plant himself down there where we said we'd sit."

I kept my eyes off her and when I looked up it was to see Destordi looking straight at me. He didn't have his eyes on me more than a second but I could see he knew I was dirt. He nodded back at the manager chap, who fairly scrambled round the chairs to come up with him.

"That's all right, Lou." Then he said something in dialect to the black-coated manager and they both looked at me. Then the two toughs and Destordi and his woman waited with the unconcern of people who might be watching a servant remove a dead cat from a narrow path.

The manager came up to me with a bow, that had in it nevertheless all the cheap importance he could muster. He meant to show what a great lad he was, and he took everything so for granted that he infuriated me.

"Pardon, m'sieur, mais toutes ces places – ci sont commandées." He showed his teeth like a monkey.

"Oh?" I said. "I didn't know that. There isn't any such thing here as ordering seats. Who wants it?"

He bowed and showed his teeth again. "The gentleman here wants it. He has all the seats."

"Has he?" I said, and this time in English, "Then if he wants mine perhaps he'll come and ask for it."

Destordi and I looked at each other for a second, then he nodded to the stocky man. He slouched over to me at once, and I noticed the other draw up close to Destordi with his back towards him.

"Say you, what's the idea? Didn't you hear this guy tell you to beat it?"

Where the sudden courage came from I don't know but I looked him straight in the eye and told him to go to hell. I hadn't quite got the last word out when he took a step nearer, brushing the manager aside with one hand. It was the hand that remained in his pocket that scared me.

"Beat it!" he said. It was more of a growl and his mouth twisted the way I'd seen mouths twist on the movies. I know I got to my feet and tried to look dignified, but I must have cut a remarkably poor figure. And I hadn't the faintest idea what to say. All I did was to scowl at him and make my way through tables with an assumption of indifference, and all the time I listened for the roar of a gun at my back. When I got to the trellised gate affair that led from the restaurant I glanced back but the party was already seated and paying no more attention to me than the dead cat I might have been.

All the way back to the villa I was fuming with rage and cursing myself for a fool. I thought of all the wonderful things I might have done and my brain seethed with subtle ironies that I ought to have uttered and crushing looks that I ought to have cast. I must have been almost at the door when I recovered my sense of proportion and gave my first smile. It was just then that the wonderful scheme dawned on me, and I remember I quickened my step and fairly flew into the house. Madame Moulines gave a startled look at me as I went by her and up the stairs to Prargent's room. He was lying on the bed, reading a local paper.

"Hallo!" he said. "What's biting you?"

"Just had an idea," I told him. "Any chance of seeing – er – Gimbolt some time to-day?"

He looked interested. "Why not? . . . What's the idea?"

I drew myself up a chair. "You people'll all think it silly, but I know the way to get Destordi."

Chapter X
THE WHEELS MOVE

It was about ten o'clock that night when Gene Larkin came in through the front garden. I was in Prargent's bedroom which had been made into a kind of additional lounge, and he shook hands with me as if we hadn't seen each other for weeks. Hobart was with him but Marcel had gone down to the other villa.

"Now what's all this?" he said. "Prargent tells me you've got some scheme or other and you won't tell it to him."

"I thought I'd get it off my chest once and for all," I said. "It's fifty to one it won't come to anything in any case."

In my capacity of valet I got out the long drinks and as soon as we were all comfortable in our chairs I began to unburden my soul.

"Before I tell you the scheme," I said, "I'd like a little information. The head of the government here is General Fournier; isn't that so?"

"That's right," said Gene. "And an affable old boy he is – once you're in the swim."

"And he's really the Dictator? I mean, what he says, goes?"

"Good heavens, no!" He laughed. "You've been rusticating since you've been here."

"If you mean I've had damn little time to study native politics, then you're right," I said. "And who would you say was the big noise, if Fournier isn't?"

"Gabrisson, Minister of the Interior; he's the local Pooh-Bah. A big, fat chap with a belly like an alderman's. Haven't you seen him driving about in an open car with half a dozen musical comedy troopers round him? One of the sights of Montelle, my dear chap."

"It's a pleasure in store," I said. "And what are his morals like? Would he be insulted if the bribe was big enough?"

"Them guys are all alike," said Hobart, switching his cigar stub to the other corner. "The sight of a ten-spot sure makes them itch in the palm. But one thing you was forgettin', Gene. Gabrisson's in heavy with Tony. Didn't he drive up there yesterday in that swell outfit of his, and them little yellow-legged soldiers and all?"

"That tears it then," I said. "If he's a pal of Destordi, my scheme's off."

"Not necessarily," said Prargent. "If the graft was ample enough, you bet your life Gabrisson'd double-cross Destordi like a shot. Destordi here under a cloud. People like Gabrisson knew perfectly well why he came and Destordi had to pay through the nose to get where he is now. He wouldn't strut about as he does if he didn't know he had Gabrisson behind him."

"Them dagos is all double-crossers," said Hobart.

Gene smiled. "You'd better be careful how you use that word in front of Marcel. He'd slip a knife in your ribs, Spider, as soon as look at you."

"Marcel's all right," said Spider, shifting the stub back again. "Don't he call 'em dagos himself?"

"If you think he'd be amenable to a little tip," I cut in, "then the scheme might work. But there's just one other question. Are you dead sure the American Federal Authorities want Destordi as badly as you said?"

"They want him badly enough," said Gene. "But if you've got a scheme for luring him over the frontier, there's nothing doing – unless you can lure him as far as back home again."

"There won't need to be any luring," I said. "Here's my scheme. I take it it'd satisfy your ideas of justice if you sent Tony Destordi to the chair? Suppose you did that, then you could come out into the open and tell the world why you did it. It'd do a power of good to a few other crooks in your country."

"I don't know what you're getting at. How do you mean, send him to the chair?"

"This way," I said. "Here's a comic opera republic which ever since the so-called Revolution, has refused to come into line with the rest of the civilised world on the question of Extradition Treaties, the reason being that it has some high-flown ideas about Levasque being the real land of liberty. The National Debt, Prargent told me when I sounded him this morning, is seven million pounds, and that shows roughly the value of money here. You admit possessing two million pounds or so in English money. What I say is, all you have to do is to bribe Gabrisson sufficiently and he'll introduce and carry a Bill which brings Levasque into line with the rest of the world on the extradition question. As soon as that bill is law, your diplomatic representative applies for a warrant and Destordi's arrested. In fifteen days he'll be handed over to the representatives of the American Authorities."

He gave Prargent a quick look and they nodded to each other.

"What's more," I went on, "your name will go down in American history. It may be a spectacular thing to do, but it'll certainly catch the popular fancy. Instead of your being a man who's come here virtually to commit a murder, you'll be the symbol of all constituted authority. If you'll pardon my being flamboyant, you'll avenge the outraged majesty of American law by showing that a man like Destordi can't spit at it with impunity. When the American nation learns the facts about the death of your father and what you've done to get Destordi, you'll be a greater hero than Lindbergh."

He gave a wry smile at that but I could see that he was struck by the idea. Spider Hobart was looking like a man who's had bad news.

"As for Spider," I said, "he'll have this consolation. You bet your life Destordi'll get word that the Bill's going through, and as soon as he sees it's inevitable, he'll bolt. That's where you can kill him for resisting arrest. The bribe'll cover that. You can do a little private justice by collaring him when he does bolt, and you'll get all the publicity as well."

"By God, it's a great scheme!" and he gave a sideways nod of satisfaction. "What do you say, Prargent?"

Prargent smiled. "I think it shows genius. If it does nothing else it'll drive Destordi out into the open where we can get at him. He's for it in any case, and we run no risks."

"Risks!" He laughed. "We'll be sittin' pretty. And what about you, Spider? You ought to be pleased. You'll get your rake-off just the same. The State gets Destordi and all you'll have to do is collect."

Hobart shook his head and looked real grieved. "You got me all wrong. I didn't come over here for the dough. No sir! I come over here because I saw your old man on the grass with them bullets in his guts and Destordi was the one who done it. And didn't he try to railroad me?" He shook his head perplexedly. "And what for do you want to go workin' in with all them guys? The law don't cut no ice with me. If you're droppin' out, Gene, me and Marcel can handle that egg."

Gene smiled at him. I think somewhere deep down he had a tremendous liking for Spider.

"That's all right, Spider. You let me get this thing figured out my own way. You'll get a good kick out of it when he bolts."

"Then if you think there's something in the scheme," I broke in, "there's something else I'd like to put up." Then I told them about Feuermann's pal, the editor and publisher of *La Terre*, and how I'd been invited to become a contributor to the paper. "Now what I was thinking, was this," I went on. "I'll see this bloke who runs the underground newspaper and tell him I'm prepared to write an article for him. But I'll double-cross him to this extent. The article I propose writing is one on extradition, and what a disgraceful thing it is that the world's criminals – and I'll mention some of them – should sully the fair name of Levasque, and I'll say that if the country had a decent government, the first thing it'd do would be to come into line on extradition; and I'll end by saying that that'd be too much to expect from the present gang in office. When the paper comes out – if Gene stands the expense – I'll arrange to flood the country with copies."

"And where'd the double-crossing come in?" asked Prargent.

"This way," I said. "Nothing would be done till after Gene had seen Gabrisson and he'd be told that such an article was going to be written. As soon as the country had had time to read it, Gabrisson could come along and say, 'So we – the so-called present gang – won't do anything, won't we? Now I'll show you. If it's for the good of Levasque, I'll sacrifice my private feelings and bring in such a Bill, etc., etc. That'll put him in right with everybody and find him with a good excuse. Or if you prefer it we can have the article published first and that'll give you a good excuse for approaching him."

"It's good either way," said Gene. "Once we're agreed on the principles we can settle details later. Only what makes you so frightfully keen all of a sudden?"

I told them what had happened to me that morning in the garden of the Granard. As soon as I mentioned the stocky bruiser, Spider cut in.

"Spud Mason, that'd be, Gene; him what was bouncer at Spike Rafferty's place. I got plenty on him . . ."

"You lay off," Gene told him. "We don't want any private quarrels in this. Tony's our man."

"Don't I know it?" asked Spider plaintively. "Them other guys is pikers. But you wasn't thinkin' of hoggin' them too. Don't me and Marcel get nothin'?"

I had to laugh because he was just like a boy who thinks he's being put too low down in the batting order. But when I came to the end of my story I never saw a man so furious with anger as Gene was.

"Told you to beat it, did he? And poked his gat at you."

"Now don't you start nothin', Gene," said Spider ironically. "A guy like that's too tough for a society feller like you." He sighed. "Gosh, I wisht I was peddlin' peanuts like I was the day your old man give me my first job."

"He's your meat," said Gene. "Once we get the main guy, you and Marcel can have the pickin's."

Spider's lean face lit up. Prargent cleared his throat and poured himself out another tot.

"If I might make a suggestion, it'd be this. Why shouldn't you play up what happened to Donald for all it's worth? Take him along if necessary, to see Gabrisson and let him be an English pressman who's been insulted here in Montelle and who's going to give the English papers an account of it. Let him say there'll probably be such a commotion – seeing who Destordi is – that the League of Nations'll be asked to take action and bring pressure to bear on Levasque. Then you can tell Gabrisson that it'd be much better for him to do of his own accord – taking the boodle as well – what he may have to do by compulsion."

"It's a good idea," said Gene, "but don't rush me. This is going to be a big thing and it wants figuring out."

"And how much did you think of offering Gabrisson?" I asked.

"Don't know yet," he said. "I'm going to have a limit and I'll let him know he can't hot-stuff me. I shan't go over half a million and he'll have to share that with his gang."

"Dollars?"

"Good God, no! Pounds. This is big business, not piking. What's more I'll have him so tied up that he doesn't get a bean till Tony's handed over."

"He'll double-cross you," said Prargent. "He knows the ropes here and you don't."

"Don't you believe it. That money'll never leave Paris."

"And how're you going to see him?"

"That's easy," said Gene. "Remember that tall guy with the little, black imperial we saw dancing at the Cap d'Or? That's his secretary. He's the bloke I'm going after first. The rest'll be easy."

"They'll sure have you tailed," came Spider's gloomy voice. "I don't mean them dumb dicks in the yeller pants. No, sir! Them guys are a mighty peaceable lot, but if this Gabrisson is ace high in this country he'll sure have a Pinkerton outfit hangin' around. Remember that guy I told you about what was buzzin' me in the Granard?"

"Oh, shut up!" snapped Gene. "The way you talk you'd think I was just a big sap." He looked round at us. "What about a short conference? Draw your chairs in and let's get down to it."

*

The following morning at ten o'clock found me on the way to the flower shop in Cathedral Square and I posted at a handy wall-box a letter I'd written to Munro Burnside, telling him – as we'd arranged overnight – that I was proposing some time to send along something on the extradition question, and giving him a short account of the affair in the Granard that had prompted me to rush into print. We thought that'd be a good move in case Gabrisson should be minded to make enquiries through a representative in London.

I liked that old part of the town much better than the Place Granard. All round it were stalls with gaudy, striped awnings, and people marketing, and everywhere was the homely smell of onions. In the middle was a bandstand with seats round it, and the usual old men were sitting there under the few trees reading their newspapers. A wasp-like sentry was lounging before the heavy door of the jail and I could see nothing of it, but its stone walls and barred windows. The shop I wanted was easy enough to spot with its flowers piled on the pavement outside, and at the door was the crippled man in a chair which he handled so dexterously that he moved it back in a flash and then followed me across to the counter. A woman was there, buying flowers for a funeral.

"I want three white roses," I said. "And with long stalks."

He gave me a quick look, then nodded at the back of the woman in black.

"At your service, m'sieur, in one moment."

He twirled the wheels of his chair and disappeared somewhere behind the counter, but as soon as the shop was empty again he reappeared.

"This way, m'sieur."

I followed him into a living-room where he opened the door of what looked like a cupboard but turned out to be the landing for a flight of steps. It was all very mysterious and I felt a bit of a fool but I made my way down as instructed and tapped at the door at the bottom. Before I'd finished tapping, the door opened and a face appeared. It was most uncanny there in the gloom, till something happened that was really extraordinary, for my eyes opened wide all of a sudden and the other eyes opened too, and we recognised each other. Then the door opened and there stood my friend of the Nancy road who'd aired his English to me and saved my life with a cigarette.

"Monsieur Crevelle?" I asked, and handed him Feuermann's card.

He looked at it and then again at me. In a couple of minutes we were seated in his cellar room, talking away with all the ease in the world – though not in pidgin-English.

"What were you doing so far afield as Nancy that morning?" I asked him.

He took me to the window and pulled back the curtain. A few feet away ran a line of warehouses, through which one could see barges and the river. Away to the right was the tall, bare, windowless wall of the jail.

"Ostensibly," he said, "I'm an agent for Rastiers, the wine firm, and I travel about all over the place. That gives me an excuse for the car and the car carries our paper, or we send bundles on the barges by trusted men. I've actually got an office just over there and I can get in here without using the shop. Feuermann planned it all. He knows Rastier, who's one of our best friends."

"And you really expect to start a counter-revolution one of these days?"

He seemed more amused at that than anything else. "That won't come in our time. Only somebody's got to do the educational work, or it'll never come at all. Feuermann tells me you've come to help us."

I smiled modestly. "I don't know about that. He had the idea that an article or two on England might do some good and I said I'd do what I could. May I see your apparatus?"

He showed me round. It was a smelly, cheap sort of place, that gave you an immediate amazement that anything at all could ever be done in it. There were two primitive hand presses and a small binding machine worked by a treadle, and the lot looked as if Noah had sold it second-hand. The paper itself, judged by the copy he showed me, wasn't too bad, though it wasn't much more than quarto size and consisted of only the double sheet. He looked so pleased with it all himself that I had to be pleased too.

"Of course it's not like an official paper," he said, watching me like a junior clerk who entertains the head of the firm. "And naturally as time goes on and we get more support we shall do better."

That gave me my chance, and you ought to have seen his eyes bulge when I told him the news.

"I've found a sympathiser for you," I said, "but he wishes to remain anonymous. He's interested in these articles I'm willing to write, and his own pet subject is extradition. He thinks it a disgrace to this lovely country of yours that you should allow known criminals to use it as a kind of refuge. He proposed to me that I should begin the series by writing about that particular subject and then going on to whatever you people thought might do most good."

He was so bubbling over with excitement that all he could keep doing was making clucking noises. And when I counted out twenty thousand-franc notes into his hand, he suddenly gave an ecstatic " Ah! M'sieur!" and had his arms round me in a dash, and as he embraced me I had a good whiff of the oil that plastered down his long, black hair.

"That's all right," I said, when I'd disentangled myself. "There's more to come when we want it, only we've got to show our friend what we can do. You can get help if you want it?"

"But certainly!"

"And if you got some sort of an edition out at once, how many could you print?"

He thought for a moment, then said proudly that he could manage twenty thousand – by the next morning, working all night. The paper would have to be smuggled in after dark, but everything could be ready for printing. To tackle the question of extradition was a capital thing, he thought. He'd had it in mind more than once himself.

"Then we'll make a start," I said. "Get out your twenty thousand if you can and deliver them free. We want Montelle absolutely plastered with 'em. Got a typewriter?"

He produced quite a good one from a cupboard and while I hammered out the rough draft of my manifesto, began collecting the rest of the material to make up the edition. It took me well over an hour to do my stuff and I've never written anything with so much gusto. No patch was too purple and no cliché too outworn, and when I wasn't rhetorical I was maudlin. Then of course we had to get to work on the translation and we had a scratch lunch in the middle of it. It was well after two o'clock by the time we had it in its final shape and I must say it didn't read too badly. The trouble was that Crevelle was so enthusiastic that he produced at once a programme that would have kept me busy for months – the houses of pleasure in the rue des Suisses, the deplorable state of the university and education generally; in fact, all the pet grievances he'd had on his mind for months.

"We'll wait and see how this one goes," I told him. "If we want the continued and valued support of my friend, as many copies as you can print must be all over the country by to-morrow night at the latest, and here in Montelle first thing in the morning. And who're you going to say the proposed articles are by?"

It took some time to settle that and finally we agreed that Crevelle should preface the current one with a puff about a very famous English author and journalist – whose name for obvious reasons couldn't be disclosed – who was not only international in reputation but also from his youth one who had followed with interest the fortunes of Levasque.

Crevelle signalled upstairs to see if the coast was clear and when I left him he had donned a filthy apron and his fingers were already the colour of the murky type. I was a bit grubby in patches too but it had been a long while since I'd so enjoyed a morning. As I walked up the hill I couldn't help wondering if my name would ever appear in the history books as the only begetter of that great gesture of the Assemble Nationale Levascanne which should bring their country into line with the rest of civilised humanity, and the thought tickled me so much that I found myself laughing out loud.

There wasn't a soul in the villa when I let myself in, except the cook whose snores could be heard even in the kitchen. I didn't feel like sleep but took out a chair to the shade of the verandah and smoked and lazed the rest of the afternoon away.

That evening Gene was to make his first approaches to Pigolle, Gabrisson's secretary, and the following evening he hoped for an interview with the great man himself. I was to be kept out of it; the article in Crevelle's newspaper would be sufficient without my making a personal appearance, moreover there was that unfortunate occurrence in the tobacconist's shop of which Gabrisson might be aware, and the fact that my passport said nothing about journalism. That very afternoon too, as I was sitting there, Gene was probably arranging for sufficient credit at the Paris bank, and Prargent was out snooping generally, with a special interest in one lady of the now dormant opera, on whom Gabrisson was said to have an amorous claim, and whose knowledge of the proposed deal might – if we thought it expedient to use her – remove any scruples which Gabrisson might summon up. In other words, the wheels were moving, and long before I drew my next month's pay we ought to have smoked Destordi from his hole and done something – and there I smiled at the anti-climax – to maintain the principles of eternal justice; a well-sounding piece of clap-trap which I'd used in my article of the morning. But it hadn't looked quite so gaudy in French.

Chapter XI
A NIGHT OUT

I MADE myself a cup of tea and then amused myself by watching Destordi's house through Prargent's glasses.

I had them trained on it till I'd seen every stone in the walls and the cracks between the outside shutters, and that was all I did see. Whatever was going on inside it, the outside of that house was about as informative as the outside of the local jail, and it looked just as secure and forbidding. The garden was invisible, but, as Prargent had told me, there was a clear view of twenty yards of road, and when I thought of that bastard Destordi and the way he'd looked at me in the Granard, I could almost fancy myself lying there on the verandah, my finger crooked round the trigger of the Lewis, waiting to spatter that twenty yards with the contents of a tray.

I had one of my restless fits after that. The house seemed hot as hell and I wandered down to the kitchen to spend a half hour with Madame Moulines, but her niece had arrived and that drove me upstairs again. Then the telephone bell went – Prargent ringing up to say he wouldn't be in till ten. That was all but it cleared my mind for I knew what I had been itching to do. A quarter of an hour later saw me swinging down the hill to the Granard.

I ordered myself a safe three francs' worth of vermouth-citron and watched the perambulating crowd, a thing I could have done for hours, and then when I thought the time for the orchestra had come I went inside and actually collared my favourite pew. The hall was pretty empty for it was a swelterer, as I told you, and there was no sign of Feuermann, but before I'd been there a couple of minutes the waiter who knew me came over and spoke in a low voice.

"Will you come this way, m'sieur. A friend wishes to see you."

I followed him with a bit of a scare inside. For all I knew I was being led like a mutt to the spot of slaughter, and every corner I turned I expected to see my stocky friend of the previous morning, but I needn't have worried, for the room I was shown into was merely a private box affair through which you could see the hall when the curtains were drawn, and sitting at the table with an aperitif at his elbow was Feuermann, He got up as soon as he saw me.

"That's what comes of having influence," he said with his shy apologetic smile. "What will you drink?"

I shook hands and named my appetizer and when Maximilien had brought it, he explained. For all the raillery of his remark I could see he was disturbed.

"Well, young man, what were you up to after I left you yesterday morning?"

I gave him my version, though it was a job requiring a diplomat rather than a journalist. He nodded away when I'd finished.

"I've heard one version already and I thought it couldn't be right. What's your idea of Monsieur Destordi?"

"Whether you like it or not," I said, "I think he's one of the biggest swine I ever ran across. As for those two bruisers of his –" I realised I was getting into deep water and ended that with a shrug. "I'd heard of him before," I went on. "We get to hear all sorts of things in Fleet Street."

He cocked his ear at that. "Fleet Street?"

"Yes," I said. "The place which stands for the English Press. Tell me," and I looked at him. "Didn't you know he was wanted badly by the American police?"

He smiled dryly. "It doesn't matter what I know, but I'll tell you this. I didn't know it when I took on the job I now have." He looked down at his drink, then all at once he looked up again with a quick little gesture. "I believe I can trust you."

I hardly knew what to say. "I'm sure you can," was what I managed to get out. "And I know I could trust you." It sounded very lame as I said it, but he nodded at me and then drew his chair closer.

"A man can't quarrel with his living," he began, "but things aren't what they used to be up there. First he got in an American woman – not the one you saw this morning; she's the second. Then queer sorts of people used to come – that man who was shot the other day was one – and other women, and there used to be noisy drinking and card games going on till all hours." He shook his head. "I ought to have left then, but it was the old story – the money was too good and he was always all right with me. You see there aren't any aristocracy of the old school in Levasque and if I stayed here all my life I couldn't aspire to anything better. Then a month or so ago he changed for the worse. He told me there was some sort of conspiracy going on and knowing what I did I had to laugh to myself when he said it, but he had the house made like a fortress and he had those two Americans in for protection, and even the servants are grumbling and saying it's like looking after pigs. Someone told him this morning I'd been seen with you and he asked me all sorts of questions about you. He knows you were in the shop when Berousse was killed and he wants to know just who you are. I told him I knew nothing; that you were a casual acquaintance in whom I was interested because we could talk English together, and then he told me he expected me to make you talk. I told him perfectly respectfully that I couldn't do a thing like that. I wasn't engaged for it. Then he turned nasty. He told me I was getting impudent – that was the expression he used. You see he always talks American with me; perhaps that's why he first wanted to engage me. Finally he ended by saying that he insisted I kept out of your way, and what was more he didn't want me out of the house so much. A half hour in the evening before dinner he said was plenty. I said, 'Very good, sir,' as I always do, and that seemed to make him still more annoyed." He shrugged his shoulders and smiled. "What's going to happen next I don't know."

"But you mustn't run any risks for me," I began.

"No risk at all. Maximilien's all right. Nobody else knows we're here. All the same if we want to meet I'll see you at Crevelle's. It'll only be for about half an hour this time of an evening. If you drop in, you'll be told if I'm downstairs."

Again I hardly knew what to say because I knew that something would drop out of my life if I missed seeing him, but I said I'd certainly call sometimes at the flower shop.

"It'll be all the better in a way," I said, "because we shall be able to talk freely there. Thousands of questions I want to ask you about Levasque."

Then I asked him about the woman who'd been with Destordi that morning because I wanted to see if Spider or Marcel knew anything about her.

"He got her from Paris," Feuermann told me. "He used to go there occasionally when he first came here, although even I wasn't supposed to know anything about it. But she won't be here long. He slapped her across the mouth the other night and she screamed at him like a madwoman, so I was told. Next day she came crawling to him again but she knows she's only there on sufferance."

"What happened to the other woman?" I asked.

He shrugged. "He set her up in business in the rue des Suisses, if you know what that means. One of the most flourishing places there, I'm told."

He finished his drink and rose to go. "Well," and he held out his hand, "the next time will be . . . somewhere else."

Some extraordinary impulse must have seized hold of me because I blurted out the words before I'd had time to think.

"You'll keep a secret? A life and death secret?"

He smiled down at me. "I've got a dozen of them in my head already."

I realised he was still standing and I got to my feet and whispered in his ear.

"If you see the chance of another job, take it! All sorts of things might be happening."

He nodded. "What sort of things?"

I shook my head. "That I can't tell you. Read *La Terre* when it comes out to-night and have a word with Crevelle."

"Thanks," he said and nodded again. Then he smiled at me and shook hands and I watched him go. A few seconds later Maximilien appeared again and took me down to where I could slip into the hall unnoticed When I sat down I hardly knew where I was for a minute or two and I mopped away the perspiration that soaked my collar and looked round me as if afraid that everybody should know me for some sort of conspirator. But nobody, not even a waiter, was paying the least attention to me and with the same restless fit that had seized me earlier that evening, I picked up my hat again and went out to the front tables where I had a bock.

In a few minutes I heard a woman singing and noticed the movement of the people behind me, but somehow I didn't feel like moving. Then I had a sudden idea and asked for writing material. And when I had written my note and sent it by a waiter, I knew I shouldn't get an answer. But I did. In five minutes another waiter brought my own note back and scribbled on the bottom was:

"SIDE DOOR IN TEN MINUTES."

I didn't know where the side door was but I found out. She was there dead on time and when I went to shake hands like the big lummox that I felt, she merely smiled at me and said we'd better hurry. All Montelle seemed to be out of doors that night and we dodged our way in and out along the pavement towards the river. Twice we stopped at shops and she made some purchases, and it was just short of the Pont l'Abbé where the funny little trams rejoined us, that we turned off into a narrow street and a few yards along it she entered an open door. She smiled at the fat concierge who was sitting there knitting, and we mounted the stairs.

I put down my parcels on the table as soon as we got inside the tiny kitchen.

"Why wouldn't you come and have dinner with me at the Granard?" I asked point-blank.

She didn't take me very seriously for she began putting the fat yellow tomatoes into a dish.

"I don't like dining at the Granard, as I work there. The management mightn't like it." She gave me a roguish look. "Don't you want to have dinner here?"

"I'd love it," I said. "Anything I can do to help?"

She made me sit down on one of the cane-backed chairs and I watched her lay the cloth and get the meal ready. Bread, butter, sausage, salad and fruit, was the menu, with sardines as hors d'oeuvre and coffee to finish with, and there was a bottle of white wine of the country. My toilet was made over the sink and then we sat down.

"How'd you come to get into the show business?"

"Oh, I don't know." She made a face. "Father killed in the war and not enough pension to go round, so being the eldest I kicked off for myself. Pierrot troupe first, then a touring company, then I signed up for the trip to Levasque – and here I am."

I was itching to tell her that she was a cut above that sort of thing but I knew the independence of the latest generation and kept my thoughts to myself. But I must have looked something of what I was thinking because she gave me quite a superior smile.

"Don't you think I'm capable of looking after myself? I'm twenty-five, you know."

"A great age." I said. "And how much longer are you staying at the Granard?"

"Only another week, then I'm going home. I've saved thirty pounds since I've been here. Isn't it wonderful?"

"Going home!" I said blankly. "I say, that's dreadful. I'll never go to the Granard again. First it's Feuermann and now –"

She broke in there and I had to tell her what Feuermann had said half an hour before.

"So I look like losing my only two friends," I said, "and I haven't known either of you half long enough."

She laughed, then suddenly looked at me and put the question in the oddest way. "You like Herr Feuermann?"

I became lyrical at once and I saw how pleased she was. And when I said there was only one thing wrong with him, I saw her stiffen at once.

"And what's that?"

I thought I'd tease her a bit. "Well, there's two things really. It's a pity he isn't English – though he might be some day."

"What's it matter what a man is?" and she turned up her nose. "And what's the other thing?"

"Far too old," I said with exaggerated contempt.

"He isn't old. He isn't fifty."

"Fifty's a Methuselah age," I said. "You see, if I were as charming as he is and he were as young as I; if we could pool our excellencies, in short – you wouldn't be going back to England."

"Is that a proposal of marriage?"

She looked so serious that it put me rather out of countenance. I took refuge in a retort.

"Seriously, though – and don't be angry with me for saying it – would you marry Herr Feuermann if he were younger?"

She made a face at me. "That'd be asking. Let's talk about you instead. Oh, and I must show you my view."

She hopped up at once and drew back the muslined shutters. The sun was getting low and its light made the river a queer emerald colour and set the old roofs below us flaming like fire. I followed the line of orange scarlet from the tiles down by a tottering chimney and then my eye caught something that made me draw back. Across the street by the back of the gardenless house was a café, and sitting there well back in the shadows was my artist pest of the Granard, and as soon as he saw me at the window he shot back out of sight leaving his half-filled glass still on the marble-topped table.

"Any view from your bedroom?" I asked.

"The same as this one. Why?"

"There's a man out there I've seen hanging about wherever I've happened to be," I said. "He's supposed to be an artist and pesters people at the Granard."

Her eyes opened. "Herr Feuermann warned me about him. He said he was a spy."

"A spy!" For a moment I was inclined to laugh. "Whose spy? And what's he spy on?"

She pushed the shutters too again though they darkened the room.

"He said he was employed by the government. All that picture business is supposed to be a fake." Then she stared at me as if surprised. "But what's he spying on you for?"

I laughed. "Imagination probably. The man's got to go somewhere. Have you got to go back to the Granard to-night?"

"Why, of course! I have to sing again at ten o'clock."

"What a life!" I said. "It isn't right for you to be out at that time of night in a place like this."

She laughed like anything at that. "If only you knew how funny you look when you try to be serious!"

I nodded portentously. "Perhaps you don't know Levasque as well as I do." I stopped short there before my tongue ran away with me and then got up and took another squint through the shutter. There was no sign of the Bohemian and there was no glass on the table. I sat down heavily and gave another portentous nod.

"I'll bet that chap has bribed your concierge. Do you ever have people up here?"

"You're the first who's ever come," she said. "And get on with your supper. I'm sure you're talking nonsense. Why should he want to spy on me?"

"You never know," I said oracularly. "Still, if you hadn't laughed at me I'd have told you what happened to me the other day."

Then of course I had to give her a carefully edited version of the death of "Greasy" Berousse and that brought us to the end of the meal. Then she washed up and I dried, and somehow I was beginning to feel that I wanted that night to drag on and on. It wasn't that I was falling in love with her. I don't quite know what it was except that we seemed to get on so well together, and there we were like two orphans in a strange land, making the most of a rare hour or two and being jolly together without thinking of the proprieties – or the lack of them for that matter.

There was a faint scent she used, something like lilac, and every time I caught it it had that same effect on me that an English garden has on a dewy summer night.

"Your father was a soldier?" I asked suddenly.

"Not a regular," she said. "He was an architect really, only he got killed in the war. My mother was French – that's why I speak the language rather well. Pallingham, we lived at. Do you know it?"

"Pallingham?" I said. "Now who lives at Pallingham? I know. 'Tubby' Howes –"

"Not Billy Howes whose father is a doctor?"

"That's the bloke," I said. "We were at Cranmer together. Do you know him?"

"Do I know him?" She laughed, and then we both laughed. "I was at school with his sisters. Helen's a topping girl. Do you know Helen?" That kept us going for quite a long while. It was gorgeously romantic sitting there well back from the open window with the hills stretching away to the horizon and all the funny smells of the streets floating in and quaint sounds, and every now and again I found myself wondering if we really were in Levasque after all.

"How'd you like to live here for ever?" I asked her.

She gave me a droll, suspicious look. "I thought we weren't going to talk about that again?"

I know now that that was when I first really thought she was in love with Feuermann but I didn't show it.

"We're not," I said. "We're talking about living in Levasque. A topping little house facing south up there in the hills, and a garden, and vines, and enough to live on. Wouldn't you like it?"

She was silent for a moment. "I'd love it . . . but I'd like to go to England sometimes. Not often . . ."

I laughed. "I know a fairy and I'll have it all fixed up."

"A fairy?" She smiled at me. "What's she like?"

"It isn't a she," I said. "It's a he fairy; rather on the short side, brown-eyed, melancholy face –"

She jumped up laughing. "You're not a fairy. You're a gnome. And now I must get ready to go back. Just two minutes."

I lighted another cigarette when the door closed. Before the two minutes were up she stuck her head round the door.

"I've got a wonderful engagement to-morrow night. I'm putting on the frock now to try it."

The door shut again before I could turn, and I went on with my cigarette. It was five minutes before she came in and she had on a wonderful blue frock, all puckered and shimmery. I think if she hadn't looked so serious I'd have put my arms round her where she stood.

"Well? . . . Isn't it pretty?"

"It's lovely," I said. "And you're lovely too."

She shook her head and smiled. "Workaday Jane, that's me." Then she whisked on her wrap before I could help her and began to shoo me out. It was dark on the stairs and I held her arm and steered her down. Perhaps, I thought, it was all wrong about Feuermann after all.

"I didn't tell you about where I'm going tomorrow," she said when we were out on the pavement again. "Monsieur Destordi –"

I seized her arm. "You're not going there?"

It was all so quick that I didn't know how foolish I must have been looking and I let her arm go.

"Sorry. I shouldn't have done that. . . . But you're not thinking of going to a house like that, are you?" I must have annoyed her in some way for she bridled up at once.

"And why shouldn't I go to Mr. Destordi's house? It's his cabaret I sing in. He's paying me well."

I tried to make her stop. "Do wait a minute. Let me talk to you just a second. You can't go there. You really can't!"

She threw my arm off. "Don't be foolish. Besides, you're making people stare."

I followed her moodily enough, then had an idea. "Does Herr Feuermann know about it?" I asked.

"It's not Herr Feuermann's business and it's not yours."

That settled it for the moment. She walked on, head in air, and I kept a dignified silence. Then when we reached the side door of the Granard she held out her hand and she was smiling.

"Good-bye . . . And don't worry about me. I'm used to taking care of myself."

"But you don't know," I began. And that was all I said for she'd opened the door and was through it before I could get out another word. I stood there looking at that door for a minute or two, expecting something magical to happen; then I scowled at it and turned sulkily on my heel.

I sat on one of the seats in the Place Granard till the clock showed ten o'clock and then I began my journey uphill. I must have been in an abominable temper, thinking unutterable things and muttering away to myself, and it was only when I came to my senses where the pavement ended at a crossing that I began to realise I was taking far too seriously what didn't concern me in any case. All the same, I thought, I'd find some way to give Feuermann the tip, and just as I began to plan how that could be done, there was a roar from somewhere the other side of the road and a bullet spattered against the wall by my head.

I was on my belly before you could have said a word, scared cold in a flash. Then in a wild panic I scrambled up and took to my heels, tearing up the hill like a madman. Every second I thought there'd be a bullet in me, but there wasn't another sound. On I flew round the corner into the avenue, and I didn't stop till I got to the garden door. There my hand was shaking so much and I was so eager to get the door open that the damn key wouldn't go in the slot, and when I did get it open I slammed it to as if the devil were after me. Then I listened for sounds in the road but there weren't any, and I mopped my forehead with my handkerchief and flushed a more violent red as I thought of the figure I'd cut.

When I got upstairs there was Hobart rousing himself in his chair in front of the window where he'd been sleeping with his waistcoat off. He stared at me drowsily.

"Gosh," he said, "I thought it was Gene."

"What're you doing here?" I asked.

"Me?" He looked at me mildly. "The boss said for me to wait here with the telephone. Him and the Cap's gotten hold of that secretary and they're off to see the main guy rightaway. Looks as if things was pannin' out right."

I poured myself out a drink and I must have looked rather surly for Hobart noticed something wrong.

"And what's eatin' you, young man? You're not sore at me because I wasn't hot for that scheme of yours?"

"Good Lord no, Spider," I told him. "The fact of the matter is I was shot at on my way home just now."

"Shot? Sure it wasn't one of them m'skeeters what they raise round here?"

"Mosquitos be damned! Do you think I don't know a bullet when I get one half an inch from my ear?"

He sat up at that. "And who done it?"

"I don't know. But I can go out and ask him."

It took him a good minute to see that piece of heavy irony. Then he shook his head.

"Didn't I tell you? When them two guys of Tour's have put one or two of us in the boneyard, Gene'll come to life. He sure drives me nuts. I can bump off them three guys like as if I was shellin' peanuts. It's a cinch – and what's he say for me to do? Sit around and wait for him to talk on the telephone. Can you beat it?"

"Don't you worry," I said. "Your time's coming. Wait till Destordi bolts from his hole.... Have a spot of whisky and forget your troubles."

He stroked his lean jaws. "Guess I might as well. And don't go easy on the seltzer. Gene said for me to lay off the booze and what he says, goes."

I laughed at that and he looked quite upset till I showed him what he'd left of the full bottle.

Chapter XII
THE PINEAPPLE

I DIDN'T leave the house at all during the next two days. Things were moving far too rapidly for that. Indeed, so many things were happening that I ought to tell you them in some sort of order.

First of all Gabrisson had definitely bitten. It was the Thursday night when Gene had first approached him through Pigolle – or Pig-oil, as Spider would persist in calling him. On the Friday a meeting had been arranged at Nancy with a representative from the American Embassy in Paris and one of the principals of the Paris bank, and Gabrisson had attended it privately with Gene and Prargent.

As soon as the wheels had moved that far round, Marcel had had orders to put Destordi's villa under surveillance night and day, and he'd brought down three or four of his numerous relatives to help him, and the roads, so I understood, were being watched except the main road to Nancy, which was the only one Destordi would never dare to take. As far as we could figure it out, there was only one country in Europe that was reasonably safe for him, and as that was Russia, he might try a break through by Hungary. In any case, Marcel had instructions to have the car ready at a second's notice, and the guns were packed in it and I helped personally to overhaul the pair of them and fill half a dozen trays. Spider was on duty at the lower villa and I was at the Marguerite, and both of us with nothing to do but be ready for whatever happened.

What effect that first article by an eminent English journalist had had on the population of Levasque, and of Montelle in particular, I didn't know, and that was exasperating. I got hold of a copy of *La Terre* and saw myself in print, but that was nothing, for the thing that mattered was that the government organs made no reference to it whatever. What I hoped was that when Gabrisson got back they'd have the order to start moving: not that I reckoned they ever paid much attention to the fulminations of *La Terre*, any more than a couple of buffaloes in a fat pasture mind the noise of a bullfrog. But this was going to be different.

Marcel dropped in late on the Friday night and we sat up talking till lord knows when. I never cottoned to him as I did to Spider, and I don't know that I'd have trusted him far, but he was good enough company. He let out a lot that I didn't know.

"No sign of Destordi bolting yet?" I asked him.

"Bolt? All punk," he said. "Who's to wise that guy up to what's goin' on? You bet a smart guy like Gabrisson don't go givin' nothing away till he's got Gene's dough. Know what that egg was before the Revolution? A barber, that's what he was, and he didn't have his own shop neither. I'll bet a ten-spot sure looked good to him in them days, and here's him holdin' out on more'n a thousand grand. Gee! don't it make your mouth water?"

"It's a lot of money," I said, and in case that wasn't strong enough, "The hell of a lot of money."

"It sure is," echoed Marcel, then shook his head. "Gene ain't handled this thing right. Know where Gabrisson hangs out?"

I said I didn't.

"He's got a swell place up in the hills," he told me. "Back of where we are now about a coupla miles. Gene's got a dick or two hangin' around in this burg, and they tailed Tony up there and sent Gene word. And only two ways what he could get out by; one for me and one for Spider. We could have wiped out the whole outfit easy as crackin' a louse. Then Spider had him sittin' pretty in the Granard only Gene railed him off. Can you beat it?"

"Gene's paying," I said. "He's a right to have things done his own way."

Gene and Prargent came back on the Saturday afternoon, driving up to the Marguerite in a taxi as if they no longer gave a damn who knew they lived there. I was bursting to hear the news and I didn't have long to wait. Gene slapped me on the back as soon as we'd got in the room.

"Well, Machiavelli, we're on a winner!"

I grinned sheepishly. "Honestly? Everything's all right?"

"It looks good to me; don't you think so, Prargent?"

Prargent shrugged his shoulders. "I'd like it better if it weren't for what I told you."

Gene laughed. "He'll get his share of the rake-off, won't he?"

"Don't start an argument," I said. "Can't you tell a bloke what happened?"

He laughed again. "The funny thing is we don't know what happened. The old boy was scared stiff anybody should know he was there at all, though he brightened up a bit before we saw the last of him. I got Pearson of the Embassy to come along and give a formal assurance that America would be willing to make a treaty of extradition at any time, and if Levasque should see fit to do it another way by simply declaring the country no longer a non-extradition country, then application would be made at once for the extradition of certain parties."

"He knew you were driving at Destordi?"

Gene smiled. "Oh yes! the old boy knew that all right. Then the bank representative agreed to act as stake holder and I gave in to the extent of saying the money should be paid over as soon as a state of non-extradition was removed. All the old boy did was to listen to everything and nod like a fat old Arab buying carpets. But Prargent got him roused. After the formal meeting that was, just as we left him. He said if Gabrisson didn't agree to the proposal we should have no other alternative but to acquaint the Levascan people through the Press with what had been offered; in other words that for the sake of protecting his pals, Gabrisson had turned down enough money to pay most of the country's taxes for a year. That hit him where he keeps his lunch; didn't it Prargent?"

"But just a minute," I said. "I thought Gabrisson was to have the money."

"So he is, if he comes in the scheme. At the moment everything's secret as hell. Only, if he doesn't come in, the offer'll be made public. You see we've probably got him either way."

"It certainly looks good," I said. "And what was that you and Prargent were arguing about?"

Gene shrugged his shoulders. "He doesn't trust Pigolle. Neither do I – but what's it matter? He'll get his share if Gabrisson comes in. It's to his interest to push the scheme on."

"That's just where I say you were wrong," put in Prargent. "Pigolle either knows too much or too little. As it is we're almost sure he knows nothing of the real scheme, but then, on the other hand, we've given him cause for the devil of a lot of suspicion. He knows something big is in the wind. Also we're not sure old Gabrisson'll play fair when he gets the money. If you remember he enquired about the channels through which we proposed to pay it. That means he's going to hog practically the lot, and Pigolle'll be bound to talk –"

"Let him," said Gene airily. "We'll be away and gone long before that. Once we've done our job, they can wash their dirty linen where they like."

Prargent shook his head. "I don't like it. We ought to have taken Pigolle into our confidence first, then he'd have kept Gabrisson up to scratch for his own sake. Still, you're the boss – and I hope I'm wrong."

Gene laughed. "Of course you're wrong. Still, we'll know by the morning which way the cat's going to jump."

"Gabrisson's letting you know then?"

"That's right. He returned to Montelle yesterday evening for the Fête Nationale. Which reminds me. You haven't been out for a bit. You'd better take the evening off and have a look at the sights. Where's Marcel? And has he had that place well covered?"

"He and Spider ought to be down at your place," I said. "And what's this about a Fête?"

He clapped me on the back – or he would have done if I hadn't dodged. "Didn't I tell you? The Fête-Nationale – celebration of the famous revolution. All the streets are lousy with bunting; aren't they, Prargent? There'll probably be free drinks tomorrow."

"Why not to-day?"

"To-day's the preliminaries," he said. "Tomorrow's the show day. Dancing in all the Places, heaps of girls, plenty of bands, processions – gawd knows what. We're going to-morrow, aren't we, Prargent?"

"Right-ho then," I said. "I think I will take a peep. I shan't be in late though."

"You run off and have a good time," Gene told me. "Maybe after to-night we'll all of us be on duty all the time. Tony's got to be watched night and day from now on. Come along, Prargent; we'll go and hear what Marcel's got ready for us."

I had a bath and togged myself out, and no sooner did I get out of the rue Paulette than I knew something was happening in Montelle. Nearly every private house had a flag out and there were arches of bunting here and there across the road, and somewhere in the distance could be heard cheering, and there was the sound of a band. The further down the hill I got, the yellower the town became, with that ghastly national flag spawning everywhere, and the yellow draperies of the Granard statue and the windows of the hotels. People were swarming like ants and every seat in the Restaurant Granard seemed taken, for all I could see was heads.

However, I thought I'd chance my luck and I made my way across the road and wriggled through the opening, with a push here and a "Pardon, m'sieur!" there, till I got to the back of the ground verandah and there I was wedged tight. Then the sound of a band was distinctly heard from somewhere behind us. Everybody began to chatter; there was a movement in front and then a kind of stampede. From my perch I could see the crowd flocking towards the Cathedral Square, and in less than a minute I had a seat plumb in the front above the pavement.

That was good going, and I stretched my legs luxuriously and then looked round for a waiter. There wasn't one in sight.

"The service is terrible," remarked a voice. "As soon as anything happens, they lose their heads."

Before he had finished I knew the old gentleman was talking to me. He was an extraordinary old chap, straight out of a book, with his sober black; thick felt hat; pallid face and enormous white beard that began at the middle of his chin and then ran down to the middle of his waistcoat as thick as a man's wrist all the way. The rest of his face was clean shaven except for a white moustache that brushed his ears.

"What was the excitement, m'sieur?" I asked. "Where has everybody gone to?"

It was the President who had gone that way to the Hotel de Ville to read an address inaugurating the Fête, he explained. Everybody had thought he was coming through the Place Granard, but evidently the arrangements had been altered, but the procession would be coming back this way in about an hour. As for processions, he *fiched* himself of them, he said.

Just after that we got our drinks and then we began talking. He was a shrewd, old bird, and he spotted me for an Englishman at once. I don't know if it was real but he spoke with admiration of England and he kept me busy answering questions. I had more than a suspicion that he was one of Crevelle's supporters but I hadn't too much to go on except that he said he *fiched* himself of governments, a remark with which I wholly agreed.

But I must say it was very jolly sitting there and I began to feel something of what all those people were feeling as they promenaded the streets and chattered merrily and gesticulated – quite different from the rather sober, pre-occupied lot they'd always seemed to me. I had a sense of satisfaction too at securing the front seat for the forthcoming show, and as people began more and more to flock back to the Granard and the Place I kept telling myself I was a lucky fellow. Then I thought of what I'd planned for the evening. I'd go along to the flower shop to see if Feuermann was there, and if he wasn't, then I'd have a yarn with Crevelle and maybe I'd get him to come to the Granard for dinner. Most of all I wanted to see Lucy Brock, and I told myself that as soon as the procession had passed I'd phone up to the Villa Marguerite and tell Prargent I'd perhaps be out a bit later than I'd thought. Perhaps on her last night, I thought, I might get her to have dinner with me somewhere, and then I wouldn't say anything to Crevelle. I wanted to know too what had happened when she went to Destordi's, and just then happening to see a waiter coming our way I thought I'd make sure the Fête hadn't disorganised things.

"Mle. Brock is singing here to-night as usual?" I asked him.

"*Oui, m'sieur,*" he said. "There are special gala performances to-night."

I think he was going to tell me more about it but somebody collared him with an order. My friend at the table knew nothing of the details either except that he'd heard there was a tenor coming from Paris. I expected him to conclude that he *fiched* himself of tenors, but he didn't.

A thin line of spectators was now beginning to form along the pavements, and the verandah of the Granard began to get uncomfortably full again. There was the sound of tremendous cheering from the direction of the Hotel de Ville and five minutes later the crowd was ten deep along the street and the windows everywhere were packed. All at once the old gentleman cocked an ear and remarked: "*Ça commence!*" At the same time I heard a band strike up.

The procession emerged from the rue Pont l'Abbé, well to our left, and from where we sat we had the finest view in Montelle, well clear of the heads on the pavement. First came a squadron of what looked like cuirassiers, trotting slowly and keeping the crowd well back on the pavements. Next were about a hundred infantry, and they must have been sweltering in their yellow coats, drawn back at the knee like the French ones they'd been modelled on. Then, with a roar from the crowd and a fluttering of handkerchiefs, an open car came into sight. All I could see at the moment was that a man and a woman were in it, the woman carrying a parasol and the man in uniform with a vivid yellow sash across his middle.

"That the President?" I asked.

"*Ah oui,*" said the old gentleman unconcernedly. "*C'est papa!*"

The President was certain popular enough judging by the way the crowd hollered and cheered. We all stood up with our hats off as he passed, and he and madame were bowing right and left in best royalty fashion and it was all very colourful and exciting, though where he earned the breastful of medals which covered his tunic was more than I could figure out.

The cheering passed by us and then came more cuirassiers, followed by infantry and a band, and it was funny how they had to mark time when the procession was held up just opposite where we were sitting. When it moved on again another open car came in sight and I knew I was seeing Gabrisson for the first time. He was lying back in the corner of the car and he looked fat to the point of grossness. Nearly a hundred yards away I could see his gold chain across the vast area of his white waistcoat, and all the time he was lifting his silk hat while the crowd cheered him. By his side was a dark, sinister looking individual, who sat bolt upright and did nothing. Then I caught what sounded like "Vive Gabrisson!" coming from the crowd.

"That's Gabrisson, is it?" I asked the old man.

"Ah oui," he said with a shrug.

"And who's the man beside him?"

Another shrug. *"Ça, c'est Pigolle. Sont des . . . tous les deux."*

What the word was I didn't catch but I knew it was something pretty foul for he spat as soon as he'd got it out. I turned to look at the two unmentionables at closer quarters and I got a glimpse of yards more of procession coming round the corner – and then things happened.

I can't describe it to you except in the blur of moving people and things. All I know is that there was a terrific roar and a flash and I know I ducked my head. Then I remember a horrible shriek, and women screaming; then the crowds surged back madly and the air seemed full of people shouting and then there'd be screams again. In the middle of the road a man was staggering round with his hands over his eyes. Two others lay there, one moving his legs. Further on a horse lay kicking on its belly and another was bolting among the crowd. What was in the car I couldn't see because the police were round it in a flash, but in a minute a quite different procession began to move across to where we were and I saw the police were carrying two bodies, and some soldiers were shouting and clearing the way.

I didn't want to look at those bodies that now came through by where we were and I turned my head away. The road was a disturbed ant-hill with the crowds fighting their way to get nobody seemed to know where, and what had happened to the last quarter of a mile of procession I didn't know. I was wedged back against the wall and what had become of the old gentleman I hadn't any idea but he was nowhere to be seen.

Then all at once the meaning of what had happened dawned on me like a flash, and I knew I had to get back to the Villa Marguerite. To move from where I was, was impossible, and then I felt the balustrade of the verandah under my hand and I edged my way sideways till I got my legs over, and then I dropped on the pavement. I fought my way through the crowd till I reached the Square, and then I ran for all I was worth.

It was only half past four as l glanced at the clock and when I got in the house Gene and Prargent were having a cup of tea and lounging in front of the open window. Gene looked up smiling as I came bursting in, and I was so blown that I could hardly get out the words.

"Something awful's happened. . . . A bomb . . . Just killed Gabrisson."

"My God, no!"

"It's true," I said, "I've just seen it. I was as close as the end of the garden. I think it was a Mills and it dropped clean in the carriage."

I told them all about it, then they made me go over it again in detail. Spider came in while I was in the middle of it and I had to tell him too.

"My God, It's Destordi," add Gene. "The bastard got wind of what was up and queered our pitch." He got up and began prowling about the room. "Pigolle told him something. That's how it was."

"The dirty louse," said Spider. "And him a secretary."

1 think I'd have laughed at that if Gene hadn't snapped at him to shut up.

"What's the best thing to do now, Prargent?" he said. "to see the President and put the cards on the table?"

"Keep your mouth shut and say nothing," said Prargent. "If Pigolle's dead he won't do any more double-crossing, and you haven't a ha'p'orth of proof Destordi or his men had a hand in it."

"But the bomb must have been thrown from the Granard or somewhere near it," I said. "Doesn't that look like Destordi?"

"Aw, what's the good," snarled Gene. "I'm going down there to see for myself. Maybe I'll pick something up down there."

"Don't be a bloody fool," said Prargent quietly. "What good can you do there? You'll only draw attention to yourself if you go asking questions. Donald, you make yourself and Spider some tea, and then we'll talk things over."

"Right-ho," I said. "Only, you'll pardon my mentioning it, but if Destordi really was responsible for it, won't he have to bolt?"

"If he does, we'll know it," said Prargent. "A mouse couldn't get out of there without us seeing it. We can give him half an hour's start and overhaul him inside another two hours."

"Sure we can!" chimed in Spider, trying to be reassuring.

Gene, staring moodily out of the window, whipped round on him.

"Blast you, Spider! Will you shut up!"

Spider shot a look at him.

"Sure I'll shut up," and he sank back in his chair.

"No use getting rattled like this," I heard Prargent say as I shut the door behind me and went down to make the tea.

Chapter XIII
IN – AND OUT

It was a quarter to seven – I know that, for I had just looked at the clock – and I was making my longest speech of the conference.

"I agree with Prargent," I said, "that I ought to go down to the town and see if I can get hold of Crevelle. He'll have to rush out an edition of his paper, spilling the beans to the extent of saying he was dead sure Gabrisson had intended to take action, and then saying he's dead certain that Gabrisson was killed for that very reason, by men who had most cause to fear what he was doing since they ought to have been extradited long ago. If you like we'll get him to put the pertinent question about Destordi. Let him ask, for instance, if the government can guarantee where he and his two bodyguards were at the moment when that pineapple was thrown. Whatever else happens it ought to force Fournier's hand. And it'll certainly pave the way if you want an interview."

"Aw, hell!" said Spider. "Bump the bastard off."

Gene ignored that. "What I say is," he began, "we mustn't rush things —"

That was all he did say. The door flew open and without even a preliminary tap, in rushed Madame Moulines, and a whiff of garlic with her. She was wiping her hands on her apron.

"M'sieur! M'sieur! The police. At the door. A whole lorry load!"

"Christ!" said Spider and began to hoist himself out of his chair. Gene looked round as if pretty scared, then he grabbed Spider's arm.

"C'mon! Beat it like hell! You stick here, Prargent. They've got nothing on you."

He was out of the window like a flash and the last I saw of him and Spider were four hands clinging to the verandah just before they dropped down. Prargent turned to the cook who was staring goggle-eyed.

"What're you waiting there for? Let 'em in!"

The look he gave me was distinctly disquieting. "What's the idea do you think? What can they have on us?"

"Lord knows," I said, and I was a bit scared too. The police had seemed rather humorous and comic-opera at a benevolent distance, but now they assumed quite a different status.

Before we knew where we were they seemed to be all over the place; in the room, outside in the garden, and swarming into the room from the verandah. We got up and stood facing the main door, and who should I see there, with what looked like the officer in charge, but that dud artist Monard, whom I christened "the Bohemian." The bloke with the admiral's hat spoke first.

"That was the man? You identify him?"

"Yes," said Monard. "He was the man I saw throw the bomb."

The officer nodded and a couple of the wasps had me by the arms before I could stir. I was so thunderstruck that I couldn't say a thing. My French wasn't equal to the emergency. I was the sort of bloke who can sit down and argue on anything, given my own time and manner in which to do it – but this was all different. And when I did recover the use of my tongue, all I could blurt out, with a glare at the Bohemian, was: "You dirty liar!" and then: *"Il est menteur!"* and for all the effect that had I might as well have kept my mouth shut. Prargent seemed cool as ever.

"Un moment, m'sieur," he said to the officer. "Do I understand that this man says he saw my servant throw a bomb?"

The officer shrugged his shoulders. "Too late for that," he said, and I gathered he meant argument.

"You are Monsieur le Capitaine Prargent?"

"Of course I am –"

"Then you must also come with me," he said, and two men got in behind Prargent at once though they didn't lay a finger on him. I was hustled off to the door and whether I was seeing the last of Prargent or not I didn't know but I hollered back to him as they pushed me through. "Get hold of the old man with the beard I was telling you about."

I didn't have time for any more for one of the wasps put his knee into my back. They hauled me through the courtyard, with me all the while trying to tell them I'd go quietly, then out to the road where a kind of Black Maria was drawn in to the kerb, and I was jerked inside it as quick as speaking. They jammed me in the corner and in a minute Prargent was inside too at the other end. The officer and Monard followed, and we drove off at once. What the other police were doing I didn't know – probably going through our belongings.

There were no windows to that damnable van but as we went downhill I had some idea where we were going. Then I heard street noises, then the tinkle of a bell and the horn of a tram conductor, and just as I tried to catch Prargent's eye, the car drew up at the kerb again, and in the second or two it took to hustle me across, I saw we were entering the jail.

There was no sign of Prargent when I got inside the door and I was surprised to see we were in a stone-paved yard, upon which doors opened in all directions. Police seemed to be everywhere and men in plain clothes were standing about. A fat one with a black moustache came over to where I was halted just inside the door and had the handcuffs put on me. Then we marched forward and waited under a sort of covered archway, till another civilian came bustling out and said something I didn't understand, but I was marched forward, through some big doors where two men were seated at a table, and there something was written in a book.

There were more police in the room we now entered. The handcuffs were taken off and I was ordered to strip, and I don't mind telling you scowled good and plenty at having to get into my bare skin in front of a gang like that. Then when my clothes were whisked away, a sinister-looking brigand in plain clothes made me hold up my arms, and he went over me as thoroughly as if I was being deloused.

I waited there stark naked, with a mat to stand on, for a good five minutes, and then my clothes appeared again. One thing I was glad of – they hadn't got my wad. A day or two before it had suddenly struck me that I was a bit of a fool wandering about with all my worldly wealth on me, and I'd made a surreptitious cache of it in the garden of the Marguerite. When I'd dressed again I felt in my pockets and found they'd cleared me out, and when I asked for my handkerchief the sinister bloke told a policeman to swipe me across the mouth. Then they handcuffed me again and a couple of minutes after that I was marched off down a corridor and into a cell. The door was shut on me and I was left to my own devices.

The cell was about ten foot square; its walls were whitewashed and the ceiling was ten foot off. A little light came in from a tiny grating high up, and in the corner I could see a mattress on the bare, stone floor. I sat down on it, head in hands, and ran my fingers through my hair. Then I wondered something and crawled very quietly to the door and put my ear to the crack. A man was on duty outside for I could hear his breathing.

The handcuffs were still on me and damnably uncomfortable they were, but I took that as a sign that it wouldn't be long before I was hauled out of the cell again. I now began to see things more clearly and found them so much worse than they'd been in the gloom that I lay down at full length on the mattress, and then hopped up again as if the devil had clawed me, wondering who'd slept on it last and when it had been fumigated. It was funny too how I suddenly had a mad desire to keep scratching myself and how awkward it was with those damn handcuffs on my wrists.

What I thought about it all doesn't matter. Strange to say I wasn't worrying any too much, though I knew I was in what Spider would have called a jam. Virtue is always a consolation, and I knew I'd done nothing to bring me within the law, whatever that greasy bastard of an artist might testify. Besides, there was my singular friend of the afternoon, who'd certainly *fiche* himself of the police and tell what had happened; and above all, if money talked as much as people gave it credit for, then Gene would have the hell of a lot to say before anything serious happened to me.

I loafed round in that cell for nearly two hours and I knew it was getting late by the shift of light from the grating and the coolness. Then steps were heard outside and in came a couple of yellow breeched gendarmes who collared me by the arms as if I'd been a paralytic and yanked me out to the corridor where two other cops fell in behind. We went into the same large room and waited there for a bit, then a sort of usher bloke put his head round the door and beckoned.

The room into which I now went was an imposing one. Above the ornate mantelpiece was a portrait of some notability or other. At the end was a horseshoe table behind which were sitting half a dozen dignified looking gentlemen in black; grey-haired most of them and bearded, and rather like a committee of senators. Police again were everywhere, and in the chair was the official who had seen me over the affair of Greasy Berousse. I must say it was all very high-toned and impressive and I felt rather awed as I halted in front of the table.

The preliminaries didn't take long. I was asked my name, age and the usual insurance company questions, and I saw my passport lying handy. Then I was asked what Captain Prargent was doing in Levasque.

"He's a tourist," I told them. Then I gave a little shrug. "I have to obey orders. A master doesn't tell his servants everything."

I thought that was rather neat since I didn't know what Prargent himself had told them. The chairman nodded benignly, then turned to a man who looked like a clerk and I gathered that he told him to read over the charge. Before he'd read a line he was stopped and the chairman turned to me again.

"You would like an interpreter?"

I didn't want any hocus-pocus like that, and I said I didn't – if the gentleman would read slowly. The gentleman did so. You'd have thought I was deaf, and he read at a pace which resembled dictation, giving me every now and then a questioning look. When it was over I was asked if I wished to say anything.

I told them I certainly did, and might I give my statement in details. The chairman waved his hand airily as much as to say the time of the court was my own, so I waded in. I told them every detail of what I'd seen that afternoon, and most of the conversation with the man with the beard. I said I couldn't possibly have thrown the bomb or I'd have been seen and collared at once. In any case, I said, I knew nothing about bombs, and how could I have carried one on my person. Also, if the witness saw me throw the bomb as he'd described, why didn't he have me seized at once? I didn't run off –

There I was interrupted. There was a witness, I was told, who saw me running away from the Place Granard shortly after the explosion. I smiled tolerantly at that and told them why I ran – that I was anxious to give my master the news and stop his proposed visit to the town.

After that effort I was taken from the room but I saw the heads go together, and I wondered what decision they'd come to. In the ante-room I was given a chair and I must have sat there another half an hour before somebody came out and said I wouldn't be wanted any more. He was a knock-kneed, bony man with high cheekbones, who looked like a Spaniard, and I think he must have seen the relief pass over my face when I thought they were going to turn me loose, for he gave me a look that was meant to shrivel.

"Tu as mangé?"

I said I hadn't touched a bit since half past twelve.

"Right," he said to the cops. "Give him something when he gets in."

I can tell you I had the spirit knocked clean out of me at that. I stretched out my arms looking, as I remember it now, like a prodigal asking for forgiveness.

"May I have these taken off?" I said. I didn't know the French for "handcuffs" but he understood. He nodded at the cops and they marched me off to the cell again. A quarter of an hour later, in came a tin of soup. It was greasy on top and bread and vegetable and pieces of cabbage floated in it, but it tasted good, and they'd taken off my handcuffs and drawn back a grating outside so that the light from the corridor lamp trickled in and let me see what I was eating.

Perhaps it was because I'd missed my siesta but I slept that night like a dead man. I had one blanket and I risked the mattress, and when I woke in the morning it was to the sound of the opening door, when a gendarme brought in a bowl of coffee and a round of bread.

"C'est défendu d'acbeter des cigarettes?" I asked him.

He growled something that sounded like not being allowed to talk, and his pal in the doorway shut the door after him. I idled an hour or two away and then discovered the most ingenious scheme for passing the time – using the tag of a lace as a pencil and the wall as paper for the composition of cross-word puzzles. I didn't let myself think, for that wouldn't have done, but the time passed all right till lunch when they gave me a sort of rice stew affair and bread and a tin cup of sourish, red wine.

In the afternoon I tried to go to sleep but couldn't manage it, so I listened for sounds and couldn't hear any, and I did all sorts of exercises. But what I missed was tea and the long wait till the evening meal began to get on my nerves, and I had to keep a grip on myself or I'd have begun to panic. Then I rolled the mattress up and stood on it and just reached the tiny grating with my fingers, but when I drew myself up I couldn't see a thing outside but a bare wall.

When my tin of soup came in I asked if I might have some water to wash in. The man shook his head but some time later I got the water and four cops stood by while I washed. I thought I'd annoy them by stripping but they wouldn't let me get any farther than removing my shirt. That night I slept pretty badly and I would keep listening to the sounds of guards moving about, and the man outside my door would keep getting up and tramping in the corridor.

After the coffee next morning I asked for washing water again but it didn't come. I was casting about in my mind for something to do to pass the time when numerous feet were heard outside and who should come in – ushered most ceremoniously – but my old friend the chairman. Two gendarmes entered with him and they slipped on the handcuffs as a precautionary measure. I got up and politely offered him my rolled-up mattress. He refused with elaborate courtesy.

"Your story has been enquired into," he said, "and so far we're satisfied. Indeed" – and he smiled – "if you could give us certain information, there is even a possibility of your being released. When fuller enquiries have satisfied us, of course," he added.

I couldn't find anything to say to that, so I nodded.

"We're still not in agreement with you on the question of why your master came to Levasque," he said. "Would you like to revise what you told us?"

I knew what that meant, or I thought I did. Destordi was a pal of his and he wanted to know if Prargent was a pal of the New York Frank O'Brien, so I looked as ruggedly honest as possible, and as helpful, and said I only wished I could give the information he asked for.

"From which country did you come here?" he asked.

"From England," I said, and simulated surprise.

"And why did you enter the country at Belanne?"

I took refuge again in the question of the duty of servants not to reason why.

"You entered with another Englishman and an American," he said. "Where did you first pick them up?"

That had me absolutely up a gum-tree, so I looked him straight in the eye and said that in my country any accused was allowed to see a lawyer before he answered any questions at all. I don't want to bore you with what took place then; how cajoling he was and how I stood my ground – being too scared to do anything else – but at last he took his departure, and I must say he never looked the least degree ruffled. Moreover, as soon as he'd gone, in came my washing

133 | THE TRAIL OF THE THREE LEAN MEN

water, and I was grateful to him for more than that for I got myself to sleep that night going over and over everything that had taken place and getting ready the French for what I'd say next time.

The following day passed in exactly the same manner except that I didn't have any visitors. I prowled round my cell; I did my exercises, and I made up more cross-word puzzles, but every now and again I felt a bit frightened, and I wondered what was being done outside. Everybody I thought of, and I even allowed myself to think of Lucy Brock, and I wondered if I should write to Tubby when I got out of jail and find out what she was doing in England. Feuermann I thought of too, and what had happened at the Marguerite, and just where Prargent was, and a hundred other things. Then, just as I was thinking of turning in, feet were heard outside and one of the gendarmes came in. He told me to get up and follow him, and outside were three other cops who escorted me to the same old room where I'd been stripped and examined.

The head of my cops signed a book there, and then two cops only took me off. At the wicket place another book was signed and I was given my belongings, and though you'd never believe it, my money was right to a sou. I daren't feel glad for what I guessed was that I was being transferred to some other jail reserved for politicals, but this time one cop only went on with me as far as the main door. The bloke on duty there had a look at a paper my man showed him, and then the door was opened. I went through thinking the cop was with me and found the door shut on me when I turned to look for him. It took me a minute to realise I was really free!

My first instinct was to take to my heels and bolt, then I felt a tremendous surge of anger – the same thing that the fellow felt in the Acts, when he said they shoved him in jail surreptitiously and they jolly well weren't going to shove him out the same way. And while I was being heroic like that, a car drew alongside me and Prargent put his head out.

"Hop in!" he said, and he smiled sheepishly at me. I hopped in like a shot alongside him. It was Gene's car but he was alone in it. I suddenly felt very reserved and not much like talking, and he didn't talk either but drove straight on up the hill.

"Back in a minute," he said, as he dropped me at our door. I opened the old familiar door and went through. There was nobody in the kitchen and I couldn't hear madame's snores, but there was a light on the landing and then the top door opened.

Gene hauled me inside and fussed round me as if I'd done something marvellous. Spider poured me out a drink, and when Prargent came in it was with a huge bowl of soup. We chattered away like a lot of monkeys and got each others' news all mixed up.

"The reason we couldn't get you out before was your bearded friend," Gene told me. "His name's Rastier – a pal of Crevelle – and he'd just left Montelle. Also he's in pretty bad with the government and they wouldn't listen to him till we insisted. He was a great lad."

"And did you see the President?"

"Yes," he said, and scowled. "I was told, in reply to my hints as to what I'd been doing with Gabrisson, that the country was quite capable of managing its own affairs, and unless I confined my activities to those of the ordinary tourist, I'd be requested to leave the country at once. Moreover I was given a perfectly good hint that I was going to be watched."

"Watched!" I said. "That's bad."

"Don't you believe it," he said. "No more diplomacy for me. I'm keeping my dollars in my pocket – and I've made my will."

I stared at him.

"Yes," he said, "I'm going into this thing proper now. I'm bumping Tony off on sight and nobody's going to stop me. All I want is one little bit of corroborative evidence and then we're all set. You're going to help too."

"I?" I said. "I don't see what you mean."

He smiled. "That swine who swore he saw you throw the bomb. Like to get even with him?"

"My God I would!" I almost shouted that.

"Well, you can," he said. "We've had him tailed and we're waiting now till something comes through. He's going to be socked on the bean and if you like to do it, you can."

"Thanks," I said, and when I looked round at Spider everybody laughed.

Chapter XIV
EXIT MONARD

"Aw, QUIT your kiddin'!" said Spider, and twisted his lean jaws to the nearest he could get to a smile. Then he lugged out a forty-four and passed it over to me, nose first. "You sock him with this, Mr. Donald, and let him smile that one off."

I took the gun and tried it in my hand. I must have looked rather blank still for Gene laughed.

"I haven't got all this yet," I said. "How do I do the socking, and when?"

"Spider'll tell you," said Gene. "It's his racket. Do your stuff, Spider."

Spider took a bit more coaxing, then I gathered that the stoolie, as he called him, was strong for a dame who had a flat way back of the jail. How much Gene had parted with to fix this dame I didn't hear, but I reckoned it was quite enough to make her reliable. Monard was with her at the moment by special invitation, and she was going to turn him loose at about midnight when the streets would be quiet. About a hundred yards from her door was an old arch of what was once the medieval wall, and that was to be the scene of the socking. Marcel was down there with a hired car and a quarter of an hour before the dame was ready she was going to signal, and he was giving us a buzz.

"We expected you out at seven to-night," Gene told me. "That's why we staged it when we did. Still, we've plenty of time. Prargent's staying on guard here and Spider's going down to my place. We've got to look after ourselves from now on and we don't want somebody slipping in and giving us a pineapple."

"You think Destordi knows who you are?"

"Not he," he said. "I don't even think they've rumbled there's any communication between the two houses. They know Prargent's a friend of ours, of course, but we explained all that by saying we met by chance on the train."

That reminded me. "How'd you get on that night, Prargent?" I asked.

"They didn't get anything out of me," he said. "Grilled me for an hour or so and filled up about a dozen notebooks. We knew you were safe enough, or we thought you were, but we had to keep moving all the same."

"And what was General Fournier like?" I asked Gene.

"Don't know," he said. "All I saw was the bloke lower down – and that was after I'd seen one or two more." He shrugged. "What the hell? We'll do this job now as Spider wanted us to."

"Now you're talkin'," said Spider. "We've been on the sucker list long enough."

I told them all that had happened to me and the questions I'd been asked, and I wondered whether that'd make any difference to their plans.

"I should worry!" said Gene. "Once tonight's over we're all ready to do the job, and when that's done we're ready to jump the town at any minute."

"Yes, but why wait to get our own back on Monard?" I asked. "Isn't that all waste of time?"

"You'll see," he told me oracularly. "There's more in Monard than meets the eye. If to-morrow pans out all right, we'll have some backing. That's where old Spider's always too precipitate. When you make yourself a hide-out you want two doors to get out by, not one."

The telephone buzzed then and he slipped across. We heard nothing except his " O.K.," and then he hung up. He nodded over to me.

"Grab your hat," he said. "You two fellers keep an eye on things, and if we're not back by midday to-morrow, you bring the car out, Prargent, and look us up."

That was all gibberish to me, and we went down that hill so fast that I didn't like to worry him with questions. We didn't cross or skirt the Place Granard but took side streets, and long before I expected it we were at the archway, a ruined sort of place overgrown with ivy beneath which ran quite a good road.

"You stay there," Gene told me. "Keep in to the pavement and as soon as he passes, let him have it. You'll know he's coming because you'll see me coming this way. I'll get here just as you drop him and Marcel'll be following up with the car. . . . You're not scared?"

"Good God, no!" I said, and hooked my fingers round the forty-four.

He smiled. "Well, you needn't tell everybody. . . . One conk, and drop him clean. The devil of a lot depends on it."

The street lamps were a good way apart but I followed him with my eye till he was lost to sight, and then I began to feel uneasy. I took a peep round the arch and saw nothing. Then suddenly I wondered if I'd been put on the spot, and then I laughed at myself for thinking that and began to balance the forty-four in my right hand. All I could see across the road was a row of what looked like tenement buildings, or was it factories? their windows shuttered and never the sign of a light. Then I wondered what I ought to do if a stranger came by.

I was thinking that out when I caught sight of a figure coming towards me and just as I recognised it for Gene, I heard steps on the pavement. I drew back with my shoulders well into the ivy and clutched the gun. The steps came near – I saw the slouch hat – then took one step forward and struck. I remember I wondered why the thud didn't jar my wrist and how surprised I was when the man crumpled up on the pavement while I stood looking at him like a gawk.

The car was alongside in a flash and in a split second Gene had him in the back, I lending a hand with his legs. Before Gene and I were properly in, Marcel had the car moving; then Gene stooped down and began tying Monard up. He was breathing all right and we made no bones about using him as a mat. I suddenly laughed.

"It is funny, isn't it," Gene said. "And you certainly made a damn good job of it. I didn't think you had it in you."

"I wasn't laughing at that," I said. "I was thinking of the day I arrived here and you had your feet on me. A lot's happened since then, what?"

He laughed. "Sure. Money's a great little fixer – the best there is."

I didn't see at the moment what money had to do with it, and before I could ask him, he craned his head out of the window and kept it there for a bit.

"It's all O.K.," he said when he put it in. "We're clear now. Another ten minutes and we'll be there."

"Where's that?"

"You should know," he said, and I think he smiled though I couldn't see his face. "Remember the farm? And Marcel's aunt?"

"Oh!" I said blankly. "You're going to keep him a prisoner there?" And before I'd finished it I knew that was a silly question. It wasn't as if Monard were the President or even a hostage.

The car gave a lurch just then and I held on to the window. Gene didn't answer my question; all he did was to bend down to see how Monard was making it. I tried to see where we were but all I knew was we had left the main roads and were up among the hills. Five minutes of that and I heard the barking of a dog. Then the car stopped and I saw we were in the yard of the farm, with the white wall of the house on our right.

There was a light in a downstair room and the door opened almost at once. A voice said something in Levascan and Marcel answered. The man came over and I saw it was the uncle, and he calmly lent a hand to get Monard out. He was a tolerable weight and the four of us carried him inside to the kitchen. No sooner were we inside the door than he was dumped down and Marcel shook hands ceremoniously with his uncle. Then Gene shook hands, and I was introduced. After that we picked up our man again and got him in a big armchair with his legs and arms lashed to it, and there he sagged like a guy while Marcel went to the pump and got a mug of water and threw it over him. He didn't come round at that and Marcel shrugged his shoulders and left him to it Then the aunt came in and there was more handshaking, and in less than no time we were sitting down to a scratch meal, and you'd have thought we were a family party who hadn't met for years. Still, as Gene had told me in the car, money's a good fixer, and it makes for good mixing, and almost the first thing I'd seen him do when the old man appeared was to pull out his roll and peel off a bill or two.

We hadn't been at the table five minutes when Marcel nodded over to the chair and there was Monard with his eyes open looking like one of those pictures of the martyrdom of St. Sebastian. When he caught sight of me he looked worse still. Somehow I didn't like it. Unless Gene was going to hold him pretty fast I could see trouble ahead when that guy opened his mouth in Montelle. But he wasn't opening his mouth now. Marcel hollered something at him in dialect and the old man and woman laughed. Then the old man picked up a knife and ran his fingers suggestively along the blade. Monard closed his eyes.

The meal didn't go so well with me after that and when it was over and the remains piled by the sink the old woman went off and we didn't see her again. The uncle stayed on and though it was a hot night he wanted to light a fire. Gene wouldn't let him but he brought in a couple of sheepskin rugs and a mattress.

"I'm taking the chair," Gene said to me. "You get down to it and have a good night."

"But what about him?" I said, indicating Monard.

"He stays where he is," said Gene in French.

"What's more, if he makes a sound we'll cut his throat." He picked up a dirty knife from the sink and laid it handy on the mantel-shelf, but I caught his wink. "Don't you let your heart overflow with sympathy for him," he said. "Think of what the bastard tried to do to you."

Well, Gene put out the light and I got down to it though I couldn't sleep for ages. The air that came through the open window was different somehow and the scents were different, and every now and again there would be noises of *cigales* and the scampering of mice, and frogs were making the devil of a noise in a nearby pool. I was wondering too what was going to happen to Monard – and what was going to happen ultimately to me.

Then I suddenly opened my eyes and saw it was light. Thanks to a night or two's practice on a mattress I'd slept like a top. Gene was stirring too and in five minutes I'd washed at the sink and was getting outside a bowl of coffee and a hunk of bread and butter. Then I washed Monard's face while Gene regarded me amusedly.

"What's the French for shroud?" he asked me.

"Damned if I know," I said, "but *robe blanche* will do. Why?"

He told Monard why. In England, he said, the custom is to wash the dead before burial, and we wouldn't keep him waiting long, but madams was getting the shroud ready so that we could do things in style. Anything particular wanted on the tombstone?

"Leave the poor swine alone, Gene," I said. "He's half dead now by the look of him."

He laughed, then Marcel came in with a spade.

"Everything O.K., chief."

"Right," said Gene. "Get him untied but lash his arms behind him."

He nodded to me to come outside. In the yard he lowered his voice.

"Don't go weakening or doing anything silly. Follow my lead and keep your mouth shut."

I nodded.

"What you're going to see are the preliminaries," he said. "Act one doesn't start till later."

Outside the door Monard began to jabber away excitedly, though his knees were so groggy he could hardly walk. Marcel slapped him over the mouth and shook him like a rat, and where the skinny little devil got the strength from I don't know, unless it was that Monard hadn't any. Gene went on ahead and I with him. We turned to the left and followed a track through the undergrowth and were out of sight of the farm almost at once. Then we stopped – at the bottom of what was a dried-up pool. Gene took over Monard and pushed him down.

"Lend Marcel a hand," he said to me, and we took turn and turn about to dig. The soil was soft and reddish and the hole we made was seven foot long and three wide, and when we got down a couple of feet Gene gave a pointed look at Monard and said it'd be deep enough. You ought to have seen Monard's face at that. Then he began to talk and his French was so fast that I couldn't follow it. Then he whined and he was just going down on his knees when Gene yanked him to his feet. Then Gene produced a nasty looking forty-four from his hip pocket, and Monard began to squeal like a rat. "Shut up, you!" He clapped his hand over his mouth and kept it there. "You translate, Marcel, and no monkey tricks. Tell him what he's got to do if he wants to keep out of that hole."

Marcel grinned like a monkey. His French was a bit too fluent for me and I knew there was some dialect in it, but I gathered what it was all about.

"Why did you accuse this man of throwing the bomb?" was the first question. You don't want to know all that happened in between questions and the answers, and how he prevaricated and how Gene once gave him a reminder with the nose of the forty-four, but at last he wanted to know what would happen to him if he talked.

"Tell him he's got to sign a statement," said Gene, "and then I'll give him ten thousand francs, or you will, when he's over the frontier. If he ever comes back we'll shoot him on sight."

He began to haggle over that till Gene hit him over the skull again, and then he talked. Destordi had employed him to keep an eye on any Americans that came to Montelle, he said, and after the affair of Berousse he'd been told to look after me closely. That afternoon when Gabrisson was killed he'd seen me in the Granard and had reported the fact to Destordi who'd put him up to accusing me. So far so good.

"Now get the other thing out of him," said Gene, and pulled out his watch. "If we haven't the information in two minutes, he's for it."

In two minutes we heard all he had to say and I honestly believe he was telling the truth. He didn't know who threw the pineapple, but he'd had orders from Destordi to be at the Granard and he'd reported; what had happened, and he'd also swear that Spud Mason had been in the Granard not long before the outrage, and he was sure the manager of the Granard knew something if he could be made to open his mouth.

It was enough to make a man sick to see him slobbering and grovelling there, and I was glad when Gene yanked him to his pins again and we moved off back to the house. Gene and I went into the kitchen and Marcel disappeared with Monard.

"Where's he taken him?" I said. "To the frontier?"

"Not yet," said Gene. "We're trussing him up till we're ready for him to sign the statement. Like to have a stroll round?"

We spent a couple of hours out there in the open. It was a wonderful morning; the sort of thing you see in the picture books, with hill lavender coming into flower and bees humming in the wild thyme, and goats, with dull tinkling bells on them cropping the stunted grass on the hillside. All you wanted was a bloke playing a pipe and it'd have been an illustration for Theocritus or an extract from *William Tell*, I was lying with my back to a pine tree when Gene pricked his ears up. Then I heard the sound of the car too, and sat up.

"Who's that? Prargent?"

"Friends of yours," he said, and got to his feet. When we got to the court-yard, who should be there but old Rastier, and with him a most imposing looking man in black. Rastier shook hands with me most effusively, though I didn't follow all he said.

"But for you," I told him in my best and most careful French, "I shouldn't be here." I wanted to say I was profoundly grateful but the right words wouldn't come. I think he guessed, however, and he patted me on the back and I thought for a moment he was going to embrace me. Then he spat – and shrugged.

"*Sont tous des salauds. Faut s'en ficher.*" Which, as Spider would have interpreted it, meant that the government were bastards and could go plumb to hell.

Uncle appeared then and ushered the whole collection of us into the house. The bottle and glasses were produced in less than no time, and we made a regular apéritif hour of it. Then Rastier looked up.

"Well, gentlemen; to business."

I now began to see what was in the wind —or I thought I did. Gene told Rastier and his friend what Monard had owned up to and then the old chap set about drafting out a formal confession in honest-to-God French. When that was done the old uncle produced an antiquated brace and auger and a couple of peep-holes were bored in the door that led from the kitchen to a pantry place. Then Rastier and the other man went inside, and the uncle was told to fetch Marcel and the prisoner.

They took his cords off just before they let him in, and Gene told him to sit down at the kitchen table facing the pantry. Marcel stood just behind and I was at the end, and what the two in the pantry couldn't see was that Gene had his gun on the table in front of him where Monard could see it good and plenty.

Monard gave us all a hang-dog look and Gene shoved the confession under his nose and told him to read it. He gave us another uneasy glance first and when he'd finished he spread out his hands like a bargaining Armenian and began a protesting, *"Mais, m'sieur."*

Gene touched the handle of the forty-four and lugged out his watch without a word. Monard gave a resigned shrug and signed on the dotted line. Gene had a look at it.

"You see," he said, "that you admit you've signed this of your own free will. In that room there are two gentlemen, members of the unofficial police."

He raised his voice as he said that and Rastier's friend showed himself for a moment.

"You see what's in store for you if you're caught in Levasque," he went on. "Now take him to the frontier and let him make his own way over. When he's through the wire, chuck him the dough."

He peeled the notes off his wad and whether Monard ever got the whole of them I shouldn't like to say. Marcel shoved a gat in his ribs and that's the last I saw of him. Then Rastier and his pal came out of their cubby hole and we had another drink.

When everybody had gone and we two were there alone, waiting for Marcel to get back with the car, I ventured to outline our future as I rather cocksurely saw it.

"That's the end of Destordi," I said. "The country'll be too hot to hold him as soon as Crevelle's news-rag spreads the news."

"It'll spread the news all right," said Gene. "Rastier's seeing to that."

"And who was his pal?" I asked. "Anything really to do with the police?"

Gene looked at me. "Sometimes I think you're the world's prize simp," he said. "I heard his name the same as you did but I don't know him from Adam. Neither did Monard – and that was the point. How could Rastier have a friend in the government? And if he did, Monard'd have known him."

I felt just the least bit disturbed at that. "Still," I said, "why worry? All we've got to do now is watch Destordi's bolt-holes."

"You think so?" He smiled out of the side of his mouth. "Whether he does or not it won't make a ha'p'orth of difference to us. We're going straight after him. You don't think he or anyone else will pay a hoot of attention to that confession of Monard's?"

"I don't know," I began.

He cut me short. "Well, I do. I've spent money to know things in this goddam country. The place is lousy with Destordi's pals and he got rooted here before we did. What they'll do is pretend to make a fuss so that nothing'll happen. What's more, I shouldn't be surprised if the whole gang of us had the order to clear out in a couple of days and Destordi'll be at the frontier with his fingers to his nose."

"Bur why all this trouble about getting Monard's confession?"

"That's our other bolt-hole," he said. "If we kill Tony and get away clear, well and good. If we don't get so clear, then we can at least tell the world the sort of bastard we've bumped off. And the first thing I'm going to do when we get back to Montelle is to ring him up and say we're shooting on sight."

"My God, you're not going to be such a fool!" I said. "Kill him by all means but don't run your head into a noose by giving him any more warnings."

He gave me the same wry look. "Who's paying for this show? And it won't be your neck either."

That shut me up. He had that queer side to him and it wasn't a nice one, but as I figured it out he had a right to get nasty sometimes and it wasn't my father who'd been left lying with a belly-full of slugs.

But it wasn't a second or so before he smiled over at me, and then poured us both out another small tot.

"You're a rum little cuss, Donald," he said and slapped me on the back as he set down my drink.

"So are you, Gene," I told him. "All the same I'm not sorry I came to Levasque."

He grinned. "Well, here's to you Donald. And here's hopin' hell ain't too overcrowded."

Queer how he'd be riding you sore one minute and then have you beaming on him the next. But Marcel came in while we were sitting there handing each other the flowers, and Gene gulped off his drink and said we'd be getting back.

"Where'd you leave that guy?" he asked Marcel.

"He jumped the wire at the crossing, boss, after we'd trailed a guard. Last I seen of him he was eatin' up the trail."

"You gave him his wad?"

"Sure!" said Marcel, in a tone of injured innocence. "Didn't you say for me to give it him?" But as soon as Gene's back was turned I caught his wink.

Chapter XV
THE MAN ON THE STRETCHER

That afternoon there was no siesta for any of us. When Destordi bought that villa of his he neglected just one thing – to have a garage of his own made in the garden, and though it wouldn't take a quick mover a couple of seconds to get from the door to the kerb, it gave us time enough to see who was leaving the house, and if the other door was chosen, that could be overlooked from the bedroom window of Gene's place. One of Marcel's gang was now down there with Spider, taking turn and turn about during the daylight, and Marcel and I were doing the same at the Marguerite. For my own part I hadn't the least compunction in lying with the glasses handy to train on that stretch of road, and I'd have given quite a lot to let off a tray at either Destordi or his pals.

The car was in our garage now, the tank full and all ready to move off if Destordi made a break. Marcel had first go with the Lewis that afternoon and I was sitting yarning with Prargent, the glasses in my hand ready for a quick dekko, though that wasn't my job but part of Marcel's.

"What was your idea about Gene ringing up Destordi?" I asked him.

"I thought it was damn good," he said. "Nothing like a voice out of the dark to get a man's nerves on edge."

"Good Lord!" I said. "I thought he was going to ring up in his own voice."

He laughed. "You don't know Gene as I do. All he told Destordi – or Spud he said it was that answered the 'phone – was that Tony'd pass over as soon as he dared to pop his head outside his shell. Gene said he was a yellow quitter and dared him to come out and take his medicine. If he's got the guts of a louse after that he'll come out and bring his bodyguard with him."

"No chance of getting him on a spot?"

Prargent was very patient with me. "My dear chap, you haven't an idea what's been done since we've been here. We daren't trust a soul till we were dead sure of 'em, and now we've got enough men to watch Tony's house and the roads. We've had a go at one of his menservants and we'd have got your friend Feuermann if he hadn't turned us down. And we've got two waiters at the Granard so that if anything breaks there we can have a chance to get away. You see," he went on, "we're always apt to despise a country like this till we get to know it. You didn't feel like laughing when you were in that jail?"

"By God I didn't!" I said. "It struck me as efficient enough. But what's worrying me is what we're going to do if Destordi persists in staying where he's safe. We can't stop here for ever."

"Why not? It's a great country, ain't it?"

Marcel had been lying so quiet there on his belly that I thought he was dozing.

"Sure it's a great country," I said. "Only I don't like earning my money too easy."

"You'll get action all right," said Prargent.

"Gene's down at the Granard – or he will be. If Tony turns up there, Gene'll shoot him on sight. He's not such a good shot as Spider, but he's good enough."

It was extraordinarily hot that afternoon and though we were sitting with the minimum on we felt sticky and restless. I said I'd go and make tea early and perhaps it was just as well that I did for old Madame Moulines would have been scared stiff when the furtive tap came at the side window of the kitchen.

I wondered what it was myself after my experiences of the weekend, and when I squinted through the grimy window I didn't recognise who it was. But I did see that it was a solitary man and I opened the door and kept my knee behind it. Then I saw it was Feuermann.

I was so astonished that I opened the door wide regardless of who might be behind him. He came through at once and he took off his hat as soon as he was in the kitchen. I knew something was wrong because his English was just a bit off the track for the first time since I'd known him.

"I must ask your pardon," he said. "It was so urgent. I wished to see you and I didn't like to come here. Then I thought it was the hour for siesta and it would be safe."

"Why, certainly it's safe," I told him. "What's the matter? You're looking none too good." And he wasn't. His eyes were heavy and there were lines on his face that made him look ten years older.

He shook his head. "I shouldn't have troubled you with my affairs only I knew you'd be interested. It's a long story."

"You come up and tell it to Captain Prargent," I told him. "Wait there while I make the tea and I'll take you up. I'm assuming it's got to do with . . . with a man we both know?"

"Yes," he said. "Destordi. . . . At least, I don't know. I'll tell you and you shall judge for yourselves."

I made a large pot of tea and took up some rolls and butter and jam. Feuermann kept behind till I'd set down the tray and then I said we had a caller and brought him in. Prargent stared and then got to his feet with his hand out.

"Hallo! Herr Feuermann; what are you doing here?"

I saw Marcel roll over on his side and then I realised the Lewis was in full view. Marcel opened his mouth to speak but I got in first.

"I'll vouch for him all right," I said. "He's got something to tell us about Destordi."

Prargent always had the most charming manners and now he smiled.

"Whatever it is he may as well say it in comfort. This chair's pretty comfortable, Herr Feuermann. And you'll have some tea with us?"

As soon as I'd given them their rations, Feuermann began his tale. In the stronger light of the upstair room I could see he was looking desperately tired and upset.

"I've left Destordi," he said. "Perhaps that isn't right. It was he who got rid of me. I told Mr. Donald that things had been getting very difficult." I'm not sure of it but I think he flushed slightly before he went on. "Then he had a Miss Brock, whom Mr. Donald knows, come up to his place one night very late and only a pianist with her and he was a man I didn't trust. It was not my place of course to say anything, but I thought I'd keep my eyes open and that's just what I couldn't do. Everybody who comes to the house now is watched and one of the two Americans is always there to see who it is, and they never get past the outer door unless they're sure. If it's tradesmen, then I or someone in the house deals with them, but what I mean is that the man called Mason let Miss Brock into the house and I wasn't sent for to go to the room while she was there. I know it was rather noisy after she'd finished and Destordi tried to force her to sit down with them and drink.

"I wanted to see her the next evening – Mr. Donald knows all about how we used to meet – but I was told I couldn't go out as I'd be wanted in the house. On the Saturday morning M. Destordi came to me in what I afterwards thought a too friendly fashion and said he wanted me personally to take an important message to Lecroy, to a friend of his, and he couldn't trust anybody to do it but me. I had to start at once and I knew I couldn't very well get back till late. I asked him about that because I wanted to say goodbye to Miss Brock who was leaving Levasque on the Sunday morning and making her last appearance at the Granard on the Saturday night. He said I might possibly have to spend the night in Lecroy. You think perhaps I'm going a roundabout way in telling you this . . ."

"Tell it your own way," Prargent told him. "We're in no hurry."

He gave a little bow. "Thank you. I'm very grateful. And what I wanted you to understand was that on my way to the station I managed to get a message to a friend of mine – Mr. Donald knows him – to say that if I wasn't back personally on the Sunday morning to see him, would he see Miss Brock off at the station and take her some flowers from me and explain that I'd been called away. I may say that M. Crevelle – my friend – got the message and was at the station. Miss Brock wasn't on the Paris express as she ought to have been; at least he hunted through the train and couldn't see her. Then he thought he'd go to her flat to see what had happened. The concierge said a car had come for her things that morning and she'd gone on the Paris express as she'd said. He asked what kind of car it was and she said an ordinary taxi.

"I may say that my friend Crevelle is for various reasons a suspicious person, and he couldn't understand why he hadn't seen Miss Brock on the train, because she must have been looking out for some of us who knew her to see her off. What M. Crevelle did therefore was to telephone to a friend of his in the customs at the frontier and ask him to find out if a passport of a Miss Brock had been presented on the French side where they keep full records. The friend reported later that a lady of the name of Lucy Brock had certainly been on the train and her passport had been in order.

"In the meanwhile I got to Lecroy and delivered my letter and was told I couldn't return an answer till the next day. Actually it was midday on the Sunday when I got away and in the meantime I'd heard about the explosion in the Place Granard, and that an Englishman was being held by the police. I tell you that train went slowly, and if there'd been an aeroplane service, as you have in England, I think

I'd have taken it. What happened when I got back was perfectly inexplicable.

"I may say I had been asked to leave my key behind when I left for Lecroy and so I couldn't let myself in. The man Harris came to the *guichet* and took me straight to Destordi's room. He took the letter I gave him and then he began to abuse me. He said one of my friends – meaning you, Mr. Donald – was in jail and would be executed for killing the minister and his secretary, and that was the sort of company I kept. Then he paid me what I said was due to me and ordered me out of the house. Harris went with me and saw my luggage packed and he examined everything I had. He saw me through the side *guichet* and there was a taxi there ready for me."

Prargent smiled. "We knew all that. At least, you were seen to go in the taxi. But you left it just short of the Place Granard, didn't you?"

"Yes," said Feuermann. "I didn't want Destordi to know where I'd gone, so I stopped at the house of a friend and later that night I had my belongings moved to the headquarters of my friend Crevelle, which Mr. Donald knows." It was his turn to smile. "I was actually there, though he didn't see me, when one of your men saw M. Rastier. But the great thing is that before I went there that day I went to the Granard to see another friend and he wasn't there. I may say it was the waiter, Maximilien Allain, whom I trusted implicitly. I was told that the previous night he had done what I had always arranged for when Miss Brock was late at the restaurant – escorted her as far as the turning to her street. That was just before midnight, and he never came back as he should have done. He hasn't been seen or heard of since."

"I see." Prargent nodded. "But before we go any further, Herr Feuermann, there's one thing I'd like to know. You've finished with Destordi for good?"

Feuermann, usually so undemonstrative, spread out his hands with a gesture of tremendous finality. Prargent went on before he could speak.

"What I mean is, can we count you in with us?"

Feuermann looked at him as if summing him up.

"Yes," he said slowly. "I think I can trust *you*."

"Right," said Prargent. "So far, so good. Anything else to tell us?"

"Yes," went on Feuermann. "When I entered the house on the Sunday afternoon there seemed to be something peculiar about it. It was lifeless, if you know what I mean. I've since discovered that there's no one there now except the chef. Everybody else was sent away."

"Many, were there?"

"There was the chef and a young apprentice, two menservants and the wife of one of them, and a gardener. The chauffeur wasn't his as he hasn't a car. He always orders one when he wants it."

Prargent grunted, then thought for a bit. "What do you think of it?" he said to me. "Think he's getting ready to bolt?"

"I wouldn't like to say," I said. "I don't see why he should bolt now, before he knows how much we know. This is his home town and he's come back to it a big man. If you ask me, he'll stick."

"And what's your idea about this Miss Brock?" he said to Feuermann. "If she's crossed the frontier, what are you worrying about?"

Feuermann made an apologetic gesture. "I know. It's only that I feel something is wrong and I hoped Mr. Donald could have told me something." He seemed to be finding the words difficult. "You see, she wasn't at the station – and then there was Maximilien."

Then I had an idea. "What about that woman of Destordi's? Did you see her at the house? You see," I said to Prargent, "if he's got rid of her as he did the last one, she might be useful if we got hold of her."

Feuermann told us he hadn't seen her and Prargent said that made no difference. Destordi's house was only under our personal observation during daylight and during the weekend when all the bother was taking place over me, anything might have happened.

"Tell you what I'll do," he said. "I'll get hold of Gene and I'll find out a thing or two. You two sit tight till I get back. No telephoning from here, mind you. We never know if they've got the line tapped." He hesitated for a moment, then turned to Feuermann. "Tell me absolutely point blank. I may be very wide of the mark, especially on the evidence, but haven't you got an idea that Destordi's got hold of this English girl?"

Feuermann stared at him. "You think so too?"

Prargent gave an elegant shrug. "Now you're asking. My point's this. You're with us if it becomes necessary to break into his house by force? You'll risk that much?"

Feuermann looked at him appealingly. "Anything I will do." Then he shrugged too. "After all perhaps I'm a fool. There may be nothing."

Prargent smiled. "What do you say, Donald? Shall we give him the king's shilling and sign him on?"

"He'll be with us," I said. "He always was, though he didn't know it. Only, if he's going all the way, he ought to be told the truth. Don't you agree?"

"You're responsible," he said. "Use your own judgment."

I didn't feel like having Marcel overhear all I'd got to say, so I told him he could have a couple of hours off, and I drew Feuermann a chair alongside the gun and talked to him while I kept my eyes on that stretch of road. When I'd finished there wasn't much about us he didn't know; what's more there was a lot he hadn't understood which was a bit more clear.

"This Mr. Gene," he said, "was the friend who helped Crevelle?"

I nodded.

"And it was Destordi you were aiming at."

It was his turn to nod; then he shook his head. "It's a hard thing to take the life of a man."

"I thought that once," I told him. "But what the State won't do, private justice must. And suppose Destordi had got hold of . . . Miss Brock and had treated her like his other women. Suppose he'd turned her over to those two men of his. What would you do? Apply to the State?"

"If he's as much as touched her," he said, "I'll kill him myself."

"You won't get the chance," I told him. "You'll have to take your place in the queue with the rest of us."

We went on talking for the best part of an hour about all sorts of things. Feuermann had some money saved, he said, and he wasn't worrying about being out of a job. If he ever had money, his idea of spending it would be to get a first-class machine and make that paper of Crevelle's a real live thing. The Levascans weren't so bad; it was ignorance that was the enemy. He loved the country and that would be his contribution to its future. Like digging at a mountain with a shovel he admitted, but it'd be good work.

"How'd you come to drift into journalistic work?" I asked him.

He smiled. "I don't know. I suddenly found myself with the itch for writing – and I got to know Crevelle. The rest was easy."

It was that word "itch" that set me wondering again.

"Perfectly amazing, your English," I said. "Where'd you learn it?"

He smiled. "That's part of the past – my past. One day perhaps I'll tell you . . . I don't know." And he shook his head.

That was all very mysterious and I might have persisted and tried to worry out more but Prargent came back then. He said Gene was coming along after dark and he'd like to see Feuermann for himself. And he had some other news. Not long after midnight on the Saturday a car had dropped a woman and a man at Destordi's house and the woman had left on the Sunday morning at about half-past eight, and a man with her. Whether it was the same man and woman wasn't known, and as their instructions had been to report on Destordi himself, they hadn't mentioned it again after trying to get hold of Gene and failing to find him.

"That was when we were after Rastier," Prargent explained. "The problem is, how's it help?"

I didn't like to hurt Feuermann's feelings and I rather toned down what I thought.

"There's no reason," I said, "why Destordi shouldn't have paid her well to come up to the house again on the Saturday night, and that'd explain Maximilien too – assuming he was the man who entered the house with her."

They soon knocked the bottom out of that. It didn't explain the total disappearance of the waiter after he'd left the house the following morning, and it didn't fit in with the story of the concierge.

"I didn't like the look of that woman," I said.

"She ought to be questioned again, and that's one thing the police might do for us. They ought to be interested enough in the disappearance of one of their own citizens – let alone what's happened to Miss Brock."

"Just a minute," said Prargent suddenly. "I've got an idea. Is your friend Crevelle likely to be in his dug-out, Feuermann?"

Feuermann said he'd be there at seven for a certainty.

"Right," said Prargent. "You go down there, Donald, and see him. Get hold of that man in the passport office at the frontier and get a description, if you can, of the person with the Lucy Brock passport."

I saw what he was driving at, but I didn't like the idea of going into that flower shop and I said so. Prargent only laughed.

"Nonsense!" he said. "You've nothing to fear in Montelle. You've been inoculated against arrest if you only knew it. You could spit on old Fournier's whiskers and get away with it."

I took his word for it, and I'll tell you I didn't get much of a thrill out of passing that jail even though the sentry outside the gate didn't waste a look on me. Inside the flower shop I got a handshake from the cripple, who evidently knew all about me, and when I got down in Crevelle's cellar, I thought I was never going to get my hand loose. It was only when I delivered an ultimatum that he said he'd try to get hold of his friend. I sat on in the cellar while he disappeared in the direction of Rastier's warehouses. He was gone a quarter of an hour and when he came back he hadn't any information. All the friend had been able to say was that the woman had answered to the description of the passport.

"That might mean anything," I said. "I know from experience that they never trouble to look at the photographs, especially when there's a rush on."

I couldn't get away till I'd done my share of the ultimatum and told him all my adventures. Then I had to promise another article for his paper and he showed me what they were going to print about Monard that night. It was just as I was going, and he was saying that he was sorry he hadn't been able to get any information about the woman, that he suddenly stopped talking about that and went off at right angles.

"The woman in the tunnel. Might it have something to do with it?"

"What woman?" I asked. "And what tunnel?"

He rushed over to where he kept his papers and came back with an issue of the government *Journal*, turning the pages until he'd found the paragraph he wanted.

I didn't know what to make of it but I suddenly felt something strike me like a chill. The body of a fully dressed woman had been found on the Monday night in the Mont Crillon tunnel, and though the body had been terribly mutilated by a passing train, death was due to a stab in the heart. Nothing was found to give a clue to her identity.

"Where is the tunnel?" I asked.

He said it was just beyond the frontier and was five kilometres long. At its end was the junction of Crillon and there the train always stopped.

"Do you mind if I cut this out?" I asked him. He made me take the paper itself, and then when I'd promised again to let him have that article of mine, I managed to get away.

I stood for a moment indecisively on the pavement, wondering if I should call in at the Granard, and then all at once a feeling of tremendous hatred for the place came over me and I knew that something had gone that could never lure me back again; something I'd always refused to admit even to myself. I didn't think of Feuermann at that moment. I thought only of myself and her, and the last time I'd seen her when she turned to me at the side door after we'd quarrelled over Destordi.

I think I said out loud, "Ah, what the hell!" as I turned away, and then I became aware of an ambulance sort of car that had drawn up at the kerb and I found my way blocked by a couple of police. The car must have just drawn up for I saw the door open at the back and two other police got out. A stretcher was then pulled from the slides and the two each took an end and as they steadied themselves I saw that on the stretcher was the body of a dead man. I remember I pushed against the man who had come up to my side on the pavement and as I went to apologise I saw who it was on the stretcher – Maximilien, and his black clothes soaking wet, his face a soggy grey and his open mouth gaping aimlessly.

"They've pulled that one from the river," said the man at my elbow.

"The river?" I said. He was just an ordinary citizen who'd been held up on the pavement like myself. "And why are they taking him in there?"

He shrugged his shoulders. "All that come from the river go in there, m'sieur. *C'est la Morgue.*"

Chapter XVI
PRARGENT KNOWS

IF I HADN'T remembered what happened to me the last time I ran home through the streets of Montelle I think I'd have sprinted for all I was worth, and as it was as soon as I got away from the Place Granard I stepped out pretty lively, and I fairly flew across the courtyard and into our dining-room where the meal was going on. Prargent grabbed his napkin and got to his feet as soon as he saw me rush in like that, and you never saw a couple more perturbed than he and Feuermann when they'd heard all I'd got to tell them. Feuermann got up shaking like a leaf.

"I shall get the police," he began. "We'll make that concierge tell the truth."

"You sit down and finish your dinner," Prargent told him. "What the hell's the good of getting rattled? Besides, Gene won't stand for the police being brought into this. We can handle things our own way."

"Prargent's right," I said. "We don't know who this dead woman is. We know she can't be Lucy or Crevelle'd have seen her on the train. It's ten to one it's that woman Lou, or whatever her name was." Then I had an idea. "You saw her often enough, Feuermann. Had she got any distinguishing marks about her?"

He thought for a moment and said she had a mole just below her neck on the right shoulder blade.

"What about it?" I said to Prargent. "Any hope of finding out?"

He said he'd have a shot at it. Moreover, what Destordi's money had done with the concierge, Gene's money could buy, and he thought of having a shot at it. At any rate he left the rest of his meal and went off again. I sat down to mine and set about cheering Feuermann up, and I don't mind saying I wanted a bit of the same thing myself.

"Men like Destordi are the curse of our country," he said. "How many people would know the name of Levasque at all if it weren't for the criminals who escape here? I know they're supposed to be under government surveillance, but –" He shrugged. "And take the death of Gabrisson. Everybody knows Fournier was jealous of him and tired of being a figurehead. There are more impossible things than that Fournier was a party to that bomb-throwing. And what chance have we of getting a man like Destordi arrested? Your friend's right. We must take the law into our own hands – only we must tell the country afterwards why we've done it."

"Spoken like a first-class journalist," I said. "About taking the law into our own hands, I'm with you, but once the job's done you won't see me for dust – if you know what that means. I've had one look inside the jail and I don't want another."

Well, we sat talking till dusk and didn't get beyond relieving our feelings, and then at about ten, Gene rolled up and he had with him one of those police Alsatians. A quietly mannered sort of dog he seemed as he sniffed at me and Feuermann.

"He's running loose round the house," Gene said. "There's another round my place. They've both been trained not to pick up meat or go to strangers, and they'll save us the devil of a lot of work at night."

He took the dog in to Marcel and then disappeared with him somewhere. When he came back Prargent was with him.

"Now Herr Feuermann," he said, "we've got some news for you. Open those windows, Donald, and get some drinks out. We can see well enough without the lights."

That was another thing about Gene; whenever he was there things always looked like getting a move on, and there was a sort of confidence that took hold of even the pessimistic Feuermann, who'd been telling me we'd never get Destordi out of his shell if he chose to stay there.

"Captain Prargent's been telling me all about you, Herr Feuermann," he began. "He says you're coming in with us and I'm glad of it. You're too good a man to be on the other side. And first of all, about this Miss Brock, whom I've seen once or twice at the Granard and admired. If she hasn't got a mole like that woman of Destordi's, she's not the one that was thrown out of the train. I got hold of Santour where the body still is, and this woman has the mole you described and she's five foot six as near as we can work it out. Miss Brock wasn't that, was she?"

"She wasn't an inch more than five three," I said.

"That's all right then," went on Gene. "About the man Harris, Herr Feuermann. At what time did you see him at Destordi's house?"

"At about five o'clock," said Feuermann. "He was there when I got back."

"That fits all right," said Prargent. "He'd have had lashings of time."

Gene nodded. "This is our theory – and it's only a theory, mind you. Destordi collared Miss Brock that night and Maximilien was bumped off and dumped in the river. She was brought to Destordi's house, and the next morning Harris took Lou to the station with Miss Brock's passport, and what she probably thought was that she'd get out at Santour and come back to Tony's circuitously. What she didn't know was that Harris had had orders to get her out of the way, and when he'd done it he came back to Montelle alone. We haven't been able to make that concierge speak. A man of mine went round with a wad of notes, but she hangs on to her tale. She's scared stiff, that one. Tony's told her what'll happen if she squeals."

Feuermann looked at him; it was more of a stare than a look. "You mean . . . Miss Brock's in there with *Destordi*?"

"Don't know," Gene told him. "If she is it's up to us to get her out. One thing you've got to get into your head. You're in with us and what we say, goes. Destordi's our main line, and the other'll fit in. If she's not there, then we'll give Tony the works and make him squeal. And we're having no police interference."

159 | THE TRAIL OF THE THREE LEAN MEN

I can't say what Feuermann's face was like as he slowly shook his head, but he was like a man trapped either way.

"There's no need to take it hard," said Gene more kindly. "We're promising you action and that's more than you can promise yourself. You've got our backing up to the last man and the last cent – if you can get us Destordi. What are your own ideas?"

Feuermann didn't seem to have any ready. Somehow I couldn't imagine him as a man of action though he might have the pluck of a lion if it came to a scrap.

"Any way of entry you can suggest?" went on Gene. "Windows, doors, walls or anything?"

Feuermann still hadn't an idea. Even if we got over the walls, there'd be barbed wire to get through, and if we got through that, every window was shuttered and they could pick us off from inside and in the eyes of the law they'd have the right to do it. The doors were heavy and barred and altogether we looked like having as much chance as if we proposed to scuttle a Dreadnought. And, as Prargent pointed out, we hadn't a hope of surveying the ground. Our attack would be by night and lord knows what we might find ourselves up against.

"Any hope of putting him on the spot?" I asked. "For instance, if we could nobble the manager of the Granard, we might get him to ring up Destordi and ask him to come down there. Some of us could be ready and grab him as soon as he left the house."

I thought by the reception that got that it wasn't much use.

"We've toyed with that already," said Gene, "and we thought it a bit too risky. In the first place he's bound to have some simple code by which the man can warn him, and once we take him into our confidence that far, we never know if we're going to be double-crossed. And where would be a reason of sufficient urgency to get Tony out of the house, even if we bought up that manager?" He shook his head. "No. Things have gone too far. It's ourselves or nothing."

Feuermann's face suddenly lit up.

"An aeroplane!" he said. "Why not change your headquarters to over the frontier and buy or hire an aeroplane?"

"Not a hope!" said Gene, and laughed. "I know a bit about planes myself, though I shouldn't say it. If I registered a bull's-eye on that house, I mightn't get one of 'em. It'd take half a ton of stuff to blow that place up clean – and where'd we be if we scored a miss and blew up somebody else?"

"Where's Spider?" I asked. "He's an old hand. He might put us up to something."

"Spider's out prowling round," said Gene, "but this isn't his kind of show. How can you put a man on the spot when he knows where the spot is?" He got up and began walking restlessly round the room. "I tell you we've got to think of something new – and we've got to do it damn quick. I didn't like the way Fournier sent that message. First thing we know we'll be escorted to the frontier and Destordi'll be here for keeps."

It began to feel stuffy in that room and we went out to the balcony. The last of the afterglow had gone from the sky and there was a kind of velvety darkness, with the sky a luminous black and the stars thick as meadow buttercups. It all seemed damn silly as we sat there, talking quietly. Two hundred yards away was Destordi's house, though we could only see the darker mass that suggested it, and there we all were, most of us game enough, and quick enough on the draw; thousands of pounds to spend, friends of our own, the best car in the country, everything to make for a getaway – and we might as well have been a collection of tourists for all the good we were.

"If only we could see a crack of light out of one of those shutters, I'd go over on my own," said Prargent suddenly. "It's that deadness that gets my goat."

We heard the dog pad along down below and then a low voice, and in a couple of minutes Spider was climbing up the balcony rails.

"Nothin' doin', boss," he said. "That place is deader'n hell – and darker. Couldn't lamp a thing."

"Get yourself a drink," said Gene and by the way he said it I think he scowled. Then he rounded on us. "Haven't any of you guys got any ideas?"

Spider hadn't moved from the rails. "Now ain't that too bad?" he said. "Here's you gettin' sore at us and it's your own jam you've got yourself in. 'Hell's goin' to hit this burg!' Them was your words before you went soft, and then you muscled in with them politicians and –" He broke off.

"Aw, hell! Let's go home before Tony bumps us all off. Me, I'd hate to get a slug in the belly like your old man."

"Said all you've got to say?" asked Gene quietly.

"Sure," said Spider and I guess he was rather surprised at that.

"Then lay off!" snarled Gene. "Keep that skinny mouth of yours shut or I'll shut it for you. If you want to quit, quit! – and here's your dough right now."

I don't know what Feuermann thought of it all. He'd been sitting there quiet as a sheep, listening to what was going on, and I was glad when Prargent went over to Gene as he leaned moodily over the balcony rails, with a "Sh! We don't want to tell everybody we're behaving like children. Come and sit down, Gene. We haven't begun to talk about this thing yet."

I heard Spider moving about at the far end of the balcony, and the hiss of the soda as he squirted it, and I guess he thought it better to get out of the way for a bit. I felt sorry for Spider, even if his tongue did run out of control now and again, and I reckon he knew Gene better than any of us and just how far he could go. All the same I thought I'd cheer him up.

"Been having a look round, have you, Spider?"

"Sure!" He came over and sat down alongside.

"Which way did you go?"

He leaned forward and put out his hand as if to explain, then let it fall.

"Didn't I tell you I saw nothin'?" He turned to Gene. "Say, boss; whose is that nifty little villa north of Tony's?"

"Why?" asked Gene curtly.

"Well, it kinda struck me," said Spider modestly. "Say, don't them guys come out for a breath of air? Me, if I was sittin' on that verandah I could drop a pineapple easy as pie –"

"You could do a hell of a lot," cut in Gene, but he turned to Prargent all the same. "That villa is right above Tony's garden. Anything in it, Prargent? And whose is it, Feuermann?"

He had to explain the exact situation to Feuermann and then we all got a surprise.

"That's the Villa Florent," he said. "M. Rastier owns it. I've been there many a time. He doesn't use it at this time of the year; he goes to his place in the hills."

We talked about that for quite a time till Gene forgot his grouse against Spider, but we couldn't see anything to be made of it. Then Feuermann spoke – and tentatively enough.

"I know you decided that it wasn't practicable to bomb the house from the air, but would it be possible to drop a passenger by means of a parachute so that he could get on the roof?"

"Devil a hope," said Gene, but he said it more courteously than the way he'd used to Spider. I don't think even Gene at his grousiest could have been rude to Feuermann. "You see," he explained, "the job'd have to be done in the dark. It'd be a hundred to one chance in the light, so I leave you to guess. But why'd you ask?"

"There's one window we might get in by," said Feuermann, and everybody cocked his ears till you could almost hear them. "It's in the roof –"

"But the roof's flat!" said Prargent.

"Yes," said Feuermann, "The roof's flat and there's a balustrade all round, but there's a kind of trap-door that opens from the attic so that people can get on the roof."

"Locked, is it?"

"I'm afraid it is," said Feuermann ruefully. "There's a bolt on the inside."

"Doesn't matter about the bolt," said Prargent, "if the hinges are all right. Is it hinged inside or out?"

Feuermann thought for a bit then said he was sure it was hinged outside. You went up some steps from the attic and pushed upwards and the door went back. It was a window really because it had glass set in it of the thick, opaque kind.

"We'd get in all right that way then," said Prargent. "The trouble is we'll never get as far as the roof."

Gene got up and leaned over the railing again. In a second or so he was back.

"Black as hell out there. Still, what's the good of talking? As you say, we'll never get as far as the roof. What's the time, somebody?"

"Not far short of twelve," I told him.

"Right," he said. "I'm turning in. To-morrow morning we'll have another conference and if nobody's thought of anything by then, I'm going over to see Tony myself to-morrow night, if I have to knock at the door. Where're you going to-night, Feuermann?"

"I thought of going back to the town," said Feuermann. "I promised to lend Crevelle a hand with his paper to-night."

"Right," Gene told him. "You push off now and mind you're not tailed. Get back here bright and early before the town's awake. We have your word about the police?"

"You have my word," said Feuermann slowly. "I shall do nothing; nothing at all, without you."

Gene grunted something and then shook hands. I saw Feuermann off at the door and when I got back the other three were still sitting there.

"Queer bird, that Feuermann," Gene said to me. "Where the hell'd he learn to speak English like that? He speaks it a damn sight better than I do."

"I don't know," I said. "All I do know is he's a white man all through. I'll stake my life he doesn't let us down."

Gene did some more grunting and then I had to tell him at first hand all I knew about Feuermann, and that wasn't much. Prargent chipped in on my side and said that anybody could see Feuermann was a somebody, and he'd vouch for him too.

Gene waved his hand and laughed at that.

"Didn't I know he was white when he turned us down first?"

"I didn't know anything about that," I said.

"Nothing to it," said Gene. "We gave him a hint through a third party and showed him a wad but he said there was nothing doing. If he wasn't white he'd have broken the promise he gave and he'd have told Tony." He yawned. "You two get off to bed, and for Gawd's sake, try and dream of something. C'mon, Spider."

When they'd gone I waited for Prargent, but he poured himself out another tot.

"You push off to bed," he told me. "I do my dreaming best when I've got a drink or two inside me."

*

When I woke next morning at six-thirty, I suddenly realised I hadn't dreamed a thing. I'd yawned my way to bed overnight and I'd been asleep before I'd had time to think; indeed, it seemed incredible that I'd been asleep at all. Then I remembered about Feuermann, and I got out of bed like a streak of lightning. But Madame Moulines was already up and she'd let him in. Then I made tea for the three of us, and we had it in the kitchen.

"Any news?" I asked Feuermann.

He shook his head. "None at all. We got the paper out. Only ten thousand – mostly for Montelle." He suddenly gave a queer little smile. "Nobody makes tea in Montelle like this – except you and me. Somewhere I must have learned how you English make tea." He called over: *"C'est bon, madame; n'est ce pas?"*

She shrugged her shoulders, and I laughed to see her sitting there like any plump old cook way back home. Then I don't quite know why I said what I did. Just a mad slip of the tongue, perhaps, and because I was thinking things myself.

"You'll have somebody to make your tea for you one of these days, Feuermann."

I saw he didn't see what I was driving at and I went fatuously on.

"Wouldn't you like to marry an English girl and have her make tea for you the rest of your life?"

I saw him suddenly flush and then, as he looked down, I knew what a caddish thing I'd said. And then when I tried to put things right, I merely set my blundering foot further in.

"How old are you actually, Feuermann?"

He looked up again. "Forty-five. . . . Why do you ask?"

"I don't know," I said, and felt a bit of a fool. "But you don't look ... I mean..." Then I got up. "Time I was making Captain Prargent some tea."

He smiled. "You were going to say I looked much older. So I do. It isn't always time that makes a man old."

I'd have liked to ask him about that but I wasn't feeling any too satisfied with myself just then; I just turned the conversation on one side and tried laughing at Madame Moulines instead, though I never did get much change out of her, especially when she said things in Levascan and then laughed at them herself. Then I made a pot of tea for Prargent and got his tray ready, and told Feuermann I'd be down again in a couple of shakes. All the way up those stairs I cursed myself for a swine, letting him know what I thought about her when he'd first claim, and when I knew she didn't trouble two hoots about me. And as I tapped at Prargent's door I knew what I'd made up my mind to do for all that. If Gene went out that night to try to get Destordi, whether Lucy was in the house or not I was going with him; and if he turned me down, then I was going alone. I still had that forty-four Spider had given me, and I'd filled up with slugs from Marcel.

Prargent was in his dressing-gown and standing before the open window. He merely turned his head as I came in, then he went on with his watching the view. I set down the tray and remarked that it was a great morning.

"Doesn't matter a damn about the morning," he said, still not turning my way. "It's to-night that's going to count. You'd better do what Gene's done and make your will."

"Why?" I said, "What's the idea?"

Then he did turn round – and he was smiling.

"The idea? Don't quite know yet, but I do know we shan't be all here this time to-morrow – or we'll be damn lucky."

I stared at him. "You mean –"

"That's right," he said. "I know the way to get Destordi!"

Chapter XVII
THE CURTAIN RISES

At ten o'clock that morning we were all assembled in Prargent's bedroom for what turned out to be the last conference. I knew what was coming, but all the others knew was that Prargent had a scheme and that Destordi's house might now be left to look after itself.

"Now this wonderful idea of yours, Prargent?" began Gene. He was very genial that morning and trying to show everybody he hadn't meant anything by his overnight outburst.

"It isn't wonderful at all," said Prargent. "You people may think it damn silly. Still, come over here and don't make too much parade at the window. Some bloke may have the glasses trained on us."

We could see reasonably well through the muslin curtain and all the south-eastern slope was spread out in front of us.

"First of all, Rastier's villa," said Prargent. "Have a good look at it and get it in your mind's eye. See the height compared with Destordi's? The ground level's higher than his roof. And mark the position. Not due north but north-east by north. That's important."

He let that sink in and everybody looked wise and said nothing. Marcel was wrinkling up his brows till he looked more like a monkey than ever.

"Now," said Prargent, "take a look below Destordi's place. What's in front of it? That side road and the line of very tall plane trees. If you remember, Gene, I once suggested to you that we might climb one of those trees so as to overlook the ten foot wall in front of Destordi's house, but we agreed that it'd have to be done by night and that wouldn't be much good even if we could see through the branches. But what I suggest now is another use for that tree – that biggest one there on the right. I'm proposing that we run a stout wire from as near the top of that tree as we can get, to the roof of Rastier's villa and go along it hand over hand till we get on Destordi's roof."

Everybody craned round to look and you could see them trying to work it all out.

"But that tree's not in front of the house," said Gene. "It's off the line."

"If you'll pardon me," said Prargent, "that's just the beauty of the whole thing. I know that tree's not in front of the house. If it were we might be overlooked in some way. I've taken the angles and I make the tree forty yards along the side road to the west. Only, you'll find that as Rastier's place is north, north-east, a line from it over Destordi's will bring you to the tree."

Gene nodded. "It's a great scheme. A great scheme! I see the top part working out all right, but I'm not so sure of the south part. Have you worked the details out?"

"Not all of them," Prargent told him, but I've got them near enough. First of all we get some stout wire. Six strand stuff, I suggest, as it won't cut the hands so much. At dusk we get that fixed on the roof of Rastier's villa at the proper place to pass over Destordi's roof and arrive at the tree. Don't forget that anywhere on the roof will do, though it'd be better if we could get somewhere near the trap-door. That's in the centre, Feuermann, isn't it?"

Feuermann said it was.

"Right then. We make all fast at Rastier's end and as soon as it's dark we pay out the wire along the ground to the end of his garden. The next garden we'll have to risk but I understand there's only a caretaker there and we might do a little judicious spending if necessary. Still, we get through that garden with the wire and then we come to the tree. Here someone will have to climb with a cord and when the road's clear someone else down below can attach the end of the wire which can be drawn up. As soon as it's fast the bloke in the tree can flash a light and we at Rastier's can pull all taut. We may have to have a man or two along the route to see there's no obstruction, and we'll have to have some system at the end of Rastier's garden to keep the wire away from the side of Destordi's house till it's higher than his roof. That shouldn't be difficult – and our time's our own."

"My God! We'll do it," said Gene, and looked round at the whole gang of us. "You fellers have a good look at the scenery and if you've got anything to say you can get it off your chests when we get inside. We don't want to stand arguing here."

It was cooler in the lower room and I set the fan going and got out some soft drinks.

"You say all you've got to say first," Gene said to Prargent. "Then the rest of us can air our ideas."

"First the villa," Prargent began. "We've got to have the key and we ought to have Rastier's permission."

"I can get the key," said Feuermann. "The agent at the offices knows me and I can make an excuse. I'll answer for M. Rastier's permission to use the villa, if he's away, and that's almost certain."

"If you can arrange for Spider to have the key in his hands for just two minutes, we needn't trouble anybody afterwards," said Gene. "He'll make us an elegant repro. that'll do the trick. It's out of the way there and plenty of trees round it and we oughtn't to be noticed if we go the right way to work."

"Next we'll want leather gloves. I thought first of a sliding pulley arrangement but that might work too fast on the wire. And we'll want a screw-driver for the hinges and we ought to have a stout bar in case there's any levering. And where's that cook sleep, Feuermann?"

Feuermann said he slept at the top of the house in a room facing north, and he slept like a pig and snored like hell.

"Right," said Prargent. "What I suggest then is that we take a rag and some chloroform and keep him asleep without disturbing him. You never know what's going to happen inside that house tonight and we don't want him left as a witness. That's the lot from me, I think, except the arrangements for buying the stuff we want, and I suggest that we mustn't call any attention to that, in view of what might be found out afterwards."

Nobody had anything to say for a bit because, I think, it all seemed so unreal our sitting there in a comfortable room in broad daylight planning what we were going to do in the dark elsewhere. It wasn't even so real as it used to be in the days when we knew we had to make a raid and the chances were some of us would be for it. Besides, I don't think we, any of us, saw a lot of danger once we got inside the house. I know I thought Spider would have the whole three of them reaching for the ceiling before they knew it.

Still, there was ultimately quite a lot of talk one way and another and then it was decided that Feuermann should get a confidential letter to old Rastier and in the meanwhile he should tell the agent that Mr. Hobart wanted to look at the villa with the hope of taking it temporarily, and Prargent would go with them and survey the ground while Spider fixed the key. One of Marcel's pals was to see to the wire, and Prargent said there was enough dope in the medicine chest to settle the hash of that chef. I was chosen to climb the tree and proposed to have a good look at it during the heat of the afternoon.

"And what do we take with us to-night, boss?" asked Spider.

"There's to be no shooting, if that's what you mean," Gene told him. "There ain't going to be any inquest as far as we're concerned. Soon as guns started popping off inside there, someone'd call in the police and then where'd we be." He must have noticed Spider's consternation. "You can take a gun to hold 'em up with, and that's all the guns there's going to be. Marcel might take a coupla knives to do his throwing act if it comes to a scrap and the rest of us'll have a handy bar or two."

"Sure," said Spider cheerfully, and included the lot of us in his helpful look. "You can do a whole lot with a bar."

*

It was ten o'clock that night when we were all assembled in the top bedroom of Rastier's villa and I must say that when the morning's conference had been so airily dismissed, we'd none of us any idea of all the things we'd either forgotten or hadn't allowed for, and some of the things you may gather as we go along. At the Villa Marguerite, for instance, all the baggage had been packed, and a spare car had been bought to hold it, with an extra seat or two in case we might have to cart Destordi and his gang off. That car and Gene's were in the garage, noses facing ready, and all stoked up for a getaway. Old Madame Moulines had also been warned and Gene had paid her up, and she too in the morning would be ready if necessary to disappear back to wherever she came from.

Then there'd been the trees between Rastier's villa and Destordi's garden, through which the wire had to be tautened, but Prargent said that was all to the good. We'd run the wire through the best gap through the trees and then turn due west and that'd keep the wire away from Destordi's roof till we were ready to raise it. We did that as soon as it was dark enough and then came the ticklish business of getting into somebody else's garden.

Still, we managed that, though it was the devil of a job with the wire getting kinked as we unrolled it, and luckily for us there weren't any trees in the way, except young ones, and we had mostly grass to go over. It was a long garden with a lodge at the end that looked as if it had once been a separate place, and then came a stone wall and we had to force the padlock before we could get through the handiest gate.

Getting up the tree was the worst job because the branches didn't begin till a long way up and the trunk was too thick to embrace. But Prargent got me a double line over a bough and then I scrambled up all right. There wasn't a single hitch then. Nobody came along that secluded road and I pulled on the wire and made it fast as high as I dared go. Then Prargent dashed a quick match and I felt the wire tightening. He disappeared after that, as his job was to superintend the wire along its length, but I got down from my tree all right and then got my line concealed behind the trunk as we'd have to use it again.

Prargent had made all correct as he went back and I returned to the villa by the road. I tell you I thought all sorts of things as I skirted Destordi's house, and yet I couldn't believe that we were going in there after a man's life. I couldn't even think there was any life at all in the black mass that represented the house itself, and as for the woman who might be in it, I wouldn't trust myself to think of her at all.

When I reached Rastier's garden things were not going so well, and Prargent was trying to get the wire raised through the gap. Finally I had to get up another tree and do some steering and to cut a long story short, Prargent reported all correct at half past eleven. Then we all went upstairs for a final word.

"Understand?" said Gene. "No guns! I'll stick a knife in the one who lets one off. I go first because I'm the heaviest and then you come, Spider, then you, Donald, and then Marcel. Feuermann stays here to see everything's right, and Prargent comes with us and we let him down to the ground by the door where he knows what to do if necessary. If anything happens to me, Prargent's in charge – and after him, Spider. And don't forget your numbers if it comes to a scrap in the dark. Yours Spider?"

"Three," answered Spider.

"Marcel?"

"Five."

"Donald?"

"Seven," I said.

"Right," said Gene. "When one hollers, the rest answer and then use your judgment about ducking. All set? Come on then. We'll get it over quick." That thing about numbers was Prargent's idea. I never saw such a chap for organisation, and he had Gene beaten to a frazzle. He went into the lead as soon as Gene spoke and when we all got out on the flat roof he felt the wire and tested it. It looked uncanny to see his hand go out and hold something we couldn't see; something stretching away out there into the darkness on which our lives might hang.

"All correct," said Prargent.

Gene grunted as he took his shoes off and hung them round his neck by the laces. Then he got on his thick gloves, those leather ones the men use in the vineyards, straddled the parapet and let his weight slide. The wire held and we saw his dark jersey for a moment and then, hand over hand, he was gone though the wire swayed dangerously.

I was beginning to feel a bit high-strung and I giggled in the dark as I thought of something. I was thin enough in all conscience, and the heat had taken more off me than good living had put on, though I felt amazingly fit.

"You're for the high jump next, Spider," I said, and then to Prargent: "Remember what brought me out here? The trail of the three lean men? Well this is it. Spider and me and Marcel, and you for make-weight."

"And not a bad trail either," he said. "Ready, Spider? The wire's steady."

"Christ!" said Spider as he leaned over the parapet. "Hell's gates is nothin' to this." He felt in his hip pocket before he let himself down, and in a couple of seconds he was out swaying on the wire. I stooped down and took off my shoes and I remember how deliciously cool it was on the stone of the roof. I felt in my pocket for the forty-five I'd got there and then in my trouser pocket for the foot long spanner, and to show I wasn't scared I sat on the parapet waiting for the wire to swing steady, and I had on my gloves all ready.

"It's easier now," whispered Prargent. "They're steadying the wire the other end."

All the same I was pretty nervous when I swung loose, and then, before I'd gone two yards, I wasn't scared at all. If it had been daylight and I could have seen the ground it might have been different, but all I was concerned about now was shifting my hands along and wondering how far it'd be to the roof of Destrodi's house. It took me no more than three minutes to get there since the wire sagged downhill, and when I did get there I found my knees brushing the parapet.

"Not too much clearance," whispered Gene, as he helped me over. "Squat down there till we're all here."

I squatted down and watched him and Spider steady the wire. Another three minutes and Marcel came along like a young steam engine. Gene collared him roound the middle and lifted him over. Prargent came along like a staid and dignified old regimental at a gymnastic reunion, but he wasn't so staid when he came to get those long legs of his over.

"Got the rope?" whispered Gene.

Prargent handed it out of his pocket. A yard or so along the parapet was the spot they'd agreed on with Feuermann, and the rope was made fast and Prargent got ready to go down again. Gene shook hands with him.

"Good luck, Prargent! Don't forget the telephone wire first, and don't worry about us till we get the door open."

Prargent got astride the parapet and slowly let himself go. Gene leaned over and steadied the rope and when all was clear, hauled it up again and stowed it away in his pocket.

"May come in handy," he whispered to me. "Follow me now and take it easy."

We got down on our hands and knees and I flatter myself that even if a sufferer from insomnia had been sleeping in every bedroom under that roof he'd never have heard a sound. Then just as we got to the trap-door Spider clutched Gene's arm.

"Christ! what's that?"

I turned in my tracks in time to see something at the parapet where the wire crossed it. Spider got out his gun and began shuffling back, till Gene's arm reached out and held him. The black shape was now on the roof outlined against the stars, then it sank down and began crawling towards us. A yard away I saw the man was Feuermann.

"Say you . . ." began Spider, but Gene silenced him.

"Feuermann," he said. "I'll settle with you when we get back. Make another break like that to-night and I'll knife you where you stand."

He was so shaking with rage that his voice came thick. We didn't move from there for a minute or two and I think it was the weight of a feather that might have turned him either way. But he didn't decide to send Feuermann back and when he moved round I knew it was all right, though I didn't dare even whisper to Feuermann.

When I ventured to draw in close by the trap door, Gene was already at work on it with the screw-driver. Spider was dabbing away at the rusty screws with an oily feather and I should say it took them a quarter of an hour to get the hinges free on the other side.

"We'll be here all night if we get the others out," I heard Gene whisper to Spider. "Prise her up and see how much she gives."

They prised the door till Spider got his long arm inside and by the way he rolled on his back and the tugging I knew he was trying to draw back the bolt. It was the prising up of the door that stopped it and he had to get to work with oil on his fingers before he could make it move, and even then it grated. Still, he got it free and Gene lifted the door off and he and Marcel laid it on one side. Below us was then a black nothing with a square of blackness for entrance.

Gene pushed us back with a thrust of his hand and shot his flashlight down the hole for a split second.

"Steps are gone," he said. "Where can we make fast?"

The only spot was the parapet and then we wondered if the rope'd be long enough. Gene flashed his light again while I held my pullover round it to keep the gleam from coming up, and as I craned over I could see what looked like a stone floor and the end of the rope dangling just short of it.

Gene tried his weight at the end of the rope and then let himself down, and from where we were we didn't hear a sound. Then Spider went, and I and Marcel, and last came Feuermann. Gene flashed the light round and we saw we were in an unused bedroom, with an old bedstead in the corner and empty boxes and oddments of rubbish all over the place. Gene took a paper from his pocket and had a look at it, then he beckoned to Feuermann.

"Lead the way and you and I'll go and settle that chef."

Feuermann nodded and moved over to the door, Gene drew him back and opened the door himself, inch by inch, listening and then letting the flash play outside. When he and Feuermann had gone through I held the door so that it shouldn't slam, and there were the three of us in the dark with nothing to look at but the stars through the opening in the roof. All I know is you could scarcely hear us breathe, so intently we were listening. But the house was as still as death and so was everything outside. I put my hand out gently and touched Marcel and he shied in the dark like a bucking bronco. Then he took my arm and whispered in my ear.

"Thought you was a snake!"

We both gave a little titter at that, and I guess he was as nervy as I, or rather, in his case that is, pawing the ground and anxious to get on with it. It'd probably be ten minutes after the two had gone that I thought I heard a something outside and drew back the door. Gene's flash came through, and then his head. All he did was to nod us over, and one by one we went through the door. It was only then that I lost the feeling of unreality and knew I was in Destordi's house.

Chapter XVIII
WHAT HAPPENED

When we came out of that door a quick flash of Gene's light showed we were on a landing; the third floor according to the plan Feuermann had drawn out for us. The stairs came at once, and luckily for us Destordi's tastes in furnishing had been of the sumptuous kind, for the carpet was so thick that you felt yourself sinking into it.

Spider now took the lead and Marcel was just behind him, and as he passed me and Gene gave the light another quick flash, I caught the gleam of the knife he had in his hand. We'd all got black pullovers on and we must have looked a working-like lot as we went carefully down those first stairs, frowning away and hardly daring to breathe.

Just short of the bottom there was a traffic jam, and word was whispered back for us to sit down where we were and get our shoes on while Gene went to reconnoitre. I felt him brush past me and then all I saw was the tiny circle of light as he played the flash on the stairs that led to the ground floor. I felt for my spanner and got it out, and then whispered in the ear of Feuermann who was sitting alongside me.

"What made you come over here?"

Before he could answer, Spider prodded me in the ribs as a sign I'd got to shut up, though I'd whispered so low I thought Feuermann himself hadn't heard it. There we sat then for what seemed ten minutes, and eerie enough it was, with the house unholily quiet and my heart going like a mad thing, till I tried taking deep breaths to slow it down. Then things happened so quickly that I've hardly time to tell you.

The first thing was the opening of a door and a voice. We didn't know whose the voice was but we thought it was Spud Mason's.

"Aw! quit your kiddin'! I'll have that dame feedin' outa my hand."

At the same moment a light was turned on. It flooded all the hall and threw a beam up to where we were so that I could see every stair as far as the floor, and the main door with its heavy bars, and a table that stood by the wall. I know I drew back up those stairs of the higher storey as if I'd been shot, and so did the others. As I moved I became aware of two things; that Marcel had his knife balanced by the blade, and that from the hall was coming the sound of a rough baritone voice singing:

"You can't take your dough when you go, go, go."

What happened then sent my hair on end and a shiver all down my spine – the sound of a blow, a kind of long drawn out scream, and then with the suddenness of the crack of doom, a single shot! It echoed round the landing as if it had been a howitzer but it didn't drown Spider's voice.

"Gene's started somethin'. C'mon!"

He dashed off down the stairs and Marcel with him. I followed, so scared that I set my feet mechanically on the stairs in front of me. The light was still on in the large, stone-flagged hall, and as I reached the bottom stair I saw a door on my left. It must already have been opening for Spider had his gun out and Marcel stood like a statue with his knife poised, and we two others halted in our tracks. Then a hand came round the door and I heard the whirr of Marcel's knife. What happened to it I don't know, but the light went out!

But there were two things I'd seen in the fraction of a second as I ducked – two bodies lying on the floor by the door, six foot or so apart. I know I ducked so quick that I caught my head a glancing blow on the rail, and I heard feet pattering quietly on the floor, and then in the pitch dark – darker than ever because of the light we'd just been in – somebody brushed by me and I knew it could only be Feuermann though I crouched nearer to the stairs.

"Five!"

I nearly jumped out of my skin as the voice came from over by the door, and I forgot all about answering with my number, and when I began to shape my dry lips to get it out, Spider's voice came from where Marcel was, and the light flashed on again.

I'd seen pictures like that but I never thought they could happen. Spider was by the electric light switch, his left hand on it and crooked behind his back, and the other held his gun and his eyes were sweeping the room, beetling from under his brows.

Marcel was crouching by the table, another knife in his hand. Feuermann was at the far end by the stairs at another door which led to the kitchen. Spider spoke first and his whisper reached me as easily as if he'd hollered.

"Got a gat on you?"

It was Marcel he was whispering to but I thought it was to me till I saw his eyes shift.

"I have," I said.

"Then get in there quick and give it the onceover."

I nodded and got out my gun. Marcel nipped over to where Gene was lying and lifted his head.

"Christ!" he said. "Gene's got his!"

He picked up the gun that lay by the wall and spun the cylinder, and I felt something rise in my throat. Then as he straightened himself up and let the head fall, he caught sight of that other body just beyond where Gene lay, and not two foot from the door where I now stood. In a flash he was over, and as he raised the head this time I saw it was Spud Mason with a knife in his ribs, and I knew somehow he was still breathing. Then, while I stood there like a paralysed rabbit, Marcel gave a couple of thrusts.

"That's him!" he said out loud and then laughed as he wiped the knife on the knee of his trousers.

"Where are them other two bastards?"

I saw Spider glare at me and I opened the kitchen door and then felt for the switch. The gun was in my hand but if Destordi himself had raised a knife at me I couldn't have pulled the trigger. I stood there fumbling and then Feuermann's hand came round and the light went on. The place was empty, and it stank like hell, and was almost as hot.

I'd got a bit of a grip on myself by that time and I nodded to Feuermann to get out and then I closed the door. Spider was still at the other switch and I went over. Marcel was there too.

"Everything's all right in there," I said and my voice sounded a sort of croak.

Spider said nothing and his lips were drawn together like a blue streak.

"Them two bastards is in there," said Marcel. "Open that door, Spider. I can handle them two eggs."

He reached for his other knife that was fixed in the woodwork where it had struck, scowled at it and slipped it into his pocket.

"This is my racket," growled Spider. "I'm givin' orders and you're takin' 'em; see? Them two guys is all ready when we want 'em, only we're goin' to get 'em without us gettin' a slug in the guts."

"What about the windows?" I said. "Any way out?"

"The Cap's out there," said Spider, and left it at that. "You sure about Gene?"

Feuermann was already kneeling there and you could see by the way he laid him down again that there wasn't a hope. Spider licked his lips and then bit them. Marcel reached for the handle of the door.

"Say, what's the hurry?" said Spider. "What's inside there anyway, Fireman? Tables and chairs and things?"

Feuermann began to tell him where things were, then Spider cut him short.

"What the hell anyway? Get down to it, Marcel, and you two guys stay outa this. I'm goin' to put this light out."

Before he could press down the switch there was a scream from inside the room. A second scream, and then a gurgle as if a hand had been clapped over the mouth. The blood ran cold down my back.

"Christ!" said Marcel. "He's got that dame in there!"

Before we knew what was happening Feuermann had grasped the handle of the door and had burst into the room. There was the crack of a gun and before Spider had time to flick off the light I saw Feuermann still on his pins. I got to the floor like a streak and ran into somebody's feet as I crawled inside. Then I reached out for the wall and found it and I lay there trying to see something in the pitch dark.

The room, with its shutters tightly barred, smelt foul and it was heavy with smoke. Then I became aware of a scuffling noise away over to the right of the room, and someone moved. There was the thud of something striking dull, and the fall of a body, and then with a suddenness that was startling, the light went on. Spider, as he crawled into the room, had hooked the noose of a string over the switch and now he'd pulled it down.

A picture flashed across my brain. The room was immense and carpeted and the centre table had been drawn away to give a clear field. Plumb in the centre of the room lay a man and standing over him was Harris, and the very instant I saw him, and that was as soon as the light flashed on, there was another crack and he pitched forward. As I followed the line of the falling body I saw something that at first I couldn't understand – something white with two black bars round it, and then I saw it was the naked body of a woman which Destordi was holding as a shield. One leg was crooked round her and a hand was over her mouth, and almost as soon as Spider's shot got Harris, Destordi fired twice, and I didn't know what happened.

What gave me the pluck to do it I shall never know, but I made a leap across that room. What saved me was that Destordi held his gun in the hand away from me, and he couldn't have turned without exposing his side. The next thing I knew I was leaping on his shoulders, and he let the girl go. In that infinitesimal fraction of a second I saw her fall to the floor, I saw the folds on Destordi's fat neck and I reached desperately for the arm that held the gun. Something flashed across the room and Destordi gave a grunt. His hand fell limply, and then Marcel was on him, stabbing like a fiend, till Spider held him off.

Lucy was crouching by the chair and I remember I snatched up the rug and put it over her and as I did so I saw the cords holding her ankles to the chair. As I unfastened them and she drew them up something was in my throat and I felt an uncontrollable desire to cry, but all I did was to kneel down where she crouched, and take her head in my arms. Then before I knew it I was kissing her and I know she kissed me once, and then she fell back with a face as white as death.

"Water, Marcel!" I hollered, but he'd gone out to the hall. Spider passed me over a bottle and a dirty glass.

"Say, water ain't no good." And then as he leaned over the chair and saw her lying there and realised just what must have happened, he suddenly seized Destordi's body by the throat, hurled it down to the floor and kicked it furiously in the ribs.

"Easy there, Spider!" came Prargent's voice. Marcel must have let him in through the unbarred door, and he had to hold Spider off before he'd stop kicking. Then he had a look at Feuermann. All the time you must imagine me there, kneeling on the floor, trying to get some of the brandy down Lucy's throat, and then taking a quick look at what was happening.

"Is he dead?" I called.

"The hell of a smash on the skull." He stood up and looked round. "My God, what a show!"

I thought for a moment he was going to lose his head, then he asked me if I was all right.

"I'm all right," I said. "And come over here, will you, and see if you can do anything."

He didn't know what was behind that chair, and he flushed when he saw who I was holding.

"The filthy bastards! I thought I heard her shriek." He bent down and touched her cheek with a touch as gentle as a woman's.

"Just a faint. Stop here with her and I'll try to find some clothes."

He turned at the door. "Marcel, you get back to the Marguerite and you too, Spider, and bring the first car outside here. Don't use the lights if you're not forced."

He clicked off the hall light before they went out and then I was left alone in that room with two dead men and Feuermann, and the woman I was holding. I know I kept smiling at her like a mother holding a sleeping baby and then I'd hold her close and all the time when I thought of her and Gene lying out there, and old Feuermann,

I had that same uncontrollable desire to start blubbering – and if I had it might have done me good.

When Prargent came back he had a suitcase in his hand and some clothes under his arm.

"I'll see to her now," he said. "When she comes round she won't mind if she knows I did it. You get Feuermann comfortable if you can and then drag those two out to the hall ready."

Feuermann must have had a tremendous blow on the back of the skull from Harris's gat and the blood had seeped through and was drying on the side of his cheek, but he was breathing all right and I rolled up another of those woolly rugs and made a pillow for him, and as I did it and I thought of how he'd had the pluck to rush into that pitch black room with nothing but his bare fists, I felt such a rush of affection that I had to turn my head away.

I could see Prargent's head above the arm of the chair and I ventured on, "Is she all right?"

"She'll come round all right," he told me. "The trouble will be when she does come round. Notice the marks on Destordi's face?"

I think he said that to cheer me up. The bloated face was wealed down its length where the fingers had scratched, and when I saw him lying there like a slug, I could have kicked him in the slats as Spider had, but I lugged him by the legs across the rucking carpet and through the door to the hall, and when I let his legs drop I noticed that Marcel had taken out his knife.

I went back again for Harris, and I didn't somehow feel the same grudge against him, and when I'd laid him alongside Destordi I dragged that other slug, Mason, there to make three. Gene I didn't touch and I couldn't bring myself to look at him. When I got inside the room again, Prargent was standing in front of the fireplace with its filling of fluffy, artificial flowers, and I noticed that the gilt clock on the mantelpiece said a quarter to twelve.

"I've got a great scheme," he said. "We'll be fighting against time but we ought to pull it off. You stay here and I'll go and wait for the car. I'll have to shut this door."

I had another look at Feuermann first and then I went over to Lucy. Prargent had got a dressing-gown on her and had made her a pillow, and she was lying there, head on one side, still white as a sheet so that I didn't dare to touch her. But I stood close by her while I looked round that room for the first time, though I still couldn't visualise all that had happened. But there was blood all over the chair where Destordi had been and blood on the floor where Harris's head had been – and then I wondered what it was that Prargent was going to do and how we'd make our getaway, what with Feuermann and Lucy and four dead men on our hands.

The car came up so quietly that I didn't know it was there till the three came into the room. Prargent had a look at Lucy first, then he told us to sit down.

"You fellers agree with what Gene said – that I'm now in charge?"

"Sure," said Spider. "We're relyin' on you, Cap, to get us outa this."

"I'll get us all out all right," said Prargent, "now I know you're with me. I think we're safe as houses in here for a bit. I could hardly hear the shots from where I was outside so I don't think anyone's been disturbed. But what you've all got to remember is this. We're in ten times more danger now than ever we were from Destordi. It's the police and everybody we're up against now – and we can't make the getaway as we intended. First of all, I propose that Marcel takes Feuermann and Miss Brock back to the Marguerite. Wake up madame, and get her to look after Miss Brock, and get Feuermann to bed –"

Spider's face was showing a look of incredulity.

"But say, Cap, what are we goin' to do when the police come makin' enquiries about all this?" He waved his hand at the room generally.

"There ain't going to be any enquiries," said Prargent. "That's part of the scheme. We're going to make Destordi clear up all the mess."

Marcel got up at once, growling at Spider out of the corner of his mouth.

"Quit shootin' off your mouth! Didn't you hear the Cap say he'd get us all out?"

Prargent patted him on the back. "That's all right. We don't want any arguing. And before you go, Marcel, we'll get all Miss Brock's things together so that nobody'll ever know she's been here. Spider, you clean out the pockets of those three and lay it all on this table. It's their passports we want. If we can't get them, the scheme's bust."

He and Marcel went upstairs while Spider and I went through the pockets. We got a good wad or two but we didn't get any passports, but that didn't matter because we found them in a drawer of the table where they'd been chucked. Then we got Lucy into the large car, and Feuermann too, and Spider went with Marcel back to the Marguerite.

"I didn't want you to go," Prargent said to me, "because I've got a special job for you. Take these clippers of mine and get rid of that wire. Then close up Rastier's place and come back here."

That was the way Prargent got work done; he gave you a job to do and he didn't tell you how to do it but left you to get on with it your own way. I guess he knew it was the devil of a job too, for he didn't say anything about the time I'd take to get back. The way I did it was this. First I cut the wire above us and closed everything up on my way down from the roof. Then I cut off the wire at each end of Destordi's garden and chucked the strands into a corner. Then I made for my tree, hoping to God nobody had been about when it fell, and there I hauled it in and left it coiled up roughly on the grass behind the tree, knowing it could hardly be connected with the house that was forty yards away. At Rastier's villa I let the wire down and coiled it up as well as I could in the dark and left it in a sort of shrubbery. By the time I'd closed everything up it was well past one.

With my pliers I'd already cleared a way through the wire in Destordi's garden and marked down the spot and I came back that way because I didn't want to risk my being seen near the door by the back road. Prargent was in high fettle when I got in.

"Ten minutes," he said, "and we'll be off. We've got most of the blood off and tidied up. I'm just writing a chit in Destordi's writing, so to speak, to leave by the chef's bedside, saying he's gone away. Funny to think we're paying him really out of Destordi's own wad."

"If you don't mind my suggesting it," I said, "I'd write it with gloves on and then we can get Destordi's own prints on it. You never know how smart these police may be."

"Damn good idea," he said, and got down to it. I asked Spider how he'd left the patients and he said they were going on all right.

"We'll have a doctor round in the morning if necessary," said Prargent, looking up from the table where he was copying something that looked like a letter. He wrote another word or two, head tilted on one side, and then he must have guessed what I was thinking. "There won't be any suspicions. Don't you worry about that. If all goes well in the next hour we'll be the safest people in Montelle."

That shut me up all right, though I caught Spider's eye in a puzzled look.

"Where's Marcel?" I asked him.

"Out there in the car," he told me. "The Cap said for him to put on them chauffeur's fittin's of his."

Prargent finished his letter and told us to wait while he went up to the chef's room and fixed things.

"Damn good chap, Prargent, isn't he, Spider?" I said.

"Sure," said Spider and looked as near enthusiasm as I'd ever seen him. "The Cap's a swell guy."

"You're a great old scout too, Spider," I told him, and I meant it.

I'd almost swear he blushed, and his lean old face wrinkled to what he meant for a grin. "Last time I was told that," he said, "was a little jane in Cicero when I was nearly railroaded." He shook his head reminiscently, then suddenly looked at me in what was a queer way for him. "Say, that Miss Brock is a swell little lady."

I blushed then and I was trying to find something to say when he finished up.

"Didn't we all know you was nuts on her? Say, if she was my baby and that guy Destordi –"

"Blast you, Spider, shut up!" I snapped at him. "Do you think I want to keep wondering what Destordi did? I don't give a hell what he did!" I hollered at him. "That won't make any difference to me. And keep your mouth shut!"

Then I knew I was making a fool of myself and I felt that lump come into my throat again. "Sorry, Spider," I said, and then again, "Sorry!" and that's all I could say.

"Don't I know?" said Spider, and shook his head again. "Guess we done wrong by Tony. We shoulda bored him in the guts like he did Gene's old man." Then he burst out. "Christ! ain't it hell? Wisht I was peddlin' peanuts. First I see Gene's old man —"

I think Prargent must have heard that for he came in talking cheerfully.

"Well, we're doing fine. You get off back, Spider, after you've given us a hand to get 'em in, and we two'll chance our arm."

He gave a last look round to see if everything was all right, then shoo'd us to the door and turned out the light. He switched off in the hall too before lie opened the outside door. Then Marcel came in and the four of us got the bodies in. Somehow we didn't feel like laying Gene alongside the other three and we got him in the front between me and Marcel and covered him with a rug. Then there was some luggage put in but it wasn't ours as I knew by the bags.

"Where's our stuff?" I whispered to Prargent.

"Tell you later," was all he'd say. He stood on the path for a moment or two, peering along the road, then held out his hand.

"Cheerio, Spider. If we don't roll up by daybreak you know where to come."

He got in behind with the three dead man and then leaned over to Marcel.

"Don't stop for anybody – and drive like hell."

The car – Gene's car – moved off and where we were ultimately going I had no idea. All I could do was sit back in the dark and keep Gene's body from sagging to the floor.

Chapter XIX
DESTORDI SAYS GOODBYE

MARCEL took the law into his own hands about driving fast and it was not till we were clear of the town that he really began to hustle. I sat there holding Gene and thinking and thinking about what had happened that evening, and most of all I kept thinking of how Lucy had kissed me, and I wondered if she'd really known who I was, and then, if she'd known me, if it had been just relief from the tension and not that she was in love with me. And what was going to happen to all of us now? Would we get out of the country and back to England? And how could I ask a girl to marry me on a couple of hundred pounds and no job? True there might be that bonus Gene had promised us but I didn't like to think of that with Gene lying against my ribs, though I hadn't any scruples now about blood money.

Strange to say I was feeling no animosity against Destordi and his gang as we hurtled on through the darkness. Except for thinking about Lucy I was utterly miserable and with that literary kink of mine that still survived from the old days of comfort and civilisation, I would keep letting my mind run on what old Tennyson wrote about Arthur and Bedivere and what they thought when the whole bottom went out of things. I didn't see the incongruity of the picture, how that I was no Bedivere and Spider and Marcel weren't quite the Round Table sort, but all I knew was that our little company had broken up and this was the last time some of us'd be together.

The car gave the devil of a lurch and swung left.

I knew that lurch and that swing and where we were bound for, and sure enough, in a minute or two Marcel slowed the car down, then he got out and stuck his head through Prargent's window.

"What about goin' on ahead, Cap?"

"Yes, do," said Prargent, and got out of the car too. Marcel disappeared into the dark and I joined Prargent for company. He spoke first.

"We're going to the farm to leave Gene there. We'll bury him on the hill some time to-morrow night if all goes well. To-night, perhaps I ought to say."

"What about his people?" I asked.

"He's only got distant relations in England," he said, "and an aunt in the States. He's left the bulk of his money there – and some to his old college. He left me in charge of things."

I could tell how cut up he was by how he was talking, as if for the sake of talking and so that he shouldn't think too much.

"The time schedule all right?" I chimed in.

"Quite," he said. "Provided we're over the frontier before it's light we're safe as houses. Marcel's a godsend." Then he laughed quietly. "The last trail of the three lean men and I wish to God one of us had been fat."

Before I had time to ask what he meant, Marcel was back.

"O.K., Cap," he said as he climbed back into the car. "I've give the old man the dope."

We drew into the courtyard and Marcel's uncle was standing at the door with a light. Prargent went over to him and they talked together quietly for some time while Marcel and I stood by the car saying nothing. Then the other two came over and we carried the four dead men into the stone floored kitchen. Then the lights of the car were switched off and we carried the bags in too. Marcel's uncle got out a bottle and we all had a tot, then Prargent made us all sit down.

"I'll tell you two what's in my mind," he began, "and then you can translate to your uncle, Marcel. Tell him there's ten thousand francs for him after this night's work."

Marcel shrugged his shoulders. "Aw hell, Cap! He ain't thinkin' about the dough. Ain't he been one of us all along?"

"I know," said Prargent. "I trust him as I do you, but you tell him all the same, then he'll know how important it is."

Marcel said something in dialect and the old man nodded away. Then he spread out his hands to Prargent with a gesture that was curiously apposite. *"A votre service, m'sieur."* Then he put his hand over his ear as if that'd help him to understand our lingo.

"This is the scheme," said Prargent. "We're not quitting this country. Destordi is. He's bolting out of his hole as we hoped he would. When that chef of his wakes up he'll find a letter saying so, and we rely on him principally to spread the news. What we want really is a fat man to represent Destordi, but we haven't got one, so Destordi's going to do his own acting. We're fastening him in the corner of the car and he's going over the frontier as if he was alive. What we depend on is backsheesh and the darkness, and by hook or by crook we've got to keep the frontier guards from looking in too closely. If necessary we'll have to conduct an imaginary conversation, but that'll be settled as we go along. I'm not too unlike Harris in build and I'm now going to get into his clothes and try to get myself more like him. Donald's putting on Spud Mason's clothes –"

"My God!" I cut in. "They'll hang on me like sacks!"

He shook his head. "No they won't, when you're padded out. You're both the same height, and we'll pad your cheeks too when we get near the frontier. We've got the very luggage they'd have taken if they'd really been bolting and we don't mind if that's overhauled by the customs. We've also got the false number plates Gene had for the car and I want you to fix that now, Marcel. We found your passport at the house, Donald, and I've got mine, so that we can recross the frontier under our own names and with the car in order."

A puzzled look came over Marcel's face. "It's a great little idea, Cap," he said, "but where do I come in? Do I drive the car?"

Prargent shook his head. "Sorry, Marcel, but we want you here. You might be recognised at the frontier and we haven't got time to cross higher up. No; what you've got to do is to see these two are buried when we've finished with them, and then get Gene laid out upstairs ready for when we come back for him to-night. You and m'sieur your uncle can make some sort of rough coffin secretly so that everything's ready. If anything goes wrong with us you'll know it, because Spider'll be along here during the morning, and you better both make for the frontier or else lie low here. That all right?"

"Sure it's all right. Ain't you the big boss?" He nodded to himself. "Guess I know where to unload them two bastards where they'll feel kinda comfortable – only we'll hatta shift a hell of a lot of dung before we start diggin'!"

Prargent smiled grimly. "Get 'em where they'll stay put. That's all that matters. Now tell your uncle all about it and you and I, Donald, 'll get rigged out."

*

We worked fast and yet it was another half hour before we were ready to start. I'd been wadded out and there were a couple of pads I'd got fixed for swelling out my cheeks. Fitting Destordi's body in the back corner was the hardest job but we managed it at last, and as for Prargent, when he took the wheel I shouldn't have known him.

There wasn't any missing the road to Bélanne, even if Prargent had forgotten it since the last time we crossed the frontier, and for the first few miles I sat alongside him and we planned just what we had to do, knowing all the time that things would never break quite as we wanted them. And if they went too badly we planned to stick to our new names and say Destordi had been killed and we were smuggling him out, though that was a poor enough tale in all conscience. Still, we hadn't time for any more before I had to shift to the back of the car alongside Destordi. The first grey light was in the sky and in half an hour it'd be a faint yellow over there by the mountains.

A few hundred yards short of the twin barriers we stopped to make a final inspection and then Prargent let the car go on at headlong speed. My heart was pounding away and I was hoping to God I wouldn't have to open my mouth for I knew I'd stammer or not get a word out of it. Then, before I was ready for it, the car drew up at the barrier with a shrieking of brakes and I saw the dust fly under the arc lights. Prargent was out at once and I had the shade lowered a bit so that they couldn't see inside. There was a glimpse of the open sentry-box affair with a man sitting writing inside, and then another man came up to Prargent and I heard him say in atrocious French that he was in a hurry, and something was slipped into the man's hand. My heart stood still as I saw him stop and then when he'd had a look at the bill by the light of the lamp, he began gesticulating, and Prargent shoved the three passports under his nose, though why they should have that damfool regulation for outgoing traffic I didn't know.

He had a look at them and then he took it into his head to come up to the car, but it was on my side. I had one of Marcel's cigars stuck in the corner of my mouth and as he came up I spoke to Destordi and then growled something in reply. And I put my head out to block the view.

"He's tired," I said in French that was worse than Prargent's. "He says the sooner he gets out of your *sacré*-d country the better he'll like it."

The yellow trousered little chap drew himself up with tremendous dignity.

"Passez messieurs; passez!" and he waved us on, and as we moved forward I heard him saying things about Destordi. Twenty yards and we stopped at the other barrier, and there the one guard on duty must have seen all that had passed on the other side of the line.

The Levasque barrier gate came across and hid the little man from view, and luckily for us we knew there wasn't to be any bother about documents to do with the car because there was some sort of agreement with Levasque about that, but there was an official paper to sign. Prargent did his act with the thousand-franc bill and offered to open the bags but all the chap did was to put his chalk mark on them and leave it at that. Then Prargent went into the office place while the paper was filled in and I snored artistically to represent Destordi.

But I tell you I was scared when the chap came across with the paper for us to sign and I leaned out of the window while he explained what I had to do. Then Prargent got hold of him while I signed and then I made a great to-do rousing Destordi and telling him what he'd got to do, and he growled at me. But his name was on the bottom all right when I handed that paper back, and then, after a wait of two or three interminable minutes, while Prargent could be heard chatting inside the office in his terrible French, the whole three came out and we were waved through the second barrier.

There was the little town to get through and as soon as we were in the open country Prargent began laughing like a madman. I wondered what the devil was the matter till I realised, and then he pulled up the car and I got in alongside him with Destordi's fastenings off and his body on the floor behind us.

I felt like laughing too, or shouting at the top of my voice, but we sobered down quickly enough and Prargent kept his eyes skinned for a handy spot to draw in at, and we found it up among the hills by some pines. The dawn was just breaking as we got out, and Prargent worked that secret shutter above the tank and took out a spade. Ten minutes later we had Destordi under two foot of soil and had scattered pine needles to cover the place. Then we took the bags further into the trees and while I watched the car, Prargent found sufficient clothes to go with his own. After that I got decently dressed too, and then we buried the luggage and the three passports. We didn't stick any sort of cross at Destordi's head and there wasn't any sermon.

We pushed on after that for some miles, following the road we'd taken when we came, and just before we struck the route nationale, we got the right identification plates back again and buried the old ones, and we also got rid of the spade. When we came to the main frontier crossing we presented our passports bold as brass and got through with never a hitch.

"And what now?" I asked Prargent.

"For me – Paris," he said. "I shall stay over till to-morrow morning to see if everything's clear and our two patients are all right, then I've got to settle up Gene's affairs – mean, when we've settled Destordi's."

I looked at him. "Isn't two feet of earth good enough?"

He laughed. "Oh, I'm not afraid of his ghost. What I'm doing is to use that letter we found in his writing and send a letter – presumably from him – enclosed to a friend of mine in Paris, who'll send it on. It'll be addressed to the editor of the chief government paper – *L'Impression* – and in it Destordi will speak his mind about Levasque, and say what a lousy hole it is, and how Gabrisson tried to get him out of the country by that extradition trick, and how he's going to spend the rest of his days elsewhere. What money he's left behind – that's a shot in the dark on our part – is to go to the poor of Montelle and he also bequeaths the Restaurant Granard to the dependants of the victims of the bomb outrage. Rather neat that, what?"

"It's neat enough all right," I said, "if it's read as a tacit admission he was responsible for throwing the bomb. The trouble is it won't be legal – I mean, it isn't a deed of gift."

"Don't you believe it," he said. "Old Fournier'll get his claws on that now he thinks Destordi's gone. Legality don't count, young feller. The main chance is the thing, and that holds good most places besides Levasque. I'm going to get your friend Crevelle to spread the news too, by the way. Every little helps. That'll be a job for you, later on."

"That ought to clear up the great Destordi mystery," I said flippantly.

He laughed. "Oh, but I've not finished yet. I'm going to get in touch with Gene's friend in Paris and tell him we've definite information Destordi crossed the frontier. That means they may go as far as to apply to the French Government for his arrest and extradition. I'm also going to place in his hands confidentially that confession signed by Monard, implicating Destordi in the bomb affair. I want him to communicate it to the Press to the extent of saying he has certain information to such and such an effect. That ought to make Levasque sit up and take notice."

I looked at him admiringly. "By Jove! you're doing it thoroughly. But why take all that trouble?"

He gave a dry smile. "I want nothing even hinted against Gene for one thing, and I don't like being chivied out of a place for another. Why should we all have to scurry out of Levasque like rats when if we had our deserts we ought to have a procession and a row of statues?" He laughed. "Seriously though; I've seen nothing of this damn country and I'm going to have a look over it before I march out with colours flying. And there's Feuermann too. We've got him to look after. He stood by us and we're standing by him." He hesitated for a moment. "And there's the girl."

I said nothing to that but sat back in my corner and really saw Montelle for the first time. Somehow it was as if I owned the Place Granard as we came into it. It wasn't the feeling that we'd done something but just that I was free; free of Montelle and the nightmare of Destordi, and as I caught a glimpse of the Restaurant Granard I no longer had that feeling of tremendous revulsion that had come over me the evening I saw Maximilien's body carted into the morgue.

I was quite excited as we rolled up the hill. Prargent drove to the door as if he didn't give a damn for anybody and as soon as I hopped out and opened it, there was Spider coming from the kitchen, and looking like a fussy parent whose offspring have been allowed out for the first time.

"Gosh," he said. "You two fair gave me the willies. Everything O.K., Cap?"

Prargent clapped him on the back. "O.K. isn't the word for it. Get that garage open and we'll tell you all about it."

We waited till the car was in and the doors locked again, then Prargent took old Spider by the arm. "How's the two patients?"

"The girl's fine," said Spider, and shook his head. "Reckon old Fireman's got his. He don't do nothing but lay there and his bean's all mussed up."

Prargent's face straightened like a flash. "That's bad. I'd better have a look at him."

He strode off at once and Spider with him. I hung behind deliberately; not because I didn't worry about Feuermann but there was something I had to know. By the time I was in the kitchen they had gone through and there was madame making coffee and all dolled up as she used to be sometimes on a Sunday evening when that niece of hers came in. I sidled up, nibbing my hands tentatively.

"*Bonjour, madame.* We're back again, you see."

She gave me a look. *"Ah, c'est M'sieur Donald."* A little shrug and she went on with the coffee making.

"The young lady," I said. "Is she better?"

She began to wheeze so violently that I thought she had a special attack, then I gathered she was telling me the young lady was asleep and mustn't be disturbed. Pale as a ghost, she was, but perhaps when she'd had some of the coffee and eaten . . .

"Which room is she in?" I asked.

She rounded on me then. In my room, she said, and I'd have to sleep somewhere else. And there was no need for me to look up the stairs. There was the Captain's breakfast to get ready.

I laughed. "The Captain's breakfast? *Je m'en fiche!*" and I sauntered on towards the door, smiling away to myself. It was the thought of who was sleeping upstairs in my room that made me do childish things like that, and I halted at the head of the stairs just to have a look at the door. Then I heard Prargent's voice as he came out of his own room.

He caught sight of me. "Here you are. I say he ought to have a doctor and Spider doesn't like it."

I went with him into the room. Spider was sitting by the bed and if I hadn't watched Feuermann closely I shouldn't have known he was alive, for his face was a chilly grey. Someone – Spider probably – had cut away the hair from the scalp and had tried to dress the wound, and altogether he looked so tired and worn that when I spoke I lowered my voice to a hush.

"Why shouldn't he have a doctor?" I asked Spider.

He looked at me wearily – or was it patiently. "Ain't we had enough to do with them outside guys? All them guys is in cahoots. Next we'll have some o' them cops in the yeller pants buzzin' us where he got that sock on the bean."

"Money'll fix the doctor," said Prargent.

"Yes," I said. "And we can tell him poor old Feuermann took a toss off the verandah in the dark."

Spider gave a shrug, but Prargent was already looking through the telephone book. "You're an old grouser, Spider," he said. "Wait till you hear how we fixed Destordi and you'll be swaggering round Montelle with a cane and a cigar."

He found his number and rang up. I stood there watching Feuermann, who seemed to be breathing and no more. I thought perhaps the morning air that came through the open window might be too much for him and I put my hand gently on his cheek to see if it was cold. Spider leaned over the back of his chair watching me and Prargent's voice was an inaudible background, and I don't know if it was the sudden touch of my hand that did it, but all at once Feuermann stirred. His head, that was lying inert on the pillow fell back limply and his lips began to move. I looked at Spider, my eyes bulging, but Spider was staring at the moving lips. There was a kind of mumble, and then I thought I recognised a word. In a flash I had my ear down and was listening with my breath held. I caught one sentence – another – and then the lips stopped moving, and I thought he was gone. But he wasn't. The breathing was as slow as before, but though I stood there with my ear bent down to listen, there was never another sound.

I became aware of Prargent at my elbow and straightened my body up. He must have seen the look of amazement on my face for he grasped my arm.

"What is it? Is he gone?"

I shook my head. "No, he's still breathing. But do you know what he did just now? Spider heard him as well as I did. He was talking – talking English!"

Spider stared at me. He hadn't seen it and neither did Prargent.

"Well, that's good," Prargent said. "It means he's coming out of his coma. The doctor's starting at once. He'll soon have him round."

"But don't you understand?" I said. "It was English he was talking. English!"

"Sure," said Spider. "That guy Fireman speaks English like you and me."

"Listen, Prargent," I said. "Feuermann's a German. When a man's unconscious I'd say it was his sub-conscious self that does the talking; his real self that is. German's his real self; his native language. Then why's he speaking English?"

Prargent shook his head. "You're chasing rainbows. Why shouldn't he be dreaming about something English?"

I looked down again at the tired face, then I shook my head too.

"I don't like it. There's something strange about him – there always was." Then I looked at him and Spider. "Do you know what he was saying there? He said, 'You stay here, sergeant. I'll get through somehow.' That's what he said."

"You stay here, sergeant." Prargent repeated the words slowly. "Hm! It's damn funny, as you say." He looked down for a good minute at the unconscious man, then gave his head another shake. Then the door opened and madame looked in.

"The young lady is breakfasting, m'sieur. You told me to tell you."

"Right," said Prargent. "Ask her if she's fit enough to see me a moment."

He went out of the room with madame, and Spider and I settled ourselves down again by the bed with our eyes on the lips of the still breathing Feuermann.

Chapter XX
THE MAN WHO BEAT THE CUSTOMS

Spider and I cleared out of the way when that doctor arrived. I had a surreptitious peep at him and he seemed a man of pretty high standing, and the car he drove up in was palatial enough to show that he was a top-notcher. After he'd been in the house a few minutes a second doctor arrived – called up by telephone to confer, as I learned later, and a few minutes after that, what should come along but a private ambulance, and I saw a couple of attendants carrying Feuermann out on a stretcher.

I waited for Prargent when he came back from the door.

"See that big white place up the hill?" He pointed to what I'd always thought to be a huge, sprawling kind of hotel up the slope a quarter of a mile behind us. "That's a private hospital-nursing-home place. They're operating at once."

"What do they think? Any hope?"

"Lord yes!" he said. "They're hopeful enough. It's something pressing on the brain they've got to get off. From what I could gather, he might have gone on lying like that for weeks. I gave them a free hand as regards expense." He laughed. "Destordi and his two pals are standing treat."

We went back to the verandah, and it seemed funny to be sitting out there in broad daylight, and every now and again that feeling of freedom came over me, and I wanted to do things to show I knew the world was a different place. As it was all I did was to put my feet up on the rail and lounge back in the chair. It was still only ten o'clock and Spider said he was thirsty as hell and he'd go and rustle up some more coffee, having been skimped at his meal.

THE TRAIL OF THE THREE LEAN MEN

"How'd you find the other patient?" I asked with all the unconcern in the world.

"Better," he said. "Mind you, I think she'll feel it for weeks. What I'd like would be to get her away with us to-morrow, out of the sight of that house." He nodded. "I'll have to sound her about it."

Something went clean across the sun as he said that. He told me afterwards he saw my face go blank.

"She's had the very devil of a time," he went on.

They shut her up in a bedroom the first night after Destordi had tried to get friendly, and the place was all locked up so she couldn't get out or make a sound. Next day Destordi tried to talk her round, and didn't do it. The same night he came in the room and she fought and scratched till he left her alone. Then they tried starving her out and the last thing they did was to drug her wine that night we got in there. What they'd have done if we hadn't got in I leave you to guess. She only knew she was there when that shot went off that killed Gene, and then she felt Destordi seizing her in the dark. Doesn't bear thinking about, does it?"

I moistened my lips as I thought back to what had happened, and there was too much to think about to say anything just then.

"We mustn't ever allude to anything yet," went on Prargent. "We've got to let her see that we take everything for granted. Later on she'll be able to think of it herself in a different way." He shook his head. "She's a damn plucky girl."

I cleared my throat with a little cough. "Any chance of seeing her? I mean, do you think she'd mind?"

He smiled as he hopped up. "You stay here and I'll see."

In a couple of minutes he was putting his head inside the door, and all he did was to nod back. I got up sheepishly and patted my hair and straightened my trousers out, and by the time I was in the corridor he was gone. I gave a tap at the bedroom door and I heard something that sounded like "Come in."

She was sitting in a dressing-gown by the window – my window that faced west. When she saw me her face went a fiery red, and I know I flushed too. Before I knew it I was sitting on the arm of the chair holding her head in my arms and all I could see of her was the hair that nestled under my chin.

"Do you love me?" My voice was like somebody else's, croaky and disjointed.

She nodded her head and I held her more closely. We sat like that till I had the courage to speak again. I remember I gave an inane little laugh.

"All the time," I said, "I thought it was Feuermann you were in love with."

She wriggled in my arms till she looked up at me. 'Oh, but I do love him. I love you both . . . only you're different."

I nodded solemnly, and then what should she do but pull down my head and kiss me. Then I kissed her too.

"When'd you know you first loved me, Lucy?"

She made a face at me. "I think it was the night when you were all so stiff and sulky. You know, when we were walking back to the Granard. . . ."

She must have suddenly remembered all that really meant, for she lowered her head and I held her tight again.

"I'm often like that," I told her. "All stiff and solemn. But I shan't be so with you again." I waited for a moment or two to get my courage to the point. "Lucy, will you marry me to-morrow? In Paris?"

"Oh, but I couldn't."

"You've got to look at me," I said, and pulled her round. "Why can't you marry me to-morrow? It'll be a civil ceremony and we can do it later again. . . . I mean, well, you know what I mean."

She blushed again. "But I haven't any money. . . ."

I knew what she'd soon be thinking of again and I kissed her. "What's money?" I said. "I've got lashings of it. I'm rolling in it."

She looked up quite startled, then she must have seen that I was either delirious or else laughing at her.

"And how much is that?" she said.

"How much?" I laughed. "Two hundred pounds – and more coming."

Then she laughed as she snuggled down again.

We buried Gene late that night on a hill under the pines looking towards Montelle. There was no one there but the four lean men and Marcel's uncle, and there wasn't any service except what Prargent remembered from the Prayer Book, and that was only a few sentences. When we let the coffin down and Prargent put on the first shovelful of earth, with a "God have mercy on his soul," it sounded pretty impressive to us, and I remember Marcel and his uncle crossing themselves, and old Spider and I said "Amen."

When the grave was filled in as we stood there for a minute or two, each thinking his own thoughts, and I know I thought that there were worse places for a man to be laid than that, with the scent of the hill lavender and the thyme and pine needles, and the air blowing free all around. I thought of a lot of things besides that as we stood there, then Spider's voice came quietly.

"He was a great guy."

"Sure he was a great guy." Marcel looked round challengingly but nobody contradicted him. Prargent nodded to himself once or twice, then turned away from the grave.

"Well, we'd better be getting back. I've got something to say to you fellows before we leave. Seems more right somehow to get it over here. Leave things behind us, so to speak."

We went back to the farm and the old uncle left us to ourselves. Prargent told us to sit down and he got out his pipe and I did the same. There was still an air of restraint about the four of us, but smoking seemed to do us good.

"It's like this," Prargent began. "To-morrow I'm going to Paris to settle up Gene's affairs and you're coming with me, Spider, and so's Marcel. I promised Gene if anything happened to him I'd see the pair of you shipped home." He smiled. "Of course if you like to come back at any time, that'd be no affair of mine. That applies particularly to Marcel. I don't think Spider's likely to get homesick about Levasque."

Spider turned his mournful eyes on him. "I've been thinkin'," he said. "Reckon it'd be a he-man's job cleanin' up that gang of grafters like that Fournier what done Gene dirt. How I've figured it, old

Fireman'd make a great little president and so'd that old guy with the whiskers – Rastier or whatever they call him."

Prargent smiled. "Well, you keep your revolutionary thoughts to yourself till you're out of the country. And that goes for the lot of us. What's happened here is dead and gone. When we leave here to-night we wipe it right out."

Spider shook his head vigorously. "Me, I don't know a thing. Neither does Marcel. Ain't that so?"

"Sure we don't. We're spillin' nothin'."

"That's all right," said Prargent. "And about business. There's a hundred thousand dollars coming to each of us, and we collect it in Paris."

"A hundred thousand dollars!" My eyes bulged. "Gawd! I didn't think there was so much money in the world."

Prargent laughed. "There'd have been more if I hadn't choked Gene off. He said we should all share that money Gabrisson was to have, only I told him I refused to take it. And by the way, when he made that will he put down the legacies as free of tax and as a personal mark of his affection and gratitude towards all of us." He shook his head reminiscently. "There weren't many fellows who'd have thought of that. What he wanted was that none of you should have any scruples about taking it. He meant it to be a personal gift."

I suddenly laughed. Spider's face, when Prargent had mentioned scruples, had been too amusing.

"Well," I said, "I'm taking mine and I'm jolly grateful to Gene for it – though I'll never tell him so."

"I think that's how we all feel," said Prargent. "But there's just one thing I want to put up to you all. What about Feuermann? He stood in and he risked his life with the rest of us. Why shouldn't he have his share?"

There wasn't one of us who disagreed with that.

"What I propose is this," said Prargent. "I've got the balance of what we found on Destordi and those two men of his, and I've got the rest of Gene's wad. Then there's the Villa Marguerite which was left to me personally, though I didn't want it. That we'll sell and it can all go in the pool. I reckon altogether there'll be best part of fifty thousand dollars. I'll so arrange it that Feuermann's given a supposed extract from the will where he's put down just as we are, for a legacy as a mark of esteem, and so on. He's the only one of us who's likely to have scruples."

Everybody agreed. There wasn't one of them who didn't wish Feuermann well.

"That's settled then," said Prargent. "And what about you, Don? Coming to Paris with us tomorrow? If so we'll close down the Marguerite."

"Sure I'm coming," I said. "Amn't I getting married there to-morrow?"

That was the first they'd heard about it. Prargent stared at me, then hopped up and nearly wrung my hand off. So did Marcel. Spider looked rather sheepish.

"Sure I always knew you was a great guy," he said. "And she's a swell little lady." Then he wagged his lean jaws. "But say, what you want to be in such a hurry for? Not that I'm sayin' –"

"You're not saying anything," laughed Prargent and slapped him on the back. "What you're going to do is roll up at the ceremony with the rest of us."

"What me?" He looked shocked. "Me, I ain't got none o' them swell pants like what they wear at weddings."

"Too ba-a-a-d!" I bleated, and everybody laughed.

Before we left next morning we had more news about Feuermann, that he'd had a good night and was doing well, and so we all went off with a good conscience. We reserved a first-class compartment for ourselves and you bet we made a great journey of it. Then, after what took place in the afternoon, Lucy and I said goodbye to Spider and Marcel and went off on our own. Spider nearly broke my fingers with his bony grip and of course he had to tell me he'd always known I was a great guy and I had to have my usual joke about its being a pity he didn't put it into practice sooner. We took an address in New York where we could get hold of them and promised to send our own as soon as we had one.

Paris is a great place for a honeymoon. We made the most of it for a week and then Prargent looked us up. He'd been settling up Gene's affairs and later on, he told us, he was going to have something done about burying Gene properly, but that couldn't be till the whole affair had simmered down. Feuermann was getting on well, so he said, and he'd given him all the news, though most of it had had to be guarded.

A week later we went back to Levasque. Prargent wanted to close down the villa for good and take away the car. The smaller one, by the way, he gave us for a wedding present. I didn't want Lucy to come with us but she insisted. Perhaps she was right. It doesn't do to run too far away from things in this life, and the sooner the facing up is done, the better for nerves and memory.

We warned Feuermann not to refer to anything that happened that night, though in a way I wish something could have been said. It was pretty sickening to have my wife regarding me as a hero who'd broken into Destordi's for the sake of rescuing her, when things hadn't been like that at all. Still, one of these days when I screw my courage up and I think she can stand it, I'm going to tell her all about that.

It was a great afternoon when we arrived in Montelle and the whole town was drowsing under the July sun. It was great too to sit back in a taxi and be driven up to that hospital place with never a thing in the world to worry about. That hospital was what Spider would have called a swell joint, and the gardens were a long slope of colour and shade.

"Twenty quid a week!" Prargent whispered to Lucy. She raised her eyebrows but she didn't know who was paying.

We came on Feuermann unawares. He was lying back in a long, wicker chair in the shade of a tree, and his thin hands held a pair of glasses through which he must have been looking. Prargent gave a little cough and then stopped him before he could rise. I looked sheepish, with a grin on my face, and then Lucy did the perfect thing by kissing him unblushingly.

He beamed at the three of us, then shook his head with the old diffident smile.

"Well, it's good to see you all again. I was watching your train come in. And you, my dear?" He took Lucy's hand. "Life's a great thing, isn't it?"

She smiled at him and couldn't say a word.

"Sure it's a great thing!" I said, and then apologised. "Living with Spider," I said, "has sure done my English no good."

He laughed. "And you, Captain Prargent," he said; "you've got the disease too?"

"Not he," I said. "If he had it wouldn't matter. He's never likely to get a living by writing."

"Neither are you," said Prargent. "Nor any of us for that matter. Unless we carry on for a hobby, as old Feuermann here used to do."

A white-coated attendant came up at Feuermann's signal and we all had tea – of sorts – there under the tree. We talked of all kinds of things and Feuermann did most of the listening. He was a different man from when we'd seen him last; there was some colour in his cheeks and his eyes were bright, and yet there was some strange reticence about him; perhaps I should call it a not unfriendly reserve. I thought he had something on his mind.

"What are you going to do now you've come into a young fortune?" I asked him.

He looked at me for quite a time before he answered – and then he turned his head away.

"I don't know. It depends." Then he gave me that old apologetic smile of his. "I wonder if I might ask you something. You were acquainted with – er Fleet Street pretty well?"

I smiled. "Well, I knew a good few people in it in my time."

He nodded. Then he leaned back in the chair. "Tell me. Did you by any chance ever hear of a man called Varlow? Tom Varlow to be precise?"

"Good Lord!" I stared at him, but he was still lying back there with his eyes closed. "If it wasn't for tiring you out," I said, "I'd tell you something amazing about Tom Varlow." I looked round at the others. "Why, if it hadn't been for Tom Varlow I shouldn't be sitting in this chair!"

Feuermann suddenly smiled. He raised himself in the chair, and Lucy darted up and put a cushion behind him.

"You won't tire me," he said. "I'd just love to hear about it."

Prargent had never heard the story at full length and Lucy hadn't any idea of it, so I waded in and told them just how I came to board the train at Victoria that morning.

"And how on earth did you get to know Tom Varlow?" I said to Feuermann when I'd finished. "Did you run across him in the war?"

"Yes," he said. "I think I knew him in the war. I wondered . . . I mean until I asked you my question, I wasn't sure if there'd ever been a Tom Varlow."

Prargent cut in with the same old truism. "The world's a small place," he said. "One thing I'll do too, when I get back in town. I'll get a chap I know to let me read some of that fellow Varlow's stuff. It sounds jolly interesting."

I laughed. "I was thinking the same thing the other day. That yarn of his Munro Burnside left so tantalisingly in the air; the one about the man who beat the customs. I'd like to know how that was done."

"My dear, I'm not going to let you smuggle *me* home any scent," said Lucy emphatically.

Prargent laughed. Feuermann leaned forward in his chair and there was the most amazing look on his face. It was the look of a man who's found something he's lost – and is almost afraid of what he's recovered. His eyes were shining too.

"May I tell you?" he said. "I mean, about this man who smuggled in the scent?" He didn't wait for us to say anything but went straight on. "You see," he said, "as far as I remember, the whole point of the story was that a famous firm of scent manufacturers specialised in flasks of rare perfume, and the flasks were of that long, thin type that look almost like daggers. So rare was the scent and so exquisite the glass that it paid them to smuggle in one at a time and this man constantly travelled from Calais to Dover for the purpose. The customs people guessed a lot, but they never caught him. You see," and there he smiled at all of us, "he happened to be a member of a rare profession – and he was a master of his art. He was a sword-swallower!"

Lucy gave a little, "Oh!" Prargent and I laughed like blazes. Feuermann sat there quietly till we'd finished, and he was still leaning forward in his chair. I think he saw my face suddenly straighten, and he certainly anticipated my question.

"Yes," he said, and waited for a moment. "You see . . . I was the man who wrote it!"

My eyes goggled. Lucy's face flushed the most violent red, and it was Prargent who burst out with the very words I'd have used, if I hadn't been too tongue-tied to speak.

"You mean you're this Tom Varlow!"

Feuermann leaned back against the cushion. We almost held our breath.

"If you'll forgive me," he said, "I'll bring the dead to life for just one minute. I didn't know what was dead and what was living till I asked a question half an hour ago. When I came round from the anaesthetic I knew I was two men, and one was so vague and shadowy that I thought he was some hallucination. I've been frightened – frightened to think. Now I know, perhaps I shall be able to work it out."

We didn't dare to speak but sat watching him as he lay back with closed eyes.

"You see," he went on, "I was captured during the chaos of the Spring of nineteen eighteen. I remember I was taken far into Germany and then I made a break for the Swiss frontier. I spoke the lingo like a native and once I'd got some clothes I saw no reason why I shouldn't get through. Then I fell in with a German deserter and he and I trekked together but just short of the frontier he was shot at and wounded. He died in the woods and I buried him there – and I took his clothes and his papers, and made my attempt at crossing alone. All I remember is falling from somewhere. I must have been already over the frontier without knowing it for when I woke up I was in hospital and I was Ernst Feuermann, a German waiter, and I knew nothing else. I thought I'd forgotten all my past as people do sometimes, and as I was a deserter I never dared go back to Germany to make enquiries about my people, and I never had much urge either.

Then, after the revolution here in Levasque I came to Montelle with a friend I'd made and I got a job in the Granard."

There seemed to be nothing we could say – it was all so amazing.

"Wonderful!" said Prargent and shook his head mysteriously. Lucy patted his hand and smiled at him. When I chimed in my voice seemed coming from a distance.

"And what are you going to do now?" I said. Then I laughed. "Why! you'll be coming back to England with us. Think of everything there'll be to see," and I gazed round at the others for confirmation.

"Why! you'll be your own scoop. Fleet Street'll go mad –"

He shook his head. "All that's dead. Didn't I tell you so? This Tom Varlow is nothing to me. I wasn't a man then. I was somebody I recollect as you remember a dream. I had an old aunt – and she must be dead long ago – and I remember I had money, but that must be gone too; and I shouldn't need it if it hadn't. No!" and he looked round at us steady-eyed. "This is my country. I feel it my country. What I am it has made me. My friends are here and they seem part of me too. Not that you're not my friends – you know what I think of all of you." He shook his head and smiled gently to himself. "Tom Varlow is dead – you must promise me that. What you see here is Ernst Feuermann – who owes you so much . . . and who thinks of you all as the first among all the friends he has."

Prargent stretched out a lean arm and shook him by the hand, and so did I, and Lucy kissed him again and said if it hadn't been for him she never . . . Then she blushed, and in the middle of all the excitement the chief doctor bloke came along and though he was decent enough, hinted that the patient had had quite enough for one afternoon. But he did let us say our farewells in peace.

"Lucy and I are going to wait here for you," I said. "Then we're all having a tour together to see the country. You're going to be the guide."

He smiled with pleasure. "I think I'd like to do that."

"And we're coming every day to see you," added Lucy.

"You mustn't do that, my dear," he said. "You must get about and enjoy yourselves. Rastier's insisting that I stay up north for a bit with him. We'll all go there together when the time comes."

THE TRAIL OF THE THREE LEAN MEN

I tried to look mysterious as I took his hand.

"And we'll all do some smuggling. Wonderful smuggling!"

"Smuggling?" He looked at me as if wondering whether I was serious or not.

"Yes," I said, and I lowered my voice. "What about that brave new printing press we're going to have up in old Rastier's country? All those set-'em-alight articles we're going to write?"

He smiled, but I saw his eyes look away to the north for all that. My eyes ran there too, where the hills receded to an indeterminate grey, and you couldn't tell which was mountain and which was cloud. I found myself wondering too just how we'd smuggle that machine in, and I was nodding away like a china mandarin when Lucy touched me on the arm.

THE END

CPSIA information can be obtained
at www.ICGtesting.com
Printed in the USA
BVHW031326290322
632742BV00001B/27